HEARTS
in
Circulation

"This charming rom-com won me over from page one. Sarah Monzon excels at writing uniquely lovable characters, and Levi Redding is definitely the type of unforgettable book boyfriend romance readers will happily fall for."

Becca Kinzer, award-winning author of
First Love, Second Draft

"A uniquely heartfelt message, lovable characters, and laugh-out-loud moments. Sarah Monzon's newest novel is a delight!"

Melissa Ferguson, bestselling author of *How to Plot a
Payback* on *An Overdue Match*

"I can always count on Sarah Monzon for romance that makes me swoon and inspiring stories that keep me fully engaged—heart, mind, and soul. I will continue to read anything she writes, forever."

Bethany Turner, author of *Cole and Laila are Just Friends*
on *An Overdue Match*

"The chemistry between the two flawed yet lovable leads sizzles, propelling the plot toward its sweet if predictable conclusion. Readers will be charmed."

Publishers Weekly on *An Overdue Match*

"Lovingly poking fun at a variety of romance tropes, Monzon delivers all the swoony feels, along with a message about true beauty and God's pursuing love."

Library Journal on *An Overdue Match*

HEARTS in Circulation

Sarah Monzon

BETHANYHOUSE

a division of Baker Publishing Group
Minneapolis, Minnesota

© 2025 by Sarah Monzon

Published by Bethany House Publishers
Minneapolis, Minnesota
BethanyHouse.com

Bethany House Publishers is a division of
Baker Publishing Group, Grand Rapids, Michigan

Printed in the United States of America

Library of Congress Cataloging-in-Publication Data
Names: Monzon, Sarah author
Title: Hearts in circulation / Sarah Monzon.
Description: Minneapolis, Minnesota : Bethany House, a division of Baker
Publishing Group, 2025. | Series: Checking out love
Identifiers: LCCN 2025007794 | ISBN 9780764243752 paperback | ISBN
9780764245695 casebound | ISBN 9781493451302 ebook
Subjects: LCGFT: Christian fiction | Romance fiction | Novels
Classification: LCC PS3613.O5496 H43 2025 | DDC 813/.6—dc23/eng/20250505
LC record available at https://lccn.loc.gov/2025007794

Cover design and illustration by Camila Gray

The author is represented by Rachel McMillan.

Baker Publishing Group publications use paper produced from sustainable forestry
practices and postconsumer waste whenever possible.

25 26 27 28 29 30 31   7 6 5 4 3 2 1

For Elijah. Sorry, kid. I saddle you with my sensory processing issues and all you get is this dedication. And my love. Always my love.

1

"You cannot be serious," I say, my voice oozing with dubiety as I take in the heap of metal littering the corner of the library's parking lot. The monstrosity looks like it's in need of a tow truck to take it to its eternal resting place in the junkyard and not at all like a vehicle primed and ready for its reincarnate life as the new bookmobile.

"I'm afraid he's deadly serious, Hayley." Evangeline breathes out the words while also staring at what has become my newest worst nightmare, dethroning my recurring irrational fear of getting stuck inside the "It's a Small World" ride at Disney World.

"Maybe we shouldn't use the word *deadly*." Martha winces from my right.

I'm sandwiched between our small town's other two librarians, the three of us in a disbelieving stupor, still trying to make sense of the . . . the . . . *thing* . . . parked cattywampus in front of us. When Marge from the town council had dropped by last week to say there would be a surprise waiting for us this morning, not in a million years would our imaginations have come up with something like this.

And our imaginations are Olympic-level, let me tell you.

We're librarians, after all. We practically marinate in the creative realms, and yet we've still been blindsided.

"Yeah, new rule. *Deadly* and all of its synonyms are no longer a part of our vocabulary when referring to . . ." I wave my hand in front of me, gesturing to the heap of metal. The paint is chipping and peeling, the seams are flaking iron oxide at an alarming rate, and I can't imagine the parts under the hood are somehow in any better condition.

It still needs a name, though.

I swipe my hand in its general direction again. "Cletus."

Martha whips her head toward me, her wide, caramel-colored eyes disbelieving. "Cletus? Really?"

Evangeline laughs softly. "Haven't you noticed Hayley's little quirk of naming inanimate objects?"

Martha shakes her head, her curly hair growing bigger by the second with the humidity in the air. "Okay, fine. But Cletus?" She huffs.

I shrug, not seeing why she's so put out with my choice. "It looks like a Cletus to me. You don't think so?"

She turns so her whole body is facing me. We are no longer the three of us united against . . . Cletus.

Okay, maybe not the best name, but I'm nothing if not stubborn, so I'm sticking with it. Especially in the face of Martha's incredulity.

"The name Cletus is of Greek origin. It means *illustrious*." Now it's her turn to wave her hand at the unwanted, not-asked-for automotive hand-me-down. "Does that thing look illustrious to you?"

I purse my lips and pretend to inspect the newly acquired bookmobile, hiding another wince by tapping my mouth with my finger. "It does have a certain *je ne sais quoi* about it."

"If *je ne sais quoi* means *tetanus shot*." Evangeline mumbles more to herself but loud enough that we all can hear.

"The definition is actually 'a quality that cannot be described,'"

Martha supplies helpfully, which is no help at all. "And *that*, ladies"—she punctuates by pointing a finger at Cletus—"can be described with a litany of negative adjectives."

"We're in the foothills of southeastern Tennessee, not the cliffs of Santorini, so of course I meant the hillbilly version of Cletus and not the Greek rendition."

"Maybe we shouldn't look a gift horse in the mouth." Evangeline's voice holds a note of forced optimism.

Optimism I'm just not seeing at the moment.

Martha's eyes brighten. "Did you know that the first bookmobiles precede anything with an engine, and library deliveries to the remote regions of the Appalachian Mountains were made with horses as the means of transportation? It was called the Pack Horse Library Project."

I cock my hip. "I'm pretty sure this is the perfect time to look a gift horse in the mouth. Because if this was the 1930s, then the proverbial horse we've just been given is an old, lame swayback nag that would probably have keeled over on the first strenuous incline to a hollow where we—so sorry, *I*— would've been left stranded to fend off wildlife and the elements or perish."

"Someone is being a bit dramatic." Martha attempts to quell her grin but fails.

I sigh as I let my chin fall to my chest. We've sorely gotten off topic. "Explain to me how we inherited Cletus."

"Without getting too mired in small-town politics, Mayor Breckenbridge made acquiring a bookmobile for the library one of his reelection campaign promises. Even though we're a part of the county library system, because of our geographical location and the fact he'd planned to donate the mobile library, it was a promise he could fulfill because he knew the county would use our branch as the bookmobile's home port. What he failed to inform the good citizens of Little Creek, however, was that when he said *bookmobile* what he really meant was

11

the beat-up, rust-bucket, ancestral remains of a Volkswagen Transporter that was sitting in his front lawn." Evangeline tsks.

"And how did the responsibility of mobile librarian fall on my shoulders again?"

"I can't drive a manual transmission," Martha answers simply.

I spin on my heel and clamp desperate fingers to Evangeline's shoulders, pinning her in place. "You can. My cousin taught you. I've seen you driving Tai's Challenger around town."

Maybe I'm overreacting, but I can't shake this queasy feeling in my stomach every time I picture myself behind the wheel. Like there should be ominous music playing in the background. Or if my life were being written by some cosmic author, this is when they'd be cackling with ill-conceived glee at laying down breadcrumbs of foreshadowing for some major event in the near future, filing them under the words *conflict* and *raising the stakes*.

Evangeline eases out of my grip, a fake-innocent smile playing at her lips. "Ah yes, but you see, it's your turn." She says that last bit in a sing-song voice.

My jaw slackens. I've never not liked my words being thrown back in my face more.

She rubs her chin dramatically. "I seem to recall a time when I asked you to help me out with a certain matter of a critter stuck in the book return receptacle. Do you remember what you told me?"

"That it was your turn," I grind out, then throw my hands up in frustration. "But this is different!"

Her tattooed eyebrows rise ever so slowly. "I could've needed a rabies shot. You might need a tetanus shot. I think we're even."

I seal my lips against the mild curse pushing to be released. Not a bad word; more like a hex. Not voodoo doll stuff, though.

We live in the South, but New Orleans south is another brand altogether.

I just sometimes wish for a tepid inconvenience to be brought down upon another person's head. Like, *May you never have matching Tupperware containers and lids.* I don't want real harm to befall anyone I'm mildly annoyed with, but the idea that they could be somewhat inconvenienced cools my negative feelings toward them in the moment.

I do not, however, wish these curses on my friends. Ever. And Evangeline is one of my best friends.

Mayor Breckenbridge, though . . . Oh yeah, he definitely deserves a curse.

My lips turn up at the sides. *Mayor Breckenbridge, may you only ever find one square of toilet paper left on the roll for the rest of your life.*

"Why does she look like she's hatching an evil plan?" Martha stage-whispers out of the side of her mouth.

Evangeline lifts a hand to shield her eyes from the sun, squinting. "Is it revenge evil or overthrow-the-government evil?"

"Um." Martha frowns. "Both?"

Evangeline lowers her hand and flicks me lightly on the forehead. "I love ya, Hayley, but I don't have money to bail you out of jail, so just don't, okay?"

"I wasn't scheming anything nefarious, thank you very much. It's nice to see what y'all truly think of me."

"I truly think you're a force to be reckoned with." Evangeline loops her arm through mine.

"Peach-pie-sweet but with a hefty splash of spicy bourbon added to the recipe." Martha links her arm with mine on the other side.

Once more, the three of us face down Cletus and the threat he poses.

I take in a deep, bracing lungful of air and let it out slowly.

"I guess Cletus and I should get better acquainted. Maybe we can come to some kind of agreement for our working relationship." I force cheerfulness into my voice. "He won't break down on the side of the road and leave me stranded, and I won't forget to put on the parking brake and secretly hope he rolls off the side of a mountain."

"That's the spirit?" Martha's voice pitches high at the end. "Okay, ladies, I'm off to get ready for preschool story time." She unhooks her arm and gracefully glides toward the library's entrance like some kind of literary book fairy. It's no wonder all the kids who come in love her.

Evangeline moves to stand in front of me. Her eyes have lost their teasing glint, and she's looking at me seriously. The early morning sun is hanging in the sky just behind her head, casting her in a slightly shadowed silhouette. "Tell me the truth. Are you really scared to drive that thing? Because if you are, you don't have to do it. I mean, you were right. I know how to drive a stick shift now too, and neither one of us needs to get a CDL. It's not exactly on my bucket list to wrestle a heap of metal masquerading as a bookmobile around narrow country roads or anything, but you shouldn't be afraid of coming to work just because of Mayor Breckenbridge's, uh, generosity."

I snort at her liberal use of the word. Mayor Breckenbridge wasn't thinking of anyone but himself if he'd planned all along to bestow this rust bucket on us. But it's not fair to ask Evangeline to shoulder the responsibility either, especially since she's technically head librarian and already has a full plate. Saying it was my turn was a diplomatic way of her assigning me the task. Besides, I may be more than a little nervous at the idea of driving Cletus farther than ten feet, but Evangeline has faced enough fears and been brave beyond measure this year. She's earned herself a nice, long reprieve.

I let my gaze roam over the beautifully artistic tattoo inking her bald scalp, taking in the lacework lines, colorful bouquet of flowers, and the striking image of a rising phoenix. A few months ago, she'd been hiding the fact she has alopecia, afraid her friends and the townspeople would see and treat her differently simply because she'd lost all of her hair to the autoimmune disease. She'd nearly given up on the idea that anyone would ever love her or find her beautiful just the way she is. Now she more often than not forgoes wearing any of her wigs, proudly displaying the new tattoo that Tai created for her. There's no way I'm going to ask her to do this instead of doing it myself. Like she said, driving Cletus isn't on her bucket list. But it is on mine.

I mean, the words *Drive Cletus* obviously aren't written down physically on a piece of paper anywhere, but I can remedy that real quick since I add to my bucket list (if that's what we're going to call it) every day anyway. Literally.

Every day starts with a blank page in the little notebook I carry around with me, looking for something to jot down and check off, all under the same heading. *Make It Count.*

I can never pay back my debt, but I'm really hoping I can pay it forward.

2

'm sitting in the driver's seat, my hands gripping Cletus's wheel, and nothing bad has happened. Granted the keys aren't even in the ignition and we're still in the library's parking lot, but still. I'm counting it as a win.

"Maybe I've misjudged you, old boy," I say as I stroke the leather stitching. "Maybe you're more of a classic that's just in need of a makeover. Not a true representation of what lies inside."

Like that awful cover of *Persuasion* that looks like the man-eating plant from *Little Shop of Horrors* is planning on having Anne Elliot as its next meal.

I turn my head and look at the bookmobile's interior. On the whole, not quite as scary as the outside. There are neat little shelves for us to display and transport books, and it has nice flooring that looks fairly new. Thankfully Mayor Breckenbridge did that much in his bequeathment. Although I'm not sure who's going to want to come inside with the outside looking the way it does.

Even though I know my initial reaction was one of obtuse disbelief and immediate denial and fear, the idea of a bookmobile is growing on me. I can be the librarian edition of Christy Huddleston, bringing books and knowledge and literacy to our own backwoods, rural communities like Cutter Gap. And who knows? Maybe there's an opinionated and painfully honest yet compassionate and sympathetic—not to mention ruggedly handsome—Scottish doctor waiting for me on my future book route. Hook me up, Catherine Marshall.

I'm catching the vision, seeing the inside of Cletus filled with tomes and paperbacks and board books. Little kids with big imaginations waiting to be swept away to places like Hogwarts and Narnia. Their parents on the hunt for new recipes, escape reads of their own, and the newest releases in nonfiction as well. People who don't currently have access to all the library has to offer now given the opportunity to reap the benefits of free Wi-Fi and media.

I turn back around in the seat and pat the dashboard affectionately. "I take back what I said and sincerely hope you won't hold my snap judgment against me. We're going to end up being a good team, you and I."

It's more reflex than conscious thought that has me reaching into my purse and pulling out a small notebook not much bigger than the palm of my hand. I flip to the next blank page and jot down the day's date. Next, in neat handwriting, I write *Drive Cletus*, then stop myself before adding a check mark since I haven't actually driven him yet or done anything that impacts someone else's life. Which means I need to be on the lookout for my Good Samaritan moment to add to my list for today.

My thumb slips, and the previous pages in the notebook fan open, marking at least one inscription on each page. I randomly select an entry and trace the words with my fingertip.

Give away my umbrella in a downpour

I grin as I remember that one. It had been raining cats and dogs when I'd come out of a store and noticed a mother with a toddler in her arms, huddled under the awning. I could tell she was weighing if she should wait the weather out or make a mad dash to her car even though it would mean both her and her child getting soaked. I'd opened my umbrella and handed it over, then raced out into the storm myself.

I flip to another page.

Take a CPR class

I haven't had to use these acquired skills yet, but knowing that I can jump in and potentially save someone's life seems like one of the bigger things I've done.

Leave coupons next to the item in the grocery store
Let someone cut in front of me in line
Give an extra tip along with an encouraging note
Play pinochle with the nursing home residents
Help Tai and Evangeline realize they're perfect for each other

My list varies in scale and weight of importance. Some days I can only manage to do something small and relatively insignificant. Other days I can almost convince myself I'm making a difference in the world.

I'm sure a psychologist would have a field day with my notebook if one ever saw it and knew when I'd started recording my acts of kindness and why. I get what it looks like when given the full picture, but I swear I'm not trying to repay a debt. How can I? It's my life. My literal life. Brain-synapses-firing, heart-pumping, breath-in-my-lungs life.

Or, I guess more specifically, blood-cleansing, bile-producing, metabolizing-proteins-and-carbohydrates life. Which, if you don't know, are the three main functions of the liver, although the underrated organ is responsible for so much more. Which someone realizes the moment it refuses to function properly.

Ask me how I know.

It was three weeks before my twelfth birthday when my liver decided to go on strike for good. Acute liver failure, the doctors had called it. Before that, I'd thought the worst thing my body was going to do was put me through the rigorous torture of puberty.

If only.

Instead of worrying about being called Rudolph because of a large pimple on the tip of my nose, or the uncomfortable development of inconvenient breasts that did nothing but get in the way when I was playing sports, or dealing with my first menstrual cycle that of course came at school when I didn't have any hygiene products in my backpack, I had to come to terms with the fact that I might not even live to be a teenager. Without a new liver, my life expectancy had been whittled down to a couple of weeks, tops.

The day I was wheeled into the operating room to receive a transplant . . .

There aren't words. Not even the most poetic of authors could describe the kaleidoscope of feelings that were contained in my pubescent body. I no longer had an immediate death sentence hanging over my head. You simply cannot repay someone for saving your life. It's impossible. Especially when that person had to die to do it.

But you know what you *can* do? You can make every day that you weren't supposed to live count. You can try every day to impact another person's life for the better, even if your attempts are only a fraction of the influence yours was given. And that's what I've been doing for the last seventeen borrowed years of my twenty-nine-year-old life.

A knock on the window scares the living daylights out of me, and I grip my throat, trying to stuff the scream leaping out of my esophagus back down.

Tai stands on the other side, a mischievous grin on his face.

I reach for the door handle, then push the door open with enough force to catch my cousin in the shoulder. The hinges give off a loud squeak in protest, allowing him time to dodge the full brunt of my attack.

"Need to apply some WD-40 on that," I say, neglecting to acknowledge he got me with a jump scare because I don't want him relishing in the pleasure of it.

Tai hooks his thumbs through his belt loops and rocks back on his heels, his gaze raking over Cletus. "By the looks of it, even submersing it in a lake of WD-40 wouldn't do much in way of improvements."

"I don't believe anyone asked your opinion." I sniff. Sure, I might've said something similar an hour ago, but that was before I'd gotten to know Cletus. Things are different now.

Tai tilts his head, studying me.

I jut my chin out at him.

He, in turn lets out an exasperated breath. "Angel says you've named it."

Angel is Tai's nickname for Evangeline. "Tai, Cletus, Cletus, Tai." I move my hand between them as I make introductions.

Tai chokes on a laugh but doesn't make any other comment. Being more like a second brother to me than a cousin, he's very familiar with this particular quirk of mine. Growing up, I had a Hula-Hoop named Leilani and a Chia Pet I called Alex. My first car I named Ruth, which I thought was clever because of the what the biblical Ruth told her mother-in-law Naomi: "Where you go, I will go." You get the point.

"Does it run?" Tai pushes against the front wheel with his toe.

"I'll have you know that Cletus holds the world record in the five-hundred-meter dash."

"Hayley." He gives me a deadpan look.

I make my face a mirror of his. "Tai."

He rakes a hand through his hair. He's nervous for me. I get it. I was nervous for me too.

Okay, fine. I'm still fairly nervous for me.

"Someone had to have driven it over here, right? I'm sure Cletus is hiding all his magic under the hood. An ugly duckling just awaiting his transformation."

Tai snorts.

"You know, I just so happen to be related to someone who does bodywork." I hop out of the driver's seat and shut the door behind me.

His eyes round, and he holds his hands up, palms out. "Get that idea out of your head right now. They are not the same thing."

"Poe-tae-toe, Poe-tah-toe."

"Potato, watermelon more like. Bodywork as in tattoos and bodywork as in car repair are not even in the same universe, and you know it."

I simply look at him. Fold my arms over my chest and look at him.

Tai and I are closer than Elliot—who is my actual brother—and I are. Part of the reason is probably an age thing. Tai and I are only six months apart, while Elliot didn't join the family until I was off to kindergarten. And part of the reason is probably the whole cheat-death thing. Tai had severe asthma growing up, and Aunt Missy worried that he would stop breathing at any second, which meant she tried to keep him in a little bubble as much as possible. When I got sick, Tai was one of the only people in my life who really got it. Who really understood the things I was thinking and feeling. We didn't necessarily have telepathy, but there were a lot of times when we'd know from a single look that the other needed a rescue.

I give that look to Tai now.

He sighs and hangs his head in defeat. "Fine. I'll see what I can do."

"You're the best." I grin and bounce on my toes, planting a kiss on his cheek.

"Yeah, yeah. I've heard that before. Usually right after you've talked me into doing something I don't want to do."

I laugh. "As if you'd have it any other way." I pat his shoulder and walk past him toward the library. The books won't reshelve themselves.

"Hey, Hales?"

I pause mid-step and turn. "Yeah?"

"Be careful when you're driving this thing around, won't you?"

I give him a reassuring smile. "Don't worry. Cletus is going to take good care of me."

3

Mayor Breckenbridge is in danger of being the recipient of another curse if he doesn't cut his shenanigans out.

I am beyond tired, which is making me irritable, but our prestigious mayor isn't helping anything. I was up past midnight last night trying to put together the bulletins for all four of Little Creek's churches. The office assistant they share came down with the flu, and someone mentioned how I'm always eager to volunteer, so when Pastor Jordan called asking if I'd be willing to help them out in a pinch, I couldn't say no, even though I really didn't have the time nor the energy. I can barely keep my eyes open now, but at least I have a nice big checkmark in my notebook next to yesterday's date.

Martha leans toward me and whispers, "How many pictures do you think he's made poor Peggy Sue take?"

I'm not sure why she's being careful with her volume. I'm beginning to think the only thing Mayor Breckenbridge can hear is the sound of his own voice.

"I really wish we'd wrapped it in a ribbon I could've cut," he complains. "Or had a bottle of champagne I could have smashed on its hull—er, fender. That would've made a splendid picture."

"Yes, sir." Peggy Sue doesn't bother removing her camera from in front of her face to answer.

Little Creek doesn't have what people outside our small town would call a newspaper, but we do have Peggy Sue Sturgis and the printer in her basement. From gossip column to classifieds to investigative journalism pieces, Peggy Sue is a one-woman, one-sheet, knows-all tells-all. No doubt our distinguished mayor is hoping for a full spread on how he's already on top of fulfilling his campaign promises so he can slack off the rest of his term.

I turn to Evangeline, swallowing down a yawn. "Next year I'm campaigning for Kitty Purry to be mayor. If the city of Idyllwild in California can have a golden retriever as mayor, Little Creek can elect your Ragdoll cat."

Evangeline snorts. "As if Kitty Purry would settle for anything less than a throne. She already thinks she's a queen. If you give her an ounce of power, she'll turn into even more of a tyrant."

"Are you sure you're capturing my good side, Peggy Sue?"

I roll my eyes and cross my arms. "Tai should be in these pictures. Cletus looked like he was about to join the zombie apocalypse before my cousin did his magic. Now he's the vehicle equivalent of Eliza Doolittle. A daytime talk show–worthy transformation that would fool anyone. It burns my britches that Mayor Breckenbridge is taking the credit when it's not due him."

"Tai is really fantastic, isn't he?" Evangeline's voice has gone off to dreamland, its new permanent residence whenever she talks about Tai.

I roll my eyes again. "I can't agree with you when you say it like that."

She smirks, and I just shake my head.

The truth is, Tai has outdone himself. Yes, he'd grumbled that the two types of bodywork weren't even remotely the same, but his finished product would've convinced anyone that they were. Instead of rust and dirt and years of grime and neglect on display, he'd put on a fresh coat of paint in the same shade of blue that covers the library card nestled in his wallet. He'd even hand-painted stacks of books with colorful bindings along the side with the word *Bookmobile* in blocky font.

Mayor Breckenbridge pivots and holds his hands out in a Vanna White pose.

"Okay, that's enough," I mumble before marching toward Cletus. I paste on my best customer service smile, the one I use with especially difficult patrons.

I tap the mayor on the arm. "Thank you so much for your generosity, Mayor. I'm sure Peggy Sue here will let all the good townspeople know just the kind of leader you are."

Mayor Breckenbridge puffs out his chest like a proud peacock.

Guess he missed the slices of sarcasm I slipped in there for him to chew on.

"But I know how much serving the neighboring communities means to you and how much vision and pride you've put into this illustrious bookmobile"—guess Martha's tidbit about the Greek meaning of Cletus has stuck in my brain—"and I know you don't want to see its maiden voyage delayed for any reason."

"No, no, of course not." He pats his ample belly, then seems to really look at me for the first time even though all us librarians have been out here watching the spectacle he's been making out of himself for the last twenty minutes.

Ryan, our supervisor who mainly works with us remotely from his office at the main regional branch, has come for his once-a-month personal check-in and offered to oversee operations inside while Evangeline, Martha, and I watch the circus in front of us. Considering the bookmobile is partially funded with county tax revenues and technically now property of the county library system, Ryan plays a role in its operations and wanted to be on site for its first route.

"Are you the librarian given the honor of steering our town's library into our community's rightful leading role?"

I grit my teeth but keep on smiling. "That's me."

His eyes light up. "Peggy Sue, get a picture of me handing over the keys to . . ."

"Hayley Holt," I supply.

"To Miss Holt." He digs around in his pocket and extracts a single key on a ring, then holds up the metal sphere of the ring in his pinched fingers, jiggling the key until I hold my hand out, palm up. He turns his head and beams for the camera.

When the hard metal connects with my palm, I curl my fingers around it. "Peggy Sue, would you be interested in some before and after photos of the bookmobile?"

Mayor Breckenbridge startles, shooting me a disquieted glance. He grumbles something under his breath, and I doubt the color staining his cheeks is from the temperatures that are rising with the sun.

"Oh!" Peggy Sue finally lowers her camera and looks at me directly. "That would be a nice—"

"Don't you have a route to get on, my dear?" The mayor bumps me toward the driver's door. "People are waiting for the books you're going to bring them, isn't that what you were saying?" He shoots Peggy Sue a sharp smile over his shoulder as he curls his fingers around my elbow.

I choke on my chuckle. Funny how he's all of a sudden concerned about a schedule. Also, he does realize I can just email Peggy Sue any pictures I have, right?

Evangeline and Martha sidle up to him like living bookends, matching looks of concern etched on their faces.

Martha hands me my bag. "The tablet and scanner are in there and fully charged."

I'll need both to sign patrons up for library cards, check out books, and show people how to use our website to request books that I can stock Cletus with and bring them on my next trip. Not to mention, I can set up a hotspot so everyone can have access to free Wi-Fi wherever I'm parked. I'll drive a route once a week, circling back to each destination once a month, so that I can also stay on top of my other duties at the library.

"Drive carefully," Evangeline adds. "It rained fairly hard last night."

Evangeline is always worried about rockslides after it rains. There are warning signs posted along the roads depicting large rocks falling on vehicles, and now she's scared one will come loose of the mountainside and crush her car under limestone and granite. The chances of that happening are probably less than finding a rare gem in one of the bags of dirt they sell at the tourist-trap mines in Pigeon Forge.

"I'll be fine," I assure her. I've been driving on these roads since before I even had a license, sitting on my daddy's lap and singing along to George Strait. I've never once had any issue with falling debris. Right now, she should be more worried about my drowsiness.

Her lips are pressed firm, but she manages to tilt them up in a semblance of a reassured gesture. She eyes me, then Mayor Breckenbridge. Me, then the mayor again. Her shoulders rise as she takes a deep breath, then turns her back to me and faces the mayor.

"You had a mechanic look the van over before you donated it, right?" She pitches her voice low to keep what she's saying from floating over to Peggy Sue. Probably in hopes that the mayor will be honest with her in case his answer would make him look bad in print.

He huffs and jerks his chin down and back, the extra skin around his jowls folding and layering over his thick neck. "Just what are you implying, young lady?"

"I'm not implying anything, Mayor. I just want to make sure Hayley is safe. That's all."

"Well, of course she is safe. Do you think I would do anything to put someone in my town in danger?"

Martha's gaze meets mine, and she lifts her brow. Did he

not see the condition Cletus was in when he first dropped the van off in the library's parking lot?

"My apologies." Evangeline turns and widens her eyes at me.

We're all wondering the same thing. Is Mayor Breckenbridge really that clueless, or is he simply being careless? Seriously, Kitty Purry for queen of Little Creek next year. I'll make her a tiny crown and scepter myself.

"I think we've got all we need, Peggy Sue. Thank you," Mayor Breckenbridge calls out. He tips an imaginary hat to Martha, Evangeline, and me. "Good day, ladies." With that, he turns on his booted heel and strides toward the municipal building one street over.

"Here, I checked this out for you." Martha hands me a paperback by Lynn Austin, with a young blond woman on the cover, a faraway look in her eyes. She's clutching a small stack of books to her chest, log cabins nestled in the woods.

I scan the title. *Wonderland Creek.*

"It's about a packhorse librarian in Kentucky during the Great Depression. Thought you might enjoy it during any downtime you have on your route. You know, a whole look-at-the-women-who've-gone-before type of thing."

I caress the cover with my thumb. "Thanks, Martha." I clear my throat and put on a brave face. "All right. I've dillydallied enough. Time to hit the road."

Evangeline and Martha take a step back so I can close the door. The key fits into the ignition, and the engine cranks up with enough coughs and sputters to put a chain smoker to shame. I take a cleansing breath, muting the ominous music starting to play in my mind and dubbing in some positive vibes instead. "You're the bookmobile Little Engine That Could, Cletus. Let's show them what you've got." *And that I've got nothing to worry about.*

I put the van into gear and pull out of the parking lot. My first stop is Turkey Grove, a community that doesn't even have a dot on a map. There's only one access road that I know of, and it's so narrow and riddled with potholes that cars need to turn sideways and suck in their guts in order to pass each other. I'm sincerely praying that I don't meet up with any vehicles coming the opposite direction.

I've only been to Turkey Grove once, to hike to a nearby waterfall. All that I remember is a mechanic's garage, a general store, a trailer park, a church, and miles and miles of uncorrupted nature. I saw laundry hanging on lines to dry and outhouses that were still in use. It was a bit like stepping back in time. Honestly, I won't be surprised if today will be someone's first time accessing the internet.

I've been driving about forty minutes, adrenaline from nerves kicking the sleepiness out of my system better than caffeine could have, when all of a sudden, Cletus's clutch slips, creating a squeaky, grinding noise.

My pulse spikes as my stomach jumps into my throat. "Don't give up on me now, Cletus. You can do this." I grip the wheel so tight my knuckles turn white.

A burning stench fills my nostrils, singeing the inside of my nose. The dashboard lights up like Christmas, then blinks with the heartbeat of a college rage party.

"No, no, no. Come on, Cletus!"

What should I do? Should I try to turn around and make it back to Little Creek? Keep going and hope to crawl our way to the mechanic before Cletus completely peters out?

Whether it's the right thing to do or not, I stop the van and pull out my cell phone. At least there's one bar of reception, which I'm surprised but thankful for. If nothing else, I can call a tow truck and get a ride back home.

Cletus gives a loud cough, a shudder that I feel all the way down my spine, then dies with a puff of smoke curling from under the hood.

Tow truck it is.

A buzz not unlike an insistent bee right next to your ear fills the space around me with a physical tremble. Something isn't right, but I can't pinpoint what's wrong exactly. The quiet hum becomes a distant rumble in the air, growing in volume until the vibrations are shaking my teeth together. An earthquake? I push open the van door and jump out of the driver's seat. Outside, the noise is even louder.

And that's when I spot the boulders tumbling down the mountainside behind me, dislodging more rubble and debris as they plummet to the ground. My hands shoot out to cover my gasping mouth, and in the back of my mind, I recognize the small voice wondering if this is what it was like for the Israelites watching Jericho's walls crumble in front of them. I'm far enough away to not be in danger of being crushed or hit with a stray rock, but it's hard to process what my eyes are witnessing.

As quickly as the whole thing started, the rockslide stops. The air is coated in a dusty haze that slowly dissipates on the gentle breeze. When the dust settles, a dam of boulders the size of cars and stacked as tall as a house lays across the section of road that I had just driven across. If Cletus had given up the ghost even thirty seconds earlier, I might have died right along with him.

4

'd been right to judge Cletus by his appearance. All his outward makeover did was allow me to be catfished. Like books with gorgeous covers that make you want to read them immediately but the product inside doesn't live up to the pretty packaging. Book catfishing is the worst.

My gaze travels over the broken-down bookmobile, smoke still curling in wisps from the seams of the hood. Okay, maybe there are worse things.

I look around at my surroundings, trying to find any landmarks that will jog my memory about how close I am to Turkey Grove. Maybe I can walk the rest of the way and see if the mechanic at the service station can get Cletus up and running again.

Although with the road blocked, getting him running again will solve only one of my current and dire problems. Until the Department of Transportation clears the boulders, there's no way that I know of to make it back to Little Creek.

I glare at Cletus, then swing open the driver's door with more force than is needed. Even though I know it's futile, I turn the key in the ignition, driven by a mounting desperation and the ill-fitting feeling of irony.

Nothing happens. Not so much as a single click of the starter.

I twist the key again. "Come on," I encourage through gritted teeth.

As expected, Cletus isn't suddenly resurrecting from the grave like some kind of vehicular Lazarus.

I sigh and let my arm lower in defeat.

My brain swings around and slaps some sense into me, reminding me that *hello, you had cell reception just a few minutes ago, dummy. You can literally call for help.*

Right. No need to jump into the deep end of the drama pool.

I pull my phone back out and check that, yes, there is still at least one bar. I tap open the maps app and note my location, zooming in and scrolling around to try and find Turkey Grove amid the green specks of trees and ridges of elevation gain. I don't find the hollow quickly, which means walking is out of the question. I'm not worried about getting lost since I can follow the road, but the strappy sandals I'm wearing weren't made for backcountry hikes, and a twisted ankle is so not what I need at the moment. But with the day I'm having, it's exactly what luck would dole out.

I click out of the app and tap on the web browser icon, waiting for it to load. After what seems like forever but is likely less than a full minute, a fresh search page opens. I type in *towing services near me* and click allow when a window pops up asking my permission to use my current location.

Another stretch of waiting, then the page changes, showing a small portion of a map with red pins and a list of the nearest towing companies. Levi's Service Center is at the top, with a pin on the map that makes me think it's the mechanic in Turkey Grove.

I click on the number and call. The phone rings, and I suppress saying the mantra playing in my mind out loud. *Pick up, pick up, pick up.* On the fourth ring there's a click on the line, and I feel a flood of relief.

"Hello?" I jump in, not even waiting for a greeting from the person on the other end. "Hi, my name is Hayley Holt. I'm a librarian from Little Creek, and I drive the new bookmobile that was supposed to be there in Turkey Grove today."

I pause out of politeness and because I realize I should at least give this person whom I'm assuming is Levi or Levi's office employee a chance to respond, even though I want to say *I need help* and *Please come and get me as fast as possible in case I lose this single bar of cell reception.*

There's a noise that sounds sort of like a grunt. Maybe the guy on the other end has a few bolts or other mechanic-y things he's holding between his lips because his hands are buried in an engine and he can't talk at the moment. I don't know. I don't even know how to change my dash clock after Daylight Savings, but the scenario seems plausible to me just the same so I'm going with it.

"Anyway," I plow on, "the bookmobile broke down, and a rockslide is blocking the road back to Little Creek, which means I'm completely stranded here. I'm so happy there's reception or I'd really have found myself in a pickle. But thankfully I was able to call you. Sorry, I know I'm rambling, but now that you know the situation, do you think you can tow the bookmobile to your shop and possibly get it running again? I don't know what the road I'm on is called, but it's the one that leads to Turkey Grove from US-64."

I've used all the breath in my lungs to push out that run-on bit of information, so I take a moment to breathe in and refill my chest with slightly acrid air due to Cletus's own dying puffs of smoke. The silence stretches, and I open my mouth to ask if he's still there before a deep, gravelly voice that doesn't sound like it's been used in hours, possibly even days, says, "Okay."

That's it. Just the one word. Two syllables. Like he's charged by the letter and budgeting his allowance. No *Oh, yes, I know where that is.* No *No problem, I'll be there in a jiffy.* No *A rockslide? Are you all right, ma'am?* Just a gruff, clipped *"Okay."*

"Okay," I answer back, too off-kilter to think of anything else to say. There's a click in my ear, and the call is disconnected without any sort of by-your-leave.

Slowly I pull the phone away from my ear, staring in bewilderment at the screen as if it's the Beast's magic mirror and I can see the man I'd been speaking to through it.

Beggars can't be choosers, and customer service is the least of my concerns at the moment. I couldn't care less if he isn't talkative and charming as long as he can fix Cletus and give me a ride into town so I can figure out what my next move is.

I tap open my contacts. I need to let Evangeline and Martha know what's going on so they don't worry when I don't show up later today. Just as my finger is about to touch the library's phone number, my single bar of reception disappears, replaced with four dots and the words *No Service*. I guess the magic of having any sort of reception vanished like the fairy godmother's did at the stroke of midnight. Now all there is to do is wait.

I pull out the book that Martha had shoved into my hands and flip it over to read the description on the back cover. I'm well into the third chapter when I finally hear the rumble of an engine and the pop of small pebbles being crunched under tires. I grab one of the library's bookmarks and slide it between the pages, closing the book.

A big blue tow truck rolls toward me, dust kicked up in a trailing cloud behind it. The driver's door protests when I open it and slide my feet to the ground to wait and watch. I'm one hundred percent blaming the weightless feeling of relief for the full-blown grin curving the lower half of my face and the small wave I give the approaching tow truck.

Who, from this day forward, I have dubbed Sir Galahad, because he has rescued a damsel in distress like any good knight would and because I'd bet money no one else has named him yet.

Sir Galahad slows to a stop about twenty feet from Cletus. His diesel engine drowns out the soft chirps of birdsong and the occasional rustle of a breeze moving through the leaves. The driver kills the engine, and a moment of loud silence stretches before an intrepid tufted titmouse lets out a high-pitched trill.

The tow truck's door opens, and I begin moving forward with a greeting at the ready on my upturned lips. A pair of steel-toed work boots plant themselves on the ground, visible beneath the bottom edge of the door. My gaze travels up, past the white-lettered decal with LEVI in blocky font, over the handle protruding from the side of the door. Said door swings closed, and I freeze. Gaze—frozen. Ready greeting—frozen. Heart? Yep, that's frozen in my chest too.

The man standing before me is . . .

Oh, for hootenannies' sake. I manage to blink, though that doesn't do much good. The man is still there. Still massively looming, towering like an oak masquerading as a mere mortal male specimen.

I've never really thought about the differences of tall when associating the description with a person. I'm an average height for a woman, a modest 5'5". Most men are taller than me by at least a few inches, but then there are those athletes in sports such as basketball, swimming, and volleyball who are known for their impressive height and dwarf anyone standing next to them.

Nuh-uh. Even they would feel miniature in this man's presence.

And it's not just his height. It's his breadth too, with shoulders that would make a lineman from a professional football team jealous. All at once, adjectives flood my mind. Huge. Immense. Enormous. Substantial.

I swallow past a lump in my throat and push my gaze up.

Yeah, no. His face is not an opposite from the rest of his body.

35

Not a soft or reassuring place to land. The hard lines that form him continue, although they are hidden beneath a scruffy layer of thick facial hair. A slash of his lips peek through between the coarse hairs, a straight nose rises above, followed by a pair of amber eyes so light they almost look like liquid gold, though in a piercing and sharp way. The melting this pair of eyes could cause is not in the romantic swoon connotation. It's more a don't-touch-if-you-don't-want-to-get-burned warning sign.

More adjectives march their way to the forefront of my brain. Danger. Peril. Threat.

Because, hello, I am a woman alone in a secluded area with a man who could easily overpower me with his pinkie finger if he wanted to. The fact that he's standing there, unsmiling, gruff, and foreboding is doing nothing at all to put me at ease. I'm sure every woman has grown up on cautionary tales such as this, and the sage advice passed down through the ages of placing your keys in between your fisted fingers to use as a weapon will do me absolutely no good. Especially since I left the keys in the ignition.

I bite the inside of my cheek hard enough that a metallic taste fills my mouth. The downside of having an active imagination is that it can run away with me pretty quickly. I take mine by the metaphorical reins and yank hard until it comes to a screeching halt.

The man before me is as big and imposing as a bear, but why does he have to be a scary, ferocious, predatory grizzly bear? Why can't he be a soft, fluffy, cuddly teddy bear?

That's it. He's nothing but a big, squishy marshmallow that looks like he could snap someone's arm in half like a twig but would really never hurt a fly.

I smile brighter and hold out my hand. "Thank you so much for rescuing me. I have no idea what I would've done if you hadn't been able to come help me out like this. I'm Hayley, by the way."

His golden gaze barely flicks to mine before returning to over my shoulder, effectively dismissing me in a fraction of a second. He does shake my hand, but like with the eye contact, his grasp is there for only a moment before it's gone again.

"Levi Redding." It's the same underused voice that I'd heard on the phone. Like the sound was pulled across a gravel road before reaching my ears.

I clear my throat and wave in Cletus's general direction. "Well, there's the culprit. I left the keys in the ignition, although I doubt they'll do you any good. Do you need help with anything, or should I just get out of your hair and let you do your thing?"

He looks down at me with an inscrutable expression, the longer strands of his dark-brown hair slowly falling across his forehead with the languidness of maple syrup. "You'd better wait in the cab."

I'm not sure what surprises me more—hearing a complete sentence in that deep and throaty voice of his or the fact that he follows the words up by walking around the hood of the tow truck and opening the passenger's door for me.

My feet slowly tread the same path as if my sandals are all of a sudden weighed down with red clay mud. I step around him and—okay, no contest, *this* is the most surprising part—he holds out one of his massive paws to help me climb up into the cab.

Definitely a big ol' teddy bear. A true southern gentleman in manners if not charm.

The last dregs of worry that had pooled in my stomach seep from my muscles. Generations of vigilance that has been ingrained into female DNA is obviously not needed around Levi Redding. While still more-than-slightly intimidating, this giant of a man isn't displaying any warning signs that he intends to physically overpower me and, as Mrs. Cline at the nursing home would say, steal my virtue.

I set my fingers in his palm, and my tiny digits are quickly swallowed. Next thing I know, I'm very nearly catapulted into the cab. One minute my feet are on solid ground, the next they aren't. I have never been so effectively manhandled in my life.

Levi's shaking out his hand where he stands to the side of the open door, wiping his palm along the leg of his washed-out blue coveralls as if trying to rid himself of my touch.

Rude!

He shuts the door in my face just as I'm sputtering in offended outrage. I watch him march back around the front of the tow truck again, and I clench my jaw. The driver's door opens, and he slides into the seat, not even having to use the runner to step up on. That loud, rumbly diesel engine is brought back to life, then he turns the truck around so Sir Galahad's back faces Cletus's front. He exits again without a word, then there's banging and movement coming from behind me as he hooks up one vehicle to the other.

I look down at my hands to see if maybe I have something on my fingers and that's the reason he'd wiped his hands after touching me. A little peanut butter left over from my sandwich at lunch, perhaps.

Nope. They're clean as a whistle.

My lips turn down as I glance at the side mirror and watch as he hefts a hook the size of my head—it probably weighs just as much as I do—as if it's nothing at all. I wait to see if he wipes his fingers after handling the greasy hook.

He does not.

Guess it's just my touch he finds repulsive.

That should relieve me, right? The fact that I repel this man instead of attract him? I'm solidified in the safe zone when just a handful of minutes before I was worried about the threat of assault. That is the normal reaction. Relief. But I must have more female pride than good sense because against all logic there's a feeling of hurt caught right behind my breastbone.

Okay, whoa. I am making way too much out of this. What does it even matter? He's just the mechanic. The tow truck guy. The only interactions I have to have with him are right now when I need a ride into town and one other time after Cletus is fixed. That's it. I don't, for any reason, need him to like me.

Even if I've done absolutely nothing for him not *to like me*, a small voice in my head whispers petulantly.

To keep any other arguing thoughts from being able to express themselves, I reach forward and turn on the radio, flicking through the channels until the chorus to "Good Morning Baltimore" streams through the speakers.

Two songs later, the driver's door opens and Levi plants himself behind the wheel.

"All set?" I ask, giving him my sweetest smile.

Okay, so I may have a problem with wanting people to like me. As far as fatal flaws go, it could be worse.

He merely grunts in response and puts the truck into gear, pulling forward.

Alright, then. I may not be a curmudgeon, but I'm beginning to suspect Levi Redding is.

I half expect him to either turn the radio off or change the channel. I can't really picture the giant burly man to be a big showtunes fan. But he doesn't make any move toward the radio knob and doesn't voice a single objection.

I study the man beside me out of the corner of my eye, trying not to be too obvious that I'm attempting to figure him out. I never want to jump to conclusions with people I meet. One never knows the backstory of another, what has happened in their life to shape them into the person they are or the circumstances that have led to their current behaviors. Fictional characters sometimes get a better deal than people in real life because readers are allowed to see the conflicts and motivations on the page, understand the reasons they are the way they are. Real people are too rarely afforded the same consideration, even though we all have backstories of our own.

Jennifer Hudson is belting out a high note when I turn to the taciturn mechanic who hasn't spared me a single glance, much less a word. "Is there another road out of Turkey Grove, by chance?"

A muscle in his jaw ticks, and he does what I thought he'd have done already. He turns off the radio, then flicks me a quick look in the ensuing silence. "No." He turns the music back on.

"Really? Not even one that would be a super long detour but would allow someone to come and get me?"

His hand reaches out and clicks the knob to kill the music again. "There's a Forest Service road, but it's impassable right now."

The lyrics to "Defying Gravity" fill the cab when he clicks the radio on.

I have so many questions. Why is it impassable? Even to a vehicle with four-wheel drive? How are the residents in Turkey Grove going to survive if everyone is trapped without the means of getting to any type of service? What am *I* going to do? If there's no way to have anyone come pick me up, then I'm stuck in Turkey Grove for the foreseeable future.

"Okay, what about a hotel I can stay at? An Airbnb or Vrbo?"

He clicks the music off again. "No."

I eye him and then the radio, my brows pulling down in confusion. A theory is developing but not fully formed.

He turns the radio back on. An instrumental interlude bangs out in the space between us.

I wait a few beats, then ask, "If there isn't a hotel or short-term rental, do you have any ideas on where I can stay? I'll settle for a hobbit house or a shoe, even though I'm not necessarily an old woman to live in it yet."

His jaw muscle ticks again, and the vein along the back on his hand bulges.

So, he doesn't like poor attempts at humor. Got it.

Slowly, almost as if the lack of speed were deliberate, he reaches out a fourth time and kills the music. He takes in a long breath, his nostrils flaring as he does so. This time when he looks at me, it's not fleeting. He pins me with his intense golden gaze. "You have to stay with me."

5

*L*evi Redding watched as the small woman's rich brown eyes widened a second time in disbelief beneath the curtain of thick bangs the color of watered-down strawberry wine.

He hadn't been surprised by her initial reaction to him, a look of shock tinted with a hint of fear freezing her features. After all, that was the same look he'd been receiving since he'd turned fifteen and shot up quicker than a stalk of corn after a good rain, finding himself towering over every other person he met.

At first, he'd tried to make accommodations to ease their distress. If people were frightened because of his size, he'd decided he'd simply try to make himself smaller. But no matter how much he willed it, he couldn't shrink, and all hunching his shoulders did was make his back ache. It was a pursuit in futility, especially when he had another growth spurt less than a year later, topping him off at 6'7" and tipping the scales toward three hundred pounds.

It didn't seem fair, the fact he'd tried so hard to make things easier for others when they never once offered him the same courtesy in return. It was about that time he accepted facts as they were: People didn't like Levi, and unsurprisingly, that was perfectly fine with him. Because the truth was, Levi Redding really didn't like people all that much either.

Levi returned his focus to the road. This stretch was fairly straight, and he doubted they'd pass another car. However, there were still potholes to avoid, and one never knew when a deer or a squirrel would dart in front of their path.

Besides, he had no idea how long it would take before the sprite in the passenger's seat would start flapping those cupid's-bow lips of hers again.

"What do you mean, I have to stay with you? And isn't that something you should discuss with your wife first?" Her wide eyes now stared at him through narrow, accusing slits.

"I mean," he said slowly, "that I have an extra bedroom you can use." He probably should have phrased it this way the first time. As an invitation instead of a demand. Then again, she really did *have* to stay with him. There weren't any other options that he was aware of. Not so much as a Best Western within an hour of Turkey Grove.

He reached up and scratched his jaw, the hairs of his beard tickling his fingers. "And I'm not married." He quickly glanced at her knitted fingers, noticing the absence of a ring there too.

"Thank you for the offer." Her voice wavered, unsteady and grasping. "But I'm sure I can come up with something."

Like what? He wanted to ask but held his tongue. Turkey Grove's population was such that the youngest of elementary school kids could be in charge of counting the census. Even then, its residents were scattered across the hills and dales. Chances were, someone probably did have another spare bedroom she could use, but he wasn't really acquainted with any of his neighbors well enough to know for sure. Unless someone needed their car serviced, he tended to keep to himself.

"There's a store, right?" she asked. "I think I recall a general store in the heart of town."

Levi grunted. Yeah, there was a building that sold things

run by Jack MacDonald, but Levi had never actually found anything he needed on the shelves. Most of the items sold were odds and ends that didn't make much sense. Instead, Levi drove over to Chattanooga once a month to buy supplies in bulk from a warehouse store. Otherwise, he just did without.

"If nothing else, I can purchase a tent. I'm sure there's a campground nearby where I can pitch it."

She was sure of a lot of things and wrong on all accounts.

With a sigh, Levi pressed on the brake and slowed the truck to a stop. He'd offered to house her, and she'd turned him down. He should leave her to her own devices.

He should, but he wouldn't.

Despite the fact that he didn't like people and having Miss Holt living under the same roof as him would be more than an inconvenience—it would be downright painful—he was a man who strived to do the right thing. Not helping when someone needed help was decidedly *not* the right thing.

"Why are we stopping?" She peered at him warily again.

It was a small mercy that whatever soap she used—thankfully nothing floral but something with a fresh subtlety to it—hadn't caused his skull to grip his head in a vice. But it was only a matter of time. Attending church as a kid had been torture because of all the ladies and their perfumes. He'd never been able to be within a few feet of a woman without the scent of her causing him a massive headache.

Sometimes in more ways than one.

He located his house key on the key ring and twisted it off the hoop of metal, holding it out to her.

"What's this?" she asked, eyeing his offering with skepticism.

"The key to my house."

Her brows pulled so low that her bangs no longer hid them. "Why are you giving me your house key?"

He averted his gaze and tossed the key on her lap. "Just take it. I'll sleep at the shop."

She seemed to consider that. "You have a bed at your garage?"

"No." He pressed his foot against on the accelerator. They couldn't get to Turkey Grove fast enough.

"Then where will you sleep?"

Instead of answering, he made a low guttural sound at the back of his throat. She could decipher the response however she wanted.

His sisters liked to tease him that he was no better than a caveman with his grunts, but he didn't care. He didn't feel the need to add to the chaos of endless chatter that was his family. He'd read a study once that said the average person spoke about fifteen thousand words a day. Multiply that by his four sisters and that's sixty thousand words. Which were often spoken on top of one another. As in, at the same time. Levi figured if there was an average number of words a person could say in a day, then there was probably an average number of words a person could hear in a day. Growing up, it had felt like he'd filled that quota by breakfast. It was no wonder he relished the quiet now that he was an adult and could control his environment.

"I'm not going to kick you out of your own home," Hayley said firmly.

Levi flexed his fingers over the steering wheel instead of tightening his grip. He'd figured from her telephone call that the librarian could give each and every one of his sisters a run for their money on daily word count. Sometimes he hated when he was proven right.

Not one to argue, he merely turned his head and pinned her with a look. Something on his face made her swallow, the columns of muscles in her elegant throat bobbing. She shifted in her seat as if she were uncomfortable with his direct regard, leaning away from him.

That time, his fingers did tighten around the wheel. "I'm not going to hurt you," he ground out as he turned his eyes back to the road, not checking to see if she believed him or not.

Likely not. He couldn't blame her. In appearances alone, she was the size of a woodland sprite and he was the giant troll, which, consequently, always got a bad rap in all the fairy tales. Words weren't going to reassure her, no matter how many times he reiterated them. Besides, the thought of repeating himself made him want to stop his ears up with some cotton.

With one hand still on the wheel, he leaned over and opened the glove compartment. The multi-tool knife he kept there lay on top. Grabbing the Leatherman, he pulled it out, then gently tossed it onto the librarian's lap. Maybe having a means of defense in her hands would make her feel safer.

"Do you always throw things at people?" she surprised him by asking.

He ignored the question. "Now that you're armed with a weapon, maybe you won't be afraid of me."

He could feel her scrutiny on his profile. Couldn't have been able to feel it more even if she'd reached out and traced the outline of his jaw, threading her fingers into his beard. It made the muscles in his back tense and an awareness wash over his skin.

One should not be able to physically feel a look like that. It went against the laws of physics.

Slowly, she reached out and reopened the glovebox, placing the multi-tool back inside, never once removing her gaze from his person. "I'm not afraid of you, Mr. Redding."

She delivered the pronouncement so simply, as if she were stating a well-known fact, that he actually believed her.

"Levi." His throat closed around the last syllable, his voice strained. The only times he talked this much were when his family forced themselves on him.

It was utterly exhausting.

She inclined her chin. "I'm not going to kick you out of your own home, Levi. So as long as this is not a one-bed situation, I'll accept your hospitality in letting me stay with you."

Maybe other guys wouldn't know what in the world this woman was pattering on about, but other guys didn't read as much as Levi did. He didn't like people, but that aversion was relegated to the real-life specimens. Fictional characters he rather enjoyed. He counted many of them among his closest friends, spending hours of his free time in their presence without a single irritation.

Which is why Levi knew the one-bed trope. A literary device authors used to throw the hero and heroine together in forced proximity, the two often finding themselves with arms and legs wrapped up in each other when the morning dawned.

Yeah, that wasn't happening.

"No one sleeps in my bed but me." The thought of having to share such a personal space so closely with someone made the muscle near his temple throb.

"I'm just teasing you, big man. But seriously, thank you for housing me. I promise you won't even know that I'm there."

She shouldn't make promises she couldn't keep. Especially ones so easily broken as this. Because there was no way on God's green earth that Levi wouldn't know every second of every day that this woman was under the same roof as him. She would be everywhere. Her voice echoing down the hall and ringing in his ears. Her scent hanging on every particle of air that he breathed into his lungs. Her presence a ghost that shadowed and haunted him, driving him slowly out of his mind.

But he only had to endure her until one of the roads got cleared. And if the Department of Transportation took their sweet time, he had a winch he could use to help them along.

6

"Shoot. Still no service." Hayley held her phone up at different angles, scowling at the screen with each change in position.

Didn't matter how she contorted her body, she wasn't going to find any reception out here. No telling how long she'd have had to wait until one of the residents of Turkey Grove happened to cross her path. Even with their limited resources with modern conveniences, the people of Turkey Grove were pretty self-sufficient and didn't venture out into the bigger cities all that often. Miss Holt could have ended up waiting for ages before anyone stumbled upon her. Truthfully, Levi was surprised she'd managed to find any reception to call him in the first place. Surprised, but mostly grateful as well.

"Hopefully no one is worried about me." She tilted her head. "Then again, no one knows about the rockslide, so why would they be? I wish I could've called and let them know what was happening when I still had signal."

Mostly grateful. The woman could talk the ears off a whole field of corn. A few more hours of being spared her idle chitchat wouldn't have hurt anybody. Especially Levi.

"Would you mind if I used your landline once we get into

town?" She placed her phone screen down on her lap and turned toward Levi.

"No."

Her mouth pursed to the side. "No, you won't mind, or no, I can't use the phone?"

Levi sighed. This woman was going to plunge to the bottom depths of his well of patience. "No, I don't mind."

"Thank you." She returned her gaze out the windshield.

The next sigh out of Levi's mouth was one of relief. Finally, a moment of reprieve. Well, as much as he was going to get with the constant hum of the engine and the high-pitched whistle from the passenger window not being rolled up all the way. There was never complete silence around him, but controlling the noise input to functioning levels was something he'd learned to be constantly vigilant with.

"So, what's your story?" Hayley pivoted in her seat so her hips faced him.

For all that was good and right, he did not want this woman's full attention on him.

"I don't have a story," he gritted out. Could she not go without speaking for longer than three seconds?

She laughed, a musical sound that, surprisingly, didn't instantly grate on his nerves. He noted the anomaly, then reflexively flinched anyway. His sister, Nova, tittered when she laughed. The sound was like ice shards pricking at his brain. He'd determined never to do anything that could be construed as funny whenever she was around just to spare himself the torture.

Now that he thought of it, he made sure not to be humorous around anyone. To be on the safe side.

When was the last time he'd truly heard laughter, even his own?

Hayley smiled at him as if he'd told an award-winning joke. He hadn't. Although he kind of wanted to now. Just to hear her laugh again. See if the sound and his reaction stayed consistent. If the soothing warmth that had filled him with the rich tones would come again.

He pressed his lips together instead.

"Everyone has a story," Hayley insisted.

Did they? Debatable. Even if they did, were they all worth telling? He doubted his was. "No."

She hummed, unconvinced. "If you don't tell me, then you're going to leave me no choice but to make one up about you, and I might get some facts wrong." Her pause was poignant as she waited for him to jump in.

Let her make up whatever story she wanted about him. People had been doing it his whole life, so what did he care? She'd probably come up with something more interesting than the truth anyway.

He glanced down at his watch. They still had at least ten minutes before he could leap out of this cab and bury himself under the bookmobile's hood. She could use the phone in the garage's office, and he could close the door on her voice and finally get some peace.

Even if hers was probably the nicest voice he'd ever heard in his life.

"Once upon a time there was a mechanic named Levi Redding . . ." She let her words drift at the end, again offering the conversation to him to pick up and carry on.

She waited.

His jaw ticked like a metronome counting the seconds. The engine rumbled. The air through the cracked window whistled.

She huffed a breath, whether from exasperation or amusement he had no idea. "You know what? I've changed my mind. I'm going to wait for you to tell me yourself."

You're going to be waiting a long time.

"Okay, changing the subject. Would you mind stopping by

the general store when we get to town? I didn't exactly plan to be stranded, so I didn't pack an overnight bag. I need to get essential things like a toothbrush, soap, shampoo and conditioner, that sort of stuff."

He still hadn't felt any fingers of a headache clench into his skull even with Hayley being only a foot away, but he knew the kind of products that Jack MacDonald stocked in his store. Like soap with actual flowers crushed inside. Just walking down the aisle where the artisan bars were shelved made his head immediately pound like a cartoon anvil had fallen on him. Levi had no reason not to assume the shampoos and conditioners would be any better.

"No."

Hayley huffed again, and again he couldn't decipher if the sound was exasperation, amusement, or a little bit of both. "I have never needed an interpreter for the simple word *no* before, but here I am. Levi, do you mean, no, you don't mind stopping by the store, or no, you won't take me?"

He slipped the thumb of his left hand into his palm, wrapped the rest of his fingers around the stubby digit, and squeezed. "You don't need to go to the store. I have everything at the house."

She raised a skeptical brow. "You have an extra toothbrush lying around?"

"Yes."

She seemed to think a minute. "What if I need . . . other things?"

Other things? Oh. Right. There were some products that wouldn't normally be stocked by a bachelor that a woman might need. Lucky for her, Levi was prepared in that department too.

"I have feminine hygiene products if you need them, and if that's what you're referring to. Sisters," he said by way of explanation. His siblings didn't visit often, but he was always prepared for when one of them decided to descend upon him.

Hayley's mouth parted. "That's the most you've spoken at one time since I've met you and it was about tampons." Laughter trickled past her lips.

A warm blanket of comfort wrapped around his shoulders at the sound, releasing some of the tension that had been gathering in his chest. Her laughter was like sunshine on a brisk autumn morning, seeping into his skin and soaking into his bones.

His gaze pulled toward her, and he stared in wonderment. In bewilderment. This woman was unarguably having a rotten day. Her vehicle had broken down. She was stranded in a backwoods town until who knew when, with none of her own things, forced to stay with a stranger who had the personality of a grumpy hermit, and she was laughing. He had made her laugh. How had that even happened?

He caught himself staring and forced his gaze back to the road. No need to make her even more uncomfortable around him by his unwanted attention.

"And look at you, you're not even a little embarrassed by talking about the functions of the female reproductive system." She tapped her chin, her eyes gleaming. "Oh, there is definitely a story, and I can't wait to hear it."

"Sisters," he reiterated.

"Mm-hmm," she agreed, more placating than anything.

Let her think whatever she wanted. Didn't matter to him as long as she didn't walk around his house smelling like some grandmother's poisonous potpourri. It had taken him long enough to figure out which men's brands and scents didn't cause him to have a reaction; he wasn't about to welcome a return experience with an unwanted houseguest staying an interminable amount of time.

Even if her laughter was the strands that sunshine danced to.

After what seemed like hours but was only the time it took to travel twelve miles, the silhouettes of Turkey Grove's few establishments dotted between the trunks of red maples and sweetgum trees. Besides his service station and Jack MacDonald's general store, there was also Aunt May's Diner, Hillman's grocer-slash-pharmacy, and, of course, the church.

"Your town is so quaint."

Levi grunted. Turkey Grove wasn't really big enough to be considered a town, but that was just semantics. Plus, he liked his community the way it was. There weren't many places left where the big cities weren't expanding, becoming obese with the growing population and spilling over into suburbs and what were once small towns. He liked the fact that cell phones didn't get reception in this neck of the woods. That Wi-Fi was a luxury and not a necessity and that some of his neighbors still referred to the internet as "the interwebs" and had zero social media accounts. He liked that instead of interstate traffic, he could awaken to soft birdcalls on a still morning with dew fresh on the ground. That instead of listening to noisy neighbors through a thin apartment wall, he could hear the twigs snap in his backyard when a young deer family came to nibble on the tender shoots of grass.

He liked that he could go days without interacting with another human being. That, he liked the most.

"How long have you lived here?"

He flicked her a glance out of the corner of his eye.

She held up her hands in surrender.

Hmm. Maybe his glance had been more of a glare.

"Sorry. My daddy says I can talk the legs off a chair, and Mama calls me Chatty Cathy."

Levi squeezed his thumb again. Her parents weren't wrong on either account.

He slowed the truck as he neared the mechanic shop, released his hold on his thumb, and returned both hands to the wheel. He watched his side mirror as he took the turn wide, making sure that the bookmobile attached to the tow rigging would clear the ditch on the side. He swung the tow truck around and lined up the rear of the bookmobile to back it into the garage bay.

"Do you need any help? Should I get out and direct you, maybe?"

Levi threw the gear into park. Hayley reached toward the seat belt clipped at her side and unfastened it while Levi jumped out of the cab and marched around the hood of the truck. He could use her help. By giving him just a few moments when he didn't have to process her unceasing chatter.

Levi opened the passenger door and offered his hand to assist her down. It was a big step for anyone who wasn't him, and he didn't want her to stumble and hurt herself trying to get out, especially since there wasn't any way to get her to a hospital with the road blocked. Deborah Smith was a retired doctor who lived in a secluded cabin farther up the mountain, and people went to her every now and again, but it wasn't like she had an X-ray machine in her living room if Hayley broke her leg.

She didn't immediately put her hand in his. Instead, she regarded him with a pinched expression, her eyes level with his from her perch in the big rig. He let himself have a moment to indulge in the richness of her irises. They truly were a decadent pleasure, chocolate infused with bursts of honeycomb delight. The way her bangs traced the outline of her face acted as a frame for a masterpiece.

Levi Redding was a man of few words, but the speechlessness he felt while looking at this woman was akin to having the wind knocked out of him. Sudden. Gripping. And utterly, completely, unequivocally overwhelming.

He took in the narrowing of her lids as her gaze jumped from his face to his outstretched hand and back again. Was she still afraid of him? Did his size really cause her that much distress?

He opened his mouth to reassure her again that he would never harm her in any way when she slipped her delicate palm into his. On instinct, his fingers curled around her hand. Just as with the first time he'd touched her to help her into the cab, a shock of awareness splintered from every point of contact where her skin touched his and shot up his arm with alarming intensity.

He sucked in a breath through his nose. Mental acrobatics were required to keep his grip gentle yet supportive instead of reflexively tightening his grasp.

What was wrong with him? Why did he keep having these out-of-character reactions to this particular woman? She was beautiful, yes, but he'd seen beautiful women before. Her laugh, her scent, her voice—none of those things were offensive to him. Being around others caused a visceral reaction within him. The same was true for Hayley, but it was different. It wasn't entirely unpleasant.

Once the soles of Hayley's shoes touched the ground, she pulled her hand back, leaving the phantom caress of her touch tickling the lines etched into his palm. It was soft and light, rippling in faint waves like a pebble tossed into a pond.

It drove him out of his mind.

With rough, swift strokes, he rubbed the palm of his hand across the outside of his thigh in an attempt to erase the imprint she'd left on his skin.

Something really must be wrong with him. Not that that was new information or anything. He'd always figured his internal wiring was faulty somehow, not all things exactly right. But this? This was altogether a very different kind of wrong.

7

ayley was in the office using the phone to call the Little Creek Library to let them know what had happened to their bookmobile. Levi assumed she'd also call any friends and family or a significant other who may worry about her when she didn't come home for the night. Or the next day. Or the next.

He rubbed his index finger hard across the span of his forehead. Hopefully the Department of Transportation would have an estimate on how long it would take them to clear the road. Hayley had said she'd make that phone call as well. He wasn't sure which of them was more anxious to hear when a crew would be sent to the rockslide site.

The answer should be obvious—Hayley. She was the one not allowed to go home, stuck with a grumpy stranger in a town so small it wasn't even a town at all, and forced to make do with a situation that too eerily mirrored being marooned on a deserted island. Hopefully, if given the choice, she'd have chosen a van full of books to be stranded with because that was what she'd ended up with.

But there was a reason Levi had chosen Turkey Grove instead of someplace closer to his family when he'd moved out. He loved his family, but he'd taken the first opportunity to escape their chaos. He'd never really been all that good at living with people to begin with, even when he was a child. He was years out of practice of putting up with the hassle of sharing space with another person. To be perfectly honest, he wasn't all that confident in his capability to coexist, let alone to do so harmoniously.

He unhooked the last of the chains from around the book-mobile's chassis. It was in position to be hoisted on the lift, if necessary. First, he needed to pop the hood and have a look underneath. The fact the engine wouldn't turn over narrowed the problem to a faulty battery, alternator, or starter, if he had to wager a guess. Of course, that could be only the beginning of any sort of mechanical issues, especially in a vehicle this age. Thankfully, he had a number of parts on hand for an array of makes and models, so chances were he could likely get the bookmobile up and running again by the time the road was cleared.

His gaze snagged on the 1968 Plymouth Barracuda he had up on the lift in the neighboring bay. His latest project car, and one he still couldn't believe he'd found in a junkyard in Hendersonville. The owner had no idea the treasure he'd had wedged between a T-boned Ford Focus and a rusted-out station wagon. Levi had been more than happy to pay the man's asking price of a couple hundred dollars to take the car off his hands. Once Levi restored the muscle car, it would be worth over thirty grand. Some people flipped houses for a living; Levi flipped classic cars. He'd have to put the project aside to work on the bookmobile, but he didn't have a buyer lined up yet, so time constraints weren't an issue.

The door that led to the office opened, and Hayley stepped out. She fiddled with the ends of her shoulder-length hair, rubbing the strands between her thumb and index finger. He waited, watching her. He didn't need to ask what she'd learned about the road clearing or if she'd been able to get through to someone in Little Creek. If he waited long enough, he was certain she'd supply the answers unprompted. After all, she hadn't been reticent with conversation up until this point. Why should that pattern change now?

She chewed on her bottom lip, then let her hands fall by her side. "The Department of Transportation is estimating a week or two of around-the-clock work to get the road cleared and repaired."

Hayley was just an itty-bitty thing, but she seemed to shrink in on herself as she stared at him through her lashes, uncertain.

Levi didn't like that look on her. He didn't like it one bit. Even when she'd shown signs of fear when he'd first stepped out of the tow truck, there had still been an iron rod of determination in her backbone. Like she wouldn't go down without a fight. Where had that gone?

"Are you sure it's okay that I stay with you?" Her voice wobbled.

He gritted his teeth. He hated that even more.

"I'm sure I can—"

"Yes," he ground out. He couldn't stand to hear her speak another word in such a small, deflated tone.

She nodded, as if trying to convince herself more than him. "Okay. Thank you. I promise you won't even know I'm there."

"You said that already."

"Oh, right." She shrugged and smiled, though the expression didn't reach her eyes. "It was worth repeating." She shifted her weight between her feet and looked around the space of the garage as if trying to find something else to focus on.

Levi should show her up to the house and let her get settled. Maybe she'd want to hide herself away in the spare bedroom for a while to adjust to her new surroundings. Then he could do the same. But now that he had a houseguest, he should probably also make something for dinner instead of heating up leftovers like he'd planned.

"This way," he barked as he turned and strode out of the

open bay. Hayley followed, and when she was outside, he shut the door and locked it. He pivoted wordlessly and stepped onto the worn trail that led up to his house. The incline was a little steep, but the woodsy trail was faster than trekking up the long driveway, which was also fairly steep.

It wasn't long before Hayley was panting behind him. He slowed his pace. Should he offer her assistance? She'd only begrudgingly accepted his help out of the cab of the truck and then appeared like she'd regretted her choice of taking his hand right after, if her pursed lips and flaring nostrils were any indication. Besides, he still felt the ghost of her touch trapped under his skin. Could he handle the intensity of her proximity again so soon? Probably not.

The back deck of his house came into view first, jutting out over the mountainside and held aloft by thick posts driven into the sloping ground beneath. Camouflaged because of the cedar siding that blended so well with the surrounding woods, his house was a retreat in more ways than one. He liked that it didn't stand out, wasn't flashy. That it quietly existed. That if you weren't looking for it, you might overlook it entirely. In fact, he hoped people did exactly that.

Once they reached the front door, Hayley's cheeks were infused with color, and a few strands of her bangs were stuck to her forehead with sweat. For the love of all things, she looked even more beautiful in this state, flushed and slightly disheveled, breaths coming out in small bursts past parted lips.

He cleared his throat and averted his gaze. He had no business entertaining such thoughts. They were new and unfamiliar and entirely unwelcome. Hayley wouldn't thank him for them either. She only needed him to get the bookmobile running again and to provide a place for food and shelter. She didn't need his unwanted appreciation nor, he'd wager, would she be receptive toward it even if he was so inclined in that direction.

Which he wasn't.

After retrieving the key he'd given her earlier and unlocking the door, Hayley stepped around him to enter his home. She paused a few paces past the entryway and turned in a slow arc, eyes wide as she took in where he lived. He tried to look at his home from her perspective. He'd picked out the furniture and set the place up with only himself in mind. The couch had the deepest seats that he could find to cradle his long legs, with an ottoman instead of a coffee table for additional length so he could stretch out. The dark gray sectional faced an open hearth of a river rock fireplace, a stack of split logs piled to the side, ready to become a roaring fire. Along the back wall, his books were shelved in handmade bookcases made from the same white oak that could be found in the woods in which his house nestled.

Like a gravitational pull tugged her, Hayley headed straight toward the bookshelves. She stopped in front of the middle bookcase, lifted her hand, and lightly traced the spine of one of the titles, laughing to herself quietly. "He's oversized and hairy and has his own personal in-home library. You will not fall prey to a Stockholm syndrome trope, Hayley Holt." She said the command under her breath, to herself.

His sisters had always hated that he could hear even their faintest of whispers, never being able to keep a secret from him. It was a superpower he hadn't asked for. "You aren't being held captive, so no need to worry about that happening."

Hayley whirled around, her cheeks pink now for an entirely different reason. "I'm sorry. I didn't mean—"

He turned his back on her apology, as it wasn't in the least bit necessary. He was big and bearded and had a bit of a beastly personality. And yes, he did have his own personal library. The collection of paperbacks and hardcovers were more than just books; they were his friends and companions. They spent long winter evenings together, and they ensured that he never got lonely, always inviting him along to another world, another place, another time. They didn't grate on his nerves or make unrealistic demands of him, requiring him to try to contort himself into someone he wasn't to better fit into their world. Fictional people were more enjoyable than any real ones had ever been to be around.

"The room you'll be staying in is this way." Levi led her down a short hall and opened the door opposite his own bedroom.

Hayley stepped into the room and looked around, a small smile on her lips. "Okay, you have to admit this is at least a little like *Beauty and the Beast*. You and the enchanted prince both just happen to have a distinctly feminine bedroom waiting for a damsel to occupy? Tell me you can't see the similarities."

Levi peered down into her upturned face. "Sisters," he said simply.

Whereas the rest of his house was set up for his comfort, this one room was arranged with his siblings in mind. The blackout curtains in a pale pink for Aliyah because she liked to sleep in when she visited. The gold-filigreed mirror on the wall by the window for Constance because she preferred putting her makeup on in natural light and there weren't any windows in the bathroom. The four-poster bed had been purchased because Trinity had always wanted one growing up, but she'd had to be content with a bunkbed and a shared room with Nova. And the reason for the many, many throw pillows that littered the bed was because of that sister. He had no idea why Nova liked throw pillows so much, but she did, so there they were.

Hayley walked into the room and perched herself on top of the ruffled duvet. "How many sisters do you have?"

"Four." He leaned his shoulder against the doorjamb. Something told him she wouldn't be satisfied with his one-word answer.

She rolled her eyes, proving him right. "Are they older or younger?"

"Yes." He pressed his lips tight to keep them from curving

into a smile. He only used as many words as were needed to get a point across or to answer a question, but he was learning the monosyllable proved a third purpose—to make Hayley's brown eyes flash in his direction. He'd never really been the type to tease, not even his sisters, so he wasn't quite sure why he was doing so now with her.

She narrowed her gaze and studied his face. There was no way she could see the muscle in his cheek twitch under his thick beard as he suppressed a rare grin.

"You're doing that on purpose," she accused.

"Maybe." He turned his face away and peered down the hall. There wasn't anything there he needed to check on, but the stillness helped settle the buzzing inside him. "I have two older sisters and two younger ones."

"So, you're the only boy? Right smack-dab in the middle?"

"Yes."

She didn't even pause to take a breath before jumping in with another question. "What was that like growing up?"

His head slowly pivoted until he pinned her with a deadpanned look. He never bothered answering stupid questions.

She laughed out loud. "That fun, huh?"

"Sure. Fun." More like torture.

Again, he loved his family, but when you were right in the middle of a lineup of five, there wasn't much room to escape or even take a deep breath amid the madness. He didn't have the benefit of being the oldest and having even a few years to enjoy a modicum of solitude, nor of being the youngest and finally being able to rest when his siblings flew the coop before him. From the day he was born until the day he'd left home, life never stopped or even slowed down. There was constant . . . everything. Noise, contact, the works. His sisters seemed to thrive in the hectic environment and had never wanted him to feel excluded, thus forcing his participation when all he'd wanted was to be left alone.

Levi took in a long inhale and let it out slowly. Sometimes just the reminder of the constant stimulation was enough to cause his muscles to tense.

"Not that you asked, but I have a younger brother. Elliot. We're semi-close, I guess you could say. Not a whole lot in common, but I love him to pieces anyway. Then there's Tai. He's technically my cousin but more like another brother. He's a tattoo artist and really talented. Do you have any tattoos?"

"No." Why was he still standing there and letting her play twenty questions with him? He pushed his shoulder off the doorjamb. "I'll go make us some dinner."

She jumped up off the bed. "I'll help."

He groaned and slammed his eyes shut. Was this how it was going to be the whole time she was there? Her following him around constantly, making conversation? He could grudgingly admit that he liked her voice, her laugh. Hearing her talk didn't set him on edge like it did with most people. There was a note to her voice that he found alluring, almost addicting. He could also admit that he liked looking at her. Her beauty was more interesting than conventional, with her slightly pointed button nose and mouth that could be considered a little too wide—especially when she smiled. He thought he could study her face for years and still find features he hadn't noticed before.

Even if Hayley wasn't all bad, there could still be too much of a good thing. The sun, for example, was an excellent source of vitamin D, but too much of it could also give you cancer.

"Stay." He winced at his own gruff command. The last time Aliyah had visited, she'd told him he needed to work on communicating his boundaries in a way that wasn't so rude. Maybe she was right. "Get settled or, I don't know, relax. I can handle dinner."

"You're sure?"

"Yes."

63

Her feet shuffled. "Would it be all right if I took a quick shower, then? I'd like to wash away the day, if I can."

The door to the only bathroom in the house was to Levi's right, so he reached out and flicked the switch, bathing the room in light. "Shampoo, conditioner, and bodywash are already in the shower. There are unopened toothbrushes and deodorants in the bottom drawer of the vanity. Towels and washcloths are in the linen closet behind the door. Need anything else?"

Her gaze skittered toward the bathroom, then up at his face. Her cheeks reddened to match the shade of her hair. She toed the carpet runner under her feet. "I don't . . ." Her voice trailed off.

"You don't what?" If there was something else she needed, she'd have to tell him outright. He wasn't about to start guessing.

"I don't . . . have a change of clothes." She dipped her chin into the corner of her collarbone, trying to hide the embarrassment painting her face.

Heat rose up his own neck. Clothes. Right. That did pose a problem, didn't it? He could offer her something of his to borrow, but there was no way her hips could hold up the waistband of a pair of his shorts. His shirts, too, would probably fall right off her shoulders.

His face flamed. *Fixate on the solution, not the problem*, Levi scolded himself. But that was hard when the problem proved to be such a vivid and alluring visual.

Think. His clothes wouldn't work, but maybe one of his sisters had left something behind. He stepped around Hayley and entered the spare room. There had to be something.

Peeking out of the slightly ajar closet door was a laundry basket. Then he remembered. Constance had brought a few loads with her just last weekend because her washer was on the fritz. She'd left a load in his dryer, and he'd put the clothes back in the laundry basket and pitched them into the closet until she came back and got them.

He retrieved the basket and returned to Hayley, shoving it into her arms. "Will this work?"

She peered down at the clothes and picked up a shirt that lay on top, inspecting it. "Let me guess—sisters?" She looked back up at him. "She won't mind if I borrow her clothes?"

"No."

Hayley smirked. "I'm beginning to think that's your favorite word, big man."

As if people had favorite words.

"Mine's *onomatopoeia*, in case you were wondering."

Of course she had a favorite word and that word had more syllables than he had fingers on one hand. Why was he not surprised? Although the better question was, why did he find that fact charming?

He turned on his heel.

Space. Maybe once he acquired some, he'd start thinking clearly again.

8

Steam fogs up the small wall-mounted mirror in front of me, a super-soft white terrycloth towel wrapped around my middle. I'd thought a shower was a good idea. A way to clear my head. Wash away the day's disasters and clean the slate of the last few hours as easily as scrubbing the road dust off my body.

Boy was I ever wrong.

If anything, my mind is as hazy as my reflection staring back at me. Why had I thought standing naked in a stranger's house with only a builder-grade door standing between me and a behemoth of a man who could probably knock the hinges off with little effort was a good idea?

Okay, fine, that's unfair.

Yes, Levi probably could knock the door down, but there isn't any part of me that's worried he'll invade my privacy to get a lookie-loo or for any other reason. Even if I was in danger and he had to barge in to save me, he'd likely do it with his eyes sealed shut, his jaw locked in place, and an air of annoyance about him thicker than his facial hair.

Is he always like this, or do I bring a special brand of curmudgeon out of him?

Ugh. Fine. Still being unfair.

Yes, it's harder to pull words out of him than winning a tug-of-war competition with a herd of elephants, a person needs sunglasses to protect themselves from his constant glares, and I'm more than half suspicious that he wishes he'd left me on the side of the road. But he didn't. Even though he gives every indication of loathing my presence—loathing *me*—he's technically been nothing but considerate, generous, and hospitable.

Technically.

The shower didn't work. I need another way to clear my head.

I'd caught Levi taking long, deep breaths, which I assume he does because he finds my personality irksome and he's collecting all his patience to deal with me.

Maybe I should try that.

I take a deep inhale of hot, steamy air.

And immediately regret my life choices.

Instead of clearing my head, Levi Redding fills my senses. I lift my arm and sniff the crook of my elbow. The soap I usually use is a subtle blend of green tea and lime that I buy at the local farmer's market. Now, instead of that familiar fragrance that has become a sensory part of my identity, I smell like a very specific mountain man in mechanic coveralls and a surly demeanor.

The container of bodywash in the shower claimed to be unscented, but there are faint whiffs of something I can't quite find the right adjective to describe. Fresh. Clean. A man who can command a space without speaking a word.

That last one might be closest to the bull's-eye of all three of them.

In the grand scheme of things, having the scent of a man who makes me feel off-kilter just by resting his expressionless, lion-like gaze on me for longer than a second shouldn't be that big of a deal. So I smell like we've been very close and very intimate and that he's imprinted himself on me or marked me as his in some similar way that species from the animal kingdom do. No big whoop. At least I was able to take a hot shower, right? At least I'll have a roof over my head and food in my belly and won't have to sleep in the bookmobile or try out my nonexistent survival skills in the Cherokee National Forest.

Perspective, right?

I'm going to keep telling myself that until I'm one-hundred-percent convinced.

I rifle through the laundry basket by my feet. I've decided I'm not going to feel weird about borrowing his sister's clothes without her permission. If the tables were turned and a woman was in need of something to wear and had access to my wardrobe, I'd want her to help herself.

Besides, I don't really have any other options.

My fingers brush against soft flannel, and I pull out a cute autumn-toned plaid dress of sienna browns, tans, and navy blues. It's still about a month away before the temperatures start dropping in earnest and the leaves begin to change colors, but Levi keeps his house so cold that I wouldn't be surprised if he told me he stored blocks of ice in his living room for an annual igloo building competition. Seriously, his energy bill must be astronomical. Either way, this flannel will keep me warm.

I'm in no way shocked when I hold the dress up to my shoulders and notice that it's probably a little bit big for me. It makes sense that Levi's sisters would be tall as well. Genetics is a beautiful thing. There's probably a belt somewhere that's supposed to cinch the waist in, but accessories are the least of my worries, and the material is so soft that I don't even care if I've done a disservice to whoever designed the dress by turning it into a shift style.

Once I get all the buttons done up and roll the extra-long sleeves to my wrists, I finger-comb the tangles out of my hair, happy again for my decision to cut off twelve inches to donate after finding out about Evangeline's alopecia. The shoulder-length strands are giving me enough trouble as it is; waist-length hair would have been impossible without a real brush.

With the toilet seat lid down, I perch precariously on the edge and set my purse on my lap. Everything I have with me is in this bag. If only I could MacGyver the contents and build some sort of tool or contraption that would solve all my problems. But, alas, I'm left with . . .

My wallet, a tube of lip balm, three pens, the refill prescription of immunosuppressants I'd picked up on my way to work this morning—thank you, Jesus—some gum, my phone charger, and my little journal of good deeds.

I put everything back inside the purse except the journal, opening the notebook to the next blank page. Goodness gracious, what am I going to put for today's entry?

I didn't kill Mayor Breckenbridge doesn't quite fit the bill. Mostly because I'd made the rule when I first started these journals that an act of omission doesn't count. I had to actually *do* something. And even if wringing the mayor's thick neck was technically doing something, he was back in Little Creek and I was stuck here, way more than an arm's length away.

Here with Levi.

Just the two of us.

I guess that narrows down my options on who to bless today pretty considerably.

I pull out one of the three pens in my purse and uncap the lid, getting my hand in position to jot down a stroke of brilliance on how I can make Levi's life better within the last few hours this day holds.

Maybe I could . . . No.

Or, how about . . . Nuh-uh.

I conjure an image of him in my mind, the scowl in place, the muscle in his jaw ticking beneath the layer of scruff on his face, the way his fingers flexed on the steering wheel and the rigidity in his body. He is the poster child for the grumpy, broody male role. Mr. Darcy would appear as affable and genial as Charles Bingley if he were standing next to Levi Redding.

I've always had a theory about Mr. Darcy's aloof and un-approachable demeanor—that he wasn't really snobbish or arrogant at all, but that, in actuality, he contended with social anxiety. That his refusal to dance at the ball was merely a defense mechanism and way to cope in an uncomfortable environment among people he didn't know well. He in fact later admitted to Elizabeth Bennet that he struggled to converse easily with people with whom he wasn't well acquainted.

Would my Darcy theory hold up with Levi as well? Could his grumpy exterior be his first line of defense against social anxiety?

I tap the lid of the pen at the corner of my lips and think. What can I do to put him at ease? Maybe if I shoulder even more of the conversation and not let any awkward pauses happen, that will help him to be more comfortable. I can be extra extroverted if I need to be and if that's what he needs me to be. I'll just fill up the silence with idle chitchat so he doesn't have to mentally strain himself on my account.

I add the plan to the journal, then close the cover with a satisfied smile. That should do it. I gather my purse and the laundry basket of clean clothes that's my wardrobe for the foreseeable future and exit the bathroom. After depositing the clothes and purse into my borrowed room, I head back toward the main part of the house, following the smells of Mexican spices wafting in the air. My stomach rumbles, reminding me that the PB&J I'd had for lunch right before the mayor showed up for his photo shoot wasn't all that filling.

"Something smells good," I say as I stand beside the kitchen island.

Levi stirs ground beef in a skillet, sets down the wooden spoon, then turns toward me. At the first glimpse he gets, his nostrils flare and his fingers flex before curling into his palms at his sides. "What are you wearing?" he growls, enunciating each word in his low timbre like it physically pains him.

Like *I* physically pain him.

I look down. What does he mean, what am I wearing? He's the one who shoved the basket of clothes at me. "It's one of your sister's dresses." I wave my hand down my front in a sort of *you have eyes, can't you see for yourself?* motion.

He must have missed the sarcasm in my gesture and instead takes my hand wave as some sort of command to get a good look. His gaze moves over me in such a way that a chill runs from the top of my head down along my spine, sending a convulsion of awareness down each of my vertebras like a Slinky descending a flight of stairs. I'm covered up more than a granny in a muumuu in this thing, the hem hitting the backs of my knees, sleeves down to my wrists, and the collar buttoned all the way up to the base of my throat, but the intensity in Levi's eyes makes it seem as if I had the audacity to come to the kitchen in some lacy negligee fit for a honeymoon suite.

"It was in the basket," I say in defense and barely resist the urge to clutch at the collar to double-check that I did, in fact, don a could-never-be-considered-sexy oversized flannel dress that hangs on my body because the belt that goes with it that would give me a hint of a waistline wasn't in the basket too.

Levi's Adam's apple bobs. He hasn't taken a single step toward me, but it feels like the distance between us is shrinking by the second. As if every deep breath of oxygen he inhales into that barrel of a chest of his is making the room smaller and him bigger.

My skin flushes, and a prickling of realization begins to dawn at the corners of my brain. "This isn't your sister's dress, is it?" I ask in a quiet voice.

He shakes his head.

Dagnabbit. "I'm wearing your shirt, aren't I?"

He doesn't say anything, but he doesn't have to. The quicksand that has become my stomach is telling me I'm right.

Because of course not only do I have to smell like this man—which must be as unsettling to him as it is to me—but now the shirt that has covered him so many times in the past is hugging every part of me, and when you think about it, that's way too intimate a thing for two almost-complete strangers. "I'm sorry, I didn't know. I'll find something else to wear."

"Don't." He stops my trajectory back to the bedroom with the single word. "I said you could wear anything in the basket. It's fine."

The firm, almost angry set of his brow by no means conveys the message of *everything is hunky-dory. I don't care one bit.* Tension makes the air heavy, and I'm weighing the pros and cons of retreating and finding something else, anything else, in that blasted basket, or staying right here because, as he said, it's fine, and I should take him at his word.

I really wish *The Price Is Right* host would appear and show me what's behind door number three right now.

Levi jerks back toward the stove, picks up the wooden spoon off the counter, and attacks the ground beef in the skillet like he's afraid the cow wasn't really all the way dead yet and he's determined to finish the bovine off himself.

"So," I say warily, "that smells good."

I'm talking to the solid wall of his back. He doesn't give any indication that he even heard me, but considering he's less than five feet away and hasn't shown any previous signs of being on the cusp of deafness, I'm going to assume he knows I'm talking to him.

This good deed of single-handedly keeping a conversation in motion is going to be harder than I thought.

"Some kind of Mexican food, I'm guessing."

"Tacos," he begrudgingly answers.

"Oh, I love tacos."

He spares me a look over his shoulder that I'm interpreting as something along the lines of *everyone loves tacos*. Which, of course, is a truth universally acknowledged, so silly me for pointing it out.

"Can I help?"

"No."

Should have predicted that response.

I look around his house, trying to find a topic of conversation. His shelves of books pull me back toward them. What avid reader, even the shiest ones, can't be tempted to come out of their shell when talking about books?

"I love your library, by the way." I pitch my voice a little louder so he can hear me from the kitchen. "Do you have a favorite author or genre?"

Plates rattle in response, then the slide of a drawer opening and the tinkle of cutlery.

"I'm a pretty eclectic reader myself. I always have both a nonfiction and a fiction book going at the same time. Usually multiple ones on different platforms, if I'm honest. People ask me how I can keep up with all the different story lines, but it's not any different than having more than one show that you're watching." I tip back a spine and slide the book out of its place. "Oh, this James R. Hannibal book looks good. Have you read it yet? Is it just me, or are you immediately reminded of Hannibal Lecter when you see the author's name? He's probably heard that a lot, although I would never say that to his face."

Something thunks behind me, and I startle, turning. Levi clanks another dish on the table.

"Dinner's ready." He retreats back to the kitchen.

The table is hardly set, what with only the skillet of beef and a jar of salsa gracing the center. I follow him to help gather the rest. I don't know what he puts in his tacos, but we still need the shells, at least, and plates to eat on. When I round the island, he's opening a top cabinet and fishing out two white earthenware plates.

"I can take those in," I offer.

He spins slowly, as if he's hoping when he gets all the way turned around, I won't actually be standing here.

It's getting harder and harder not to take these little rebuffs personally. Each time he flinches or scowls or grunts, I try to tell myself that it's not me, it's the situation, and he'd act the same with anyone. But it's getting harder to grit my teeth and keep my smile in place and my voice chipper. Because he's not the only one having a terrible, horrible, no good, very bad day here.

I've miscalculated. I'm standing too close. Levi's finished his slow-motion rotation, and there isn't even any room for him to hand me the plates he's holding near his chest. My chin tilts up as my head tips back, Levi towering above me as still as a statue.

At this proximity, I can see that his eyes aren't actually liquid gold but the lightest shade of amber that I've ever seen. With as hard as the rest of him is and as unapproachable as he makes himself, his eyes betray him. They aren't hard at all but soft and nearly entreating, juxtaposing beneath the strict slashes of his thick brows and the coarse hair beneath the ridge of his cheekbones.

I'm not sure why I'm still standing here when I should be taking a step back. For that matter, I'm not sure why he hasn't barked at me to move. It's almost as if we're caught in some sort of *Twilight Zone* vortex and I can't look away, break away.

Levi's lips part, and his eyes slam shut. He makes a sound that, if it were a word, would only consist of four letters. "You have freckles," he says by way of an accusation. Like, how dare I, a redhead, have freckles dotting my otherwise porcelain-doll skin.

Like I had a say in the matter, buddy.

"And you smell . . ." That sound again.

Hey, if he doesn't like that I smell like him then he should have let me stop by the general store to pick up something else.

His eyes and the muscle in his jaw bulge. "And you're wearing . . ." The air around him practically vibrates as he makes the sound a third time, the reverberations pinging around my chest cavity like a trapped pinball.

He sounds pained. Angry. At himself or me?

Wait. Is he angry because he *likes* my freckles and the fact I smell like him and I'm wearing his shirt? Mr. I-Can't-Wait-to-Get-Away-from-You? That can't be right, can it?

"You should never wear makeup," he says as he barrels past me, grabbing a box of hard taco shells and a dish of toppings all chopped and ready to go on his way to the dining table.

I should never . . .

Okay, I'm going to skip right over the initial reaction of *a man isn't going to tell me what I should or shouldn't do or what I can or can't wear* and get straight to the heart of what I *think* Levi Redding just said. Or tried to say, rather. Which is that he thinks I'm more attractive naturally and don't need to cover up or enhance anything with beauty products.

Why, Mr. Redding, I do declare. You have such a way with words.

He's taken everything to the dining room already, so I follow behind empty-handed. There's a plate set on the table, but Levi's holding the other in his hand. Not sure what's up with that but nothing has been easy to figure out with this man so why would I think that would change now?

I pull out the chair with the place setting and lower myself into the seat. Instead of taking the seat next to me or even across from me like one would expect, Levi goes to the opposite end of the table, the seat farthest away, then sits.

I hold back my snort. So much for that half of a second when I'd deliriously thought he might actually tolerate my presence, much less more than tolerate it. This seating arrangement snuffed that idea out in a jiffy.

Your Darcy theory, Hayley.

Right. If people make Levi uncomfortable, then sitting by himself would make sense. I think?

Levi folds his hands and closes his eyes. I mimic his posture and prepare for a blessing over the meal.

Nothing happens.

I peek out behind a squinted lid.

Levi mouths the word *amen* and lifts his head.

A silent prayer, then. I say my own quickly, along with a plea for a lightning bolt of inspiration on how to put my host at ease since I don't know how long we're going to be forced to be housemates and I hate the thought that I'm making him miserable by being here.

We build our tacos, and I give myself a moment of reprieve from trying to come up with something to converse over. Talking with your mouth full is poor manners, after all. I take a bite, the hard shell crunching between my teeth and the spices exploding on my tongue.

Alert! Atomic-level explosion happening! My eyes and nose immediately water, and I cough. My mouth is on fire. I finally manage to swallow the inferno, then reach for a glass that isn't there to put the flames out. "Water," I croak.

Levi leaves and comes back a moment later with a bottle of water. "Too spicy?" he asks like I didn't just eviscerate every single one of my taste buds.

I take a play out of his book and don't bother answering. Instead, I lift my plate and scoot down the table to his end, which just so happens to be where the container of sour cream is. After scooping copious amounts of sour cream on the rest of my taco in hopes that the dairy will bring down the heat level, I plant myself in the seat beside him.

He stiffens but isn't so rude as to get up and pretend that

we're playing musical chairs right now. I pick up my taco and take another loud bite, thankfully not choking this time. I peek at Levi as I chew. A taco is dwarfed in one of his massive hands. His other hand rests on top of his thigh, his thumb tucked into a tight fist. He looks like he doesn't want to be sitting at this table with me, and I know now's the time to check off that box in my journal and get him to relax, ease his anxiety.

Idle chatter commence.

"So, I don't know if you know this, but Glen Bell, you know, the founder of Taco Bell? Well, he claims that he invented the idea of the hard-shell taco. He was looking for a fast-food alternative to the ever-popular hamburger." I take another bite and chew. "He wanted to give Americans something different but familiar while also staying true to a fast-food rule—that the meal can be eaten with one hand on the go." Another bite. Chew. "He might have made the Tex-Mex taco popular, don't get me wrong, but there were patents for a metal taco mold to make your own hard shells at home before Glen Bell ever opened his first restaurant. So, he might have made the taco popular, but he definitely didn't invent the concept."

The vein that runs along Levi's temple throbs. He seems to be getting more tense beside me, not less. Maybe if I keep talking?

"Another interesting tidbit about Taco Bell is that it didn't always 'think outside the bun' like the slogan claims. A chili burger, of all things, was on its original menu. But the franchise does do a good job at innovation, I'll give them that. Did you know that it took a team of engineers over two years and over forty recipes to get the Doritos Locos Taco right?" I laugh, a sort of unhinged sound because I realize the ridiculousness of all these off-the-wall facts about a fast-food chain and the fact that I'm running out of said facts themselves. "Oh, and the first restaurants had actual mariachi bands playing. I like mariachi music. Do you like mariachi music?"

Levi shoots out of his seat, looking more like the lion I had mentally named him early. A caged one, at that. His hair is a wild mane about him and he has muscles rippling under his clothes. He glares down at me, his arms flexed and hands fisted at his sides. "Stop. Talking. Just . . . for the love, stop talking. You said I wouldn't even know you were here. You said it twice. But you haven't let up. Not once. You're here. You're everywhere, and I can't . . . just stop . . . I need . . ."

But he doesn't articulate what he needs. Instead, he makes that growl that sounds like a curse and storms toward the bedrooms at the back of the house in an angry huff. I brace for the slam of a door that never comes, stunned speechless.

9

Well, that had been a certifiable disaster.

I slump in my chair, my spine resting on the carved back of the wooden seat as I stare unseeing at the taco trimmings laid out on the table before me. My ears are ringing from the verbal slap to the face I've just taken, and I'm trying to process—

Huh. I think I'm trying to process the list of things I need to process because I haven't even been able to figure that part out yet. This day has been nothing but a whirlwind of disasters.

I should probably apologize, though. That should probably be number one on the processing list.

I rotate in my seat to peek behind me. I can't actually see the door to Levi's room and definitely don't have Superman's X-ray vision to see *through* said door to check on the man, but I stare in that direction anyway because, well, I don't really know why.

Levi's upset. Because of me. So, I should apologize.

I nibble on the inside of my bottom lip but make no move to stand, let alone walk down the short hall and knock on his door. To be honest, I'm kind of afraid to speak to him at this exact moment, even if it's to ask for his forgiveness. He's already bitten my head off. I don't want to have him chew me up and spit me out too.

I think back to everything I've said today, to everything I've done. I've never stopped trying to be optimistic and look on the bright side when I had every right to indulge in at least a little bit of complaint. I've never stopped being friendly, replying with sweetness when all I got was sour in return. I never stopped looking for opportunities or thinking up ways to try to ease the sharp edges of this situation and make Levi more comfortable.

Are those the things he wants me to stop doing? To let up on?

My arms cross over my chest, and now I'm processing in the center of a stew pot. My internal temperature is rising with my indignation.

Now I kind of want to march my heinie down that short hall and pound a fist on his bedroom door and give him a piece of my mind. He can't just erupt all over me like he's Vesuvius and I'm Pompeii. I've been a verifiable delight today. A delight, I tell you! I don't know what he has to complain about. *I'm* the one who's had to deal with his surly attitude and inscrutability. To not let it sting every time he's immediately wiped at any part of his skin that came in contact with mine or every time he's flinched for no other reason than because I've just been myself.

He's not the one who has been trying so hard to—

Nooooooo.

I blink, and I feel like I've been slapped in the face a second time, my cheeks stinging from reality's left hook. That can't be right. That cannot be what I've been doing.

Can it?

If my brain had brakes, they would be screeching right now, smoke in plumes billowing from the wheel wells. That organ in my cranium hits Rewind and then Play (because apparently my brain metaphors convert from cars to VCRs like some kind of knockoff Transformer) and I watch scenes of the day play out like a movie in my mind's eye.

The immediate crescendo of awareness that built within me the moment Levi stepped out of his tow truck. I'd chalked up the tingling sensation that ran a marathon up and down my limbs to adrenaline and mentally thanked my body for giving me the boost of chemicals that could give me the strength to lift a car, or in my case, fight off a man the size of a car.

But what if I hadn't reacted that way because of fear? What if I'd reacted that way because . . .

Oh, for hootenannies' sake. Have I been slipped a truth serum or something?

I groan and slump farther down in my seat.

Prickles of awareness. Racing heart. Dry mouth. I had never been afraid of Levi Redding, the big oaf. I've been attracted to the man from the get-go.

Which also explains why I cared one iota about his reluctance and subsequent distaste of touching me. The rejection stung more than just my feminine pride. Normally, I would have laughed something like that off. Kind of like when a little boy wipes off his mother's kiss at school drop-off.

Every time he pulled away, I just pushed harder.

I glance behind me toward his room again.

Until I pushed too hard.

It all makes sense. Except that it also really doesn't. To be frank, Levi Redding isn't my type. Line up my past flings and you'll see a trend. David Kinner, Hudson Green, Isaac Bankston . . . All sweet guys with easygoing natures who liked to flirt and banter and tease. They all had ready smiles and crinkly laugh lines and aimed to fire a witty retort at anyone who'd verbally spar with them. They were all tall without being too tall and athletic without being too bulky. And, most importantly, they all were only looking for a good time. Someone to pass an evening with. Nothing serious. No commitments.

Levi is the exact opposite of all the men I've dated in the past. There is nothing relaxed or casual about him, no carefree air or warmth that draws you in. I haven't seen him smile once, much less laugh, and heaven knows I've tried to get him to do both. He glares instead of giving flirty glances, and the man has the communication skills of a Neanderthal. To top it off, I bet he doesn't know the meaning of the phrase *no strings attached*.

So *why* am I attracted to him? It doesn't make sense.

I sigh. Logical or not, I'm not going to embody the main character vibes of a heroine who refuses to acknowledge what's right in front of her face. I can be self-aware enough to admit that I am attracted to Levi for reasons unknown—

He's ruggedly handsome, my brain interjects helpfully/un-helpfully. *He's got that mountain man, rough-and-tumble protector vibe with hands so large and strong they could—*

Okay! I interrupt myself. One reason known.

And his eyes are unlike any you've ever seen before. While he closes the rest of himself off, his eyes offer a glimpse to what's hiding underneath. In their depths you didn't find even a hint of capriciousness or provocation. They drew you in like—

Fine! I concede. Some reasons known. We can stop listing them now.

The point is, I can admit that I'm attracted to Levi, whether that attraction is logical or not. Spoiler: It absolutely is not. Furthermore, it is a terrible idea to act on said attraction when the person in question has made it abundantly clear they do not find you similarly appealing, and you are thrust into forced proximity with said person and must rely on their goodwill and hospitality.

And even if that weren't the case, his serious demeanor is an issue. Even if this spark I feel was reciprocated, I couldn't let myself go down that road. Not with him. There's no way he'd be content with casual fun, and there's no way I can be with anything else. My future—

Nope. Shutting that train of thought down right now.

Okay. Wow, that was a lot of processing. But I'm back to square one again. Back to needing to apologize.

I lift my head and am surprised—even though I shouldn't be—to see that night has fallen. A large sliding glass door leads out to the back deck that hangs over the side of the mountain. It almost looks like I'm in a tree house, the way I'm eye-level with the top branches of the woods surrounding Levi's house. Flickers of light in small specks dance in the twilight, reminding me of wood nymphs and lands of fairies. Reality is far less magical, as the flashes of amber light are coming from a smattering of fireflies no doubt searching for a place to huddle in furrowed bark or underground to survive the winter. When they reemerge in the spring to search for their mates, their lights will truly dance in a synchronized rhythm that would put any choreographer to shame.

I walk down the hall and pause in front of Levi's bedroom. Unlike outside, there isn't even a speck of light coming from under the door. It's dark and quiet. Has he gone to bed and fallen asleep already? Even though it's only—I glance at my watch—7:43? He must have, because the only other alternative is that he's sitting in there by himself in the dark—not reading or watching TV or listening to music—and that seems unlikely.

I'll just have to ask for his forgiveness tomorrow.

10

I feel like I've been robbed. In books, when a character wakes up someplace other than in her own bed, she has a moment of confusion. A brief *where am I?* slice of time where she's given a reprieve from the memory of all the events that have landed her in her current pickle.

I get none of that.

I open my eyes and know exactly where I am, exactly what led me to be here, and exactly what is awaiting me once I crawl out of this extremely comfortable bed and gather up enough courage to open the door and face Levi again. It's a good thing big-girl panties are metaphorical and therefore always packed because I need to put them on, apologize in person, and get over this inconvenient attraction I've found myself a victim of.

Let's hit snooze on that, shall we? My embarrassment will still be here in ten more minutes.

I roll over and grab my phone that I left charging on the nightstand. The screen awakens with a tap of my finger, and I'm surprised to see that not only is there reception on Levi's mountain, but I have a number of texts waiting for me.

Mom was a little worried when I'd talked to her on the phone yesterday, but after I assured her I had my medication with me and that I hadn't been hurt in the rockslide, she'd calmed down. She also double-checked Levi's claim that the Forest Service road was impassable. Their website said it was closed for maintenance and that the weather had delayed their progress. Dad had hollered from the background that he could borrow the sheriff's four-wheeler and bring along his chainsaw, then dared the rangers to stop him from saving his little girl. As sweet as the offer was, I nipped that idea in the bud. The roads will eventually reopen. I'll be fine until then.

Pulling the phone farther away from my face, I open the messaging app and tap on the group chat full of unread messages.

Evangeline:

Just checking to make sure you haven't been murdered.

Evangeline:

Ok, that was originally a joke, but you're not responding, so now I'm kind of getting worried.

Evangeline:

If you've been the victim of a vicious crime and I have to look at your homicide in miniature form in my grandfather's basement every time I visit him, then . . .

Evangeline:

I should have had a good threat ready before I hit send.

Evangeline:

I don't even think therapy would help if I had to deal with that.

I stifle a laugh. I don't know if Levi is awake, asleep, here, or at work, and even though I'm technically avoiding him (momentarily!), I don't want him to *know* I'm avoiding him, so I'd prefer if he thought I was still asleep.

I hold my phone a little tighter, oh so grateful for the ridiculousness that is my friend. Only Evangeline would jump to murderous conclusions and then worry I'd be immortalized in her grandfather's basement. Although, in her defense, her grandfather and sister's hobby of recreating crime scenes in miniature form like little macabre dollhouses is a bit unsettling. So maybe it isn't a stretch that her mind went there, especially if she's been home to visit recently.

Evangeline:

Martha, you're the one who talked to Hayley when she called the library. What specifically did she say? What was her tone? Do you think she was in trouble? I mean, more trouble than being stranded. More like, did she hide any type of secret message in what she was saying that would require a very specific set of skills à la Liam Neeson?

Martha:

You're crazy, you know that?

Evangeline:

Yes, but you didn't answer the question.

Martha:

She sounded stressed but fine.

Evangeline:

Then why isn't she answering these texts?

Martha:

It's unlikely she has cell reception.

Evangeline:

Oh. That makes sense. Well, did she say where she was staying or who she was staying with?

Martha:

Umm . . . with the tow truck guy, I think?

Evangeline:

You think?!? Hold on.

Martha:

Do I have a choice?

Evangeline:

You do not.

It's getting harder and harder not to laugh out loud. *Oh, my goodness, I needed this.*

Evangeline:

There's only one towing service she could have used. Levi's Service Center in Turkey Grove. The place doesn't even have a website. No website and no staff photo. Is this Levi guy married? Is she staying with a nice little family in a nice little cabin?

Evangeline:

OR IS HE SINGLE? Oh my word! Is this her meet-cute?

Martha:

I thought you promised everyone that you'd taken down your matchmaking shingle for good.

Evangeline:

I didn't matchmake this. Destiny did.

That's where the text thread ends. I should probably let them both know that I'm alive and well and still very much single. I set my thumbs to work.

Hayley:

Sorry for the late reply! Cell reception is spotty out here. I didn't even know I had any until a minute ago. I'm fine and not in danger of being murdered, Evangeline.

I wasn't expecting anyone to answer right away but three dots immediately appear as Evangeline types out a response.

Evangeline:

You're alive! I've been so worried!

Hayley:

I'm fine. No need to worry.

Martha:

Any word on what made the bookmobile break down?

Hayley:

No update on Cletus yet. Levi didn't get a chance to look him over yesterday, but I think he plans to today.

Martha:
Keep us posted.

Evangeline:
Speaking of Levi . . .

I have honestly never met another person so in love with love than Evangeline Kelly. Even when the woman thought no one would ever look at her with hearts in their eyes the way my cousin does, she still wouldn't give up on romance, determined instead to try her hand at matchmaking the library's patrons, unbeknownst to them. She's being about as subtle as mud right now with her leading inquiry.

Hayley:
What about him?

I smirk down at my phone. My evasiveness will really dill her pickle.

Evangeline:
Don't be obtuse.

Martha:
While this is all highly entertaining, some of us have work to do. Pete the Cat and his groovy buttons are going to help me teach number concept to the littlest patrons today. TTYL

Thank you, Martha, for that perfect excuse not to answer. Also, I didn't realize how late it is if it's already story time at the library. My little snooze from what I need to do is now over.

Hayley:

I need to go too. I'll check in whenever I have service so you're not haunted by the possibility of me being your grandfather's next basement showcase.

Evangeline:

I appreciate that.

I set my phone back down and push off the covers.

Oh! Maybe I did have a moment of character amnesia after all because I'd forgotten about not changing out of Levi's shirt before I went to bed. In my defense, the flannel is very comfortable, like it's been washed at least a hundred times with the world's best fabric softener. There's no way I'm going to step foot outside of this room in only his shirt, though. It's hard defining boundaries when you have no choice but to cross all the normal ones. I'm sleeping in the room next to him. Eating his food. Using his soap, shampoo, and deodorant. The least I can do is not crawl into his clothes as well.

For both our sakes.

I find an actual dress in the bottom of the laundry basket. This time the piece of clothing has a floral print with little pearl buttons marching in a straight line down the front. The statistical probability that this dress is another of Levi's shirts is exactly zero. I did not do the math, nor do I need to as the dress gathers under my breasts in a ruched empire waist before falling around the rest of my body in a swish of fabric.

I finger-comb my hair, wincing when my index finger snags on a particularly tangled knot. My hair is fine, which means it's soft and silky to the touch, but also means that it gets tangled really easily. If I don't get my hands on a real brush, I'm going to be well on my way to sporting dreadlocks by the time the rockslide gets cleared.

I throw on my only pair of shoes, then crack open the door, pausing. I don't hear anything coming from any other part of the house. I pad across the hall to the bathroom and quickly brush my teeth. My steps are slow but sure as I walk into the living room and then the kitchen.

No Levi. He must have gone down to his shop to start work for the day.

A sliver of disappointment wedges under my skin like a splinter. I shake my head as if the physical movement will shake off the feeling as well. No part of me should have even entertained the thought that he'd do anything other than go about his business as usual. Hadn't he made himself abundantly clear the day before?

I lift my gaze and visually trip over an envelope with my name written in sloppy, slanted letters on the kitchen counter. Trepidation skitters across my shoulders as I pick up the envelope and pluck out the college-ruled notebook paper trifolded within.

Levi wrote me a letter? I should worry that it's an eviction notice, but even though I just met the man the day before, I already know he isn't someone who would leave another person stranded, no matter how much of a burden or how much that other person gets on his nerves.

I unfold the letter and begin to read. Or try to. His hand-writing is *really* atrocious.

Hayley,

There is no excuse for the way I spoke to you. It wasn't right. No one should be treated with disrespect like that, and I hope that you accept my sincerest apologies.

Okay, wow. Can't say I was expecting this at all. First off, written Levi and spoken Levi are two different Levis. I can hardly believe the same man who barely spoke more than monosyllable replies the day before is the same man who's penned this letter. Also, disrespect? He's being way too hard on himself. I never felt disrespected. He was just vocalizing his boundaries, albeit a bit explosively.

> *I wish I could promise that I won't ever lose control of my temper like that again while you are a guest in my house, but I won't lie to you. Chances are, my grip on my emotions will likely slip again. What I can promise you, though, is that I am trying. And whenever I fail, I will be quick to apologize. For whatever that is worth.*

Uh, I'd say that's worth a whole heap of an awful lot. Who of us isn't failing at something even after giving it our best shot? It's the mark of a person's true character, however, when they can admit when they're wrong and then try to make it right.

> *Maybe I should have warned you about my lack of people skills before you took up temporary residence across the hall, but I really couldn't think of any other options of places you could stay. The thing is, unfortunately, I'm not very ~~tolerant tolerable~~ No, I guess both those words are right. It's hard for me to be around other people, and, consequently, other people find it hard to be around me. So, if at any point yesterday you thought to yourself that I'm a curmudgeon hermit, then you were correct.*

I snort a laugh because those exact words had crossed my mind. Also, who would have thought Levi Redding would have such a self-deprecating sense of humor?

> *This is going to sound cliché, and I can't even believe I'm about to write it because it's something someone says during*

a bad break-up, so obviously they aren't words that belong between us, and yet they are the absolute truth.

It's not you, Hayley. It's me.

I can't stress that enough. You did absolutely nothing wrong and, again, didn't deserve how I treated you. I wish I could be someone other than who I am. Someone who enjoys people instead of getting agitated simply by being around them.

My chest constricts. It's a good thing for him that he's not here right now or I'd be trying to give him a hug that he probably wouldn't want. No one should wish to be someone besides the person they are.

What is it about people specifically that sets him on edge?

Like it's my favorite rerun, I play again the mental reel of the previous day. Him turning off the radio every time I asked a question instead of letting it play in the background. His aversion to touch. His insistence on me using his hygiene products instead of stopping by the store so I could pick up some of my own.

Sound. Touch. Smell.

I close my eyes and groan. I'm so stupid. No wonder he flipped his lid as I prattled on about inane Taco Bell facts. I wish I'd been able to see what was right in front of my face. I wasn't putting Levi at ease at all. I was pushing him into sensory overload, the poor guy.

I look down at the letter in my hand and realize with a jolt that I haven't finished reading the whole thing yet.

~~If it makes you feel any better at all, know that, out of everyone I've ever interacted with, you are the most bearable.~~ I really wish I'd written this in pencil instead of pen so I could erase that properly.

I laugh out loud at that. Has to be the worst compliment I've ever received at face value. Who wants to be simply bearable when words like *enchanting* and *beguiling* and *irresistible* are right there, ready to be used? But I'm coming to suspect that bearable to Levi is high praise indeed.

What I mean is, instead of making me cringe, I like the lilt and cadence of your voice. Your laugh invites me to laugh too, instead of creating the urge to plug my ears. Hayley, you don't give me a headache.

Again, with the flattering compliments.
My grin widens.

My actions are probably making you doubt my sincerity, but I honestly can only stand to be around most people for an hour or so and I lasted the majority of the day with you before I snapped.

When I wouldn't shut up. His pleas for me to *just stop* are making more and more sense.

If it would make you more comfortable, I'll ask around and see if anyone nearby has a spare room or other ideas on a place where you can stay until one of the roads are opened again. Just let me know.

Well, butter my backside and call me a biscuit. I'd figured I'd finished all my processing last night, but this letter is giving me even more to unpack.

An unbidden thought shoots to the front of the queue, and I'm grateful Evangeline isn't here because she'd probably vocalize the blasted thing with a gleeful grin on her face, but . . .

Did Levi just I-hate-everyone-in-the-world-but-you trope me?

11

I need to get out of the house. Just sitting around is making me go stir-crazy. I'm a librarian, and there's a van full of books sitting at the base of this mountain. What's stopping me from doing my job? I can stuff a backpack full of paperbacks and go door-to-door or find a wheelbarrow to pile a selection of titles in and roll it down the main street for anyone in need of a good read. Who knows, maybe Levi has a directory of some sort in his office and I can call everyone in the hollow and tell them where the bookmobile's new location is. Have them come to me. Levi can still work on Cletus—he only needs to have access to under the hood, right?—while patrons enter and exit in their quest for literature.

There's no need for me to stay cooped up inside these four walls, overthinking things.

I've already put a big X over yesterday's entry in my notebook and penned in my replacement good deed—donating money to a worthy charity. Doing something so impersonal had felt more like a cop-out instead of the spirit with which I'd begun my blessing journal. But I'd run out of time and options. Leaving the page of the notebook blank had felt all kinds of wrong.

I've also already written Levi a reply letter and slipped it under the door to his bedroom. Of course, this was after I'd argued with myself on whether or not the better option was to leave the letter someplace easy to find, like he'd done, or simply walk to the shop and give it to him in person. But I figured if I gave it to him in person then he'd have to make the uncomfortable decision of whether to pocket it to read later in private or open it right then and read it in front of me. The letter's current location is purely because of my consideration for Levi, I assure you, not because I haven't figured out how to proceed with him face-to-face yet.

I grab my bag, sling the strap over my shoulder, and then step out the front door. The morning air has a little bit of a nip that I'm not complaining about at all, especially since in about an hour I know I'm going to be fanning myself against the heat. The calendar marks September, and we're nearing the official start of fall, but it'll take Tennessee a while to get with the program and really begin cooling off. Unless an un-expected cold snap hits, I'm not expecting the leaves to sport their array of colors until around Halloween. Until then, ev-eryone's sweaters are safely folded up in their chest of drawers.

The path down the mountain is easy to spot even though it's pretty narrow. I pick my foot placements carefully so I don't trip on a root and injure myself. I've played the part of damsel in distress enough in the last twenty-four hours, thank you very much.

"Jolene!" a young girl's voice rings out.

I lift my head and peer around the slender trunks of trees, but I don't see anyone.

"Jolene!"

The echo of the name rings between my ears in Dolly Parton's falsetto voice. I mean, you hear the name *Jolene* and it's impos-sible not to immediately start singing the country star's iconic hit. Tell me I'm wrong.

"Jo—Oh, hello."

A girl about nine years old materializes out of seemingly

nowhere. She stares up at me with crystal blue eyes under a hank of blond hair that is as much in need of a brush as my own. Her oversized tie-dyed shirt almost entirely covers a pair of cut-off shorts with frayed edges tickling her knees. In her hand is a leash connected to . . .

A pig in a pink tutu?

"My name's Anna Leigh, what's yours?" The pig at her heel snorts. "Oh, and this is Fancy."

First Jolene and now Fancy. Dolly and then Reba. Please don't tell me this precious little child has a pet named after a song about a teenager forced into prostitution by her ailing mother.

I push past the notion and let my lips curl into a genuine smile. "Hello, Anna Leigh. Hello, Fancy. I'm Hayley."

"Have you seen Jolene anywhere?" Anna Leigh looks around me like she's expecting the mysterious Jolene to be hiding behind my back.

"No, I haven't, sorry. Is Jolene your sister? Where's your mama? Does she know you're out here?" Now it's my turn to look around the half-pint as I try to spot an adult who belongs with this child. Why isn't she in school? Is today a holiday I don't know about? A teacher in-service day or parent-teacher conferences perhaps?

Anna Leigh laughs. "Jolene's not my sister. He's Fancy's husband. And Mama told me to get out of her hair for a bit 'cuz I was driving her up the wall with all my jibber-jabber. I brought Jolene and Fancy out to the woods 'cuz I read that pigs are good at sniffing out something called a truffle—it looks like deer turds, if you ask me—but I guess people like to eat them and will pay lots of money, so me and Jolene and Fancy are gonna be rich." Her face scrunches. "Except we haven't found no truffles, and Jolene's gone and run off." She turns her face and cups a hand around her mouth like a megaphone. "Jolene, come back!"

Fancy snorts, then plops to the ground to lay on her side.

Anna Leigh tugs on the leash. "Get up, Fancy." She looks back at me again. "She's depressed 'cuz she thinks her husband's left her for good like Tilly's did." She leans closer and whispers. "That's what I heard Mr. MacDonald telling Mama last time we were in the general store. But between you and me, I think Tilly's better off without him. At least that's what Mama said."

I nod because I'm not sure exactly how to respond. "Would you like some help in finding Jolene?"

"Yes, please." She rocks forward on her toes and marches around me to continue her search.

I have no idea how long this little girl has been away from home, and her mother might be starting to get worried about her. "Hey, Anna Leigh, hold up a second."

She pivots to look at me. "Yeah?"

"Do you think Jolene would go back home? Maybe he got hungry and he's just waiting to be let back into his pigpen for some delicious slop."

Her face brightens. "You're real smart, Miss Hayley. Are you a teacher or somethin'?"

"I'm a librarian."

"Really?" Her eyes round. "I've never been to a real library before. My classroom has some books we can read, but Mrs. Huggins doesn't let us take them home. That's where I read about pigs sniffin' out truffles."

I'm guessing she missed the part about black truffles growing wild in Europe and not in the hills of eastern Tennessee. It's easier to focus on this piece of information than the fact she's never stepped foot inside a library before. As soon as we get back to her house, I'm going to invite her and her mom over to Levi's Service Station to look around the bookmobile and she can check out all the books she wants.

Fancy grunts with each little trot step she takes beside Anna Leigh, pulling my attention down to the pig.

"Fancy's an interesting name for a pig. Jolene too, especially since he's a boy pig."

Anna Leigh glances up at me as she continues walking. "I

named Fancy after Fancy Nancy. Why else do you think she's wearing her tutu?"

Why else indeed?

"And we thought Jolene was Fancy's sister when we first got them. Boy, were we wrong. But you just can't up and change someone's name, you know? That would give them an excited crisis, and we don't want one of those."

"Existential crisis?"

"That's what I said."

A dog barks, the sound a low warning that causes my steps to slow.

Anna Leigh notices my hesitation. "You don't gotta worry about Bruno none. Especially since you're with me."

I take Anna Leigh's word for it but inch closer to her just the same. A second later, a chocolate brown hound dog, long ears flopping on either side of his head, comes bounding out of the underbrush. He barks again, this time in what sounds like a greeting, trots over, and bounces a bit in his excitement. He shakes his head, and one of his ears folds backward, exposing the inside of his ear canal and making him look more like a goofball than a guard dog.

"Have you seen Jolene, Bruno?"

The dog tilts his head to the side as he peers at Anna Leigh.

"I really wish animals could talk like in the movies, don't you, Miss Hayley?"

"Wouldn't that be something," I say.

A single-wide trailer that's seen better days comes into view. The screen door creaks open, then slaps shut. A woman who must be Anna Leigh's mother stands with one hand on her hip and the other shielding her eyes from the sun.

"Anna Leigh, where have you been?" Her voice is a mixture of exasperation and relief.

"Truffle hunting," Anna Leigh responds like this is the only obvious answer in the world.

"Truffle . . ." The woman shakes her head. She notices me for the first time, and curiosity causes her to tilt her head much like Bruno had as she walks forward to meet us in the front yard. "Hello, there. I'm Shelby Hayward, Anna Leigh's mama."

I shake her hand. "Hayley Holt, the circulation librarian from Little Creek."

Recognition dawns. "Oh, right. I heard you were coming. Although I thought that was supposed to have been yesterday."

"It was. The bookmobile broke down."

"Levi taking a look at it?"

I nod. "He is."

"Then it'll be fixed up in no time."

"I'm sure it will. In the meantime, I was hoping everyone in Turkey Grove would take advantage of the bookmobile while it's here. It's chockful of all kinds of books." I cut my gaze down to Anna Leigh. "I'm pretty sure I even have a few that feature talking animals."

Anna Leigh's blue eyes brighten. "Do you have *Charlotte's Web*? I watched the movie with Fancy and Jolene, but I just know they'd love it if I read the book to them. That is, I can bring the book home, right? I promise I won't drop it or get it dirty or nothin'."

I grin at her. "Yes, you can check the book out and bring it home."

A high-pitched squeal from the other side of the trailer interrupts us.

Anna Leigh takes off running, Fancy's stubby legs trying hard to keep up. "Jolene, you came back!"

Shelby Hayward shakes her head, a small smile on her lips. "That girl does beat all. Truffle hunting. What will she think of next?"

My smile matches hers. "I'm sure she keeps you on your toes."

She grunts an agreement but manages to make the sound ladylike somehow. "You could say that again and twice on

Sundays." After shaking her head once more, she turns back to me. "I'd wanted to stop by the bookmobile yesterday but wasn't going to be able to make it, so the fact you're still here, while inconvenient for you, I'm sure, works out perfectly for me and Anna Leigh. I can round her up and we can head on over to Levi's now, if that works for you."

"Perfect."

Today might have threatened to have a rocky start, but it's already looking brighter.

12

Levi had gotten down to the service station early to do a visual check and some diagnostic testing on the bookmobile. He probably should've waited around the house for the spritely librarian to wake up and come out of the bedroom so he could apologize for his outburst in person, but he figured she'd want to know how long she had to put up with his sorry carcass, and he couldn't tell her that until he had some answers as to what was wrong with the bookmobile. Well, that and the DOT and Forest Service timelines, but he didn't have any control over when the state would clear the roads.

It hadn't taken long after he'd popped the hood to see where the problem lay. The alternator cables were covered in green corrosion, exposing wires. The corrosion triggered electrical resistance that led to overheating, which caused the smoke she'd seen coming from the engine area. He should have asked her if there had been any type of smell that she'd noticed yesterday when she'd broken down. There could still be other problems with the vehicle as well, but he'd definitely need to replace the wiring and the alternator itself.

While he was at it, he might as well give the thing a tune-up. Replace the air filter, fuel filter, oxygen sensor, and spark plugs.

Flush the transmission, brake, and coolant fluids. Wouldn't hurt to check the serpentine belt or the transfer case fluid either. He didn't want to think about the feisty little strawberry-blond broken down on the side of the road again. What if next time someone with less honorable intentions was the one to find her alone and defenseless?

Yeah, he wasn't going to let that happen if he could help it. And he could. By making sure this old van ran better than it had when it'd first come off the production line.

"Hullo, anyone there?" A familiar voice interrupted Levi's inspection.

Jack MacDonald. General Store owner, busybody, and self-appointed town council chairman. Not that Turkey Grove had a town council to be chairman of, but Jack didn't seem to care about that little detail.

The first time Constance had come to visit, she'd gotten a huge kick out of meeting Jack. She'd laughed and gone on and on about how he was just like Taylor Doose. At her brother's confused expression, she'd just laughed some more. Then she'd made him sit through an entire season of *Gilmore Girls*, and Levi had never been able to look at Jack the same again.

Levi pulled his head out from under the hood and reached for the rag nearby, wiping what grease and gunk he could from his fingers. His cuticles sported a continuous black ring, but washing his hands with Fast Orange later would take most of the grime from his hands. For now, the rag would have to do.

"What can I help you with, Jack? Got a problem with your car?"

"Nothing like that." He hooked his thumbs through the belt loops of his faded jeans. "I just saw you towing in that fancy bookmobile yesterday and wanted to stop by and make sure everything is all right."

Translation: He was there for any gossip he could spread along to his customers.

"A vehicle gets towed to a service station means it's broken down. Not much to see, if you ask me."

Jack chuckled. "I'd normally agree with you, but a lot of folks were looking forward to that there library on wheels coming yesterday and were disappointed when it didn't show up." He reached up and scratched under the band of his ball cap. "Do you think the librarian would let us in and get a look around? Maybe get the Wi-Fi set up if she can? Check some books out? Get a library card?"

"You mean—" Levi looked around the open space of his garage, picturing people milling about. Dread filled his middle. "Here?"

Jack nodded. "Unless you've already gotten it running again and she can drive it on over to the General Store parking lot."

"No." He hadn't even finished running all the diagnostics yet.

Jack nodded again. Or maybe he'd never stopped in the first place. He had a habit of mimicking a bobblehead. Probably thought it made him appear like he was constantly mulling over something important. "So, do you think she'd be willing to open the bookmobile up to the townsfolk for a bit?"

"I—" Levi started.

"She actually had the same idea and is here to do just that."

Levi spun slowly on his steel-toed bootheel. Hayley stood in front of the open bay door, the sun shining around her like spilled light. His heartbeat caught in his throat and lodged there, making it difficult to breathe.

He'd been about to turn Jack down flat. The service station wasn't a place for people to come and go willy-nilly. It was a business, and he had work to do that couldn't be done if he had to worry about someone getting into something they had no business messing with and hurting themselves on his machinery. Everyone could check out the bookmobile *after* he was done working on it.

Except now, as he stared at Hayley, who was the epitome of everything that was good and wholesome in the world, he felt himself softening. If she asked, he had a sinking suspicion that he'd say yes. For the life of him, he didn't know why, but he wanted to keep that sweet smile on her lips. Maybe he could even make up for his boorish behavior the night before.

Hayley stepped forward. "Well, *maybe* here to do just that. I need to talk to Levi first." She gestured toward his office. "Can I speak with you for a moment?"

Levi swallowed and nodded. He walked over to the office door without a word and opened it for Hayley. When he closed the door behind him, Hayley pivoted and turned her face up. Pink tinged her cheeks, highlighting the constellation of freckles that more than just spattered across the bridge of her nose. He'd always found freckles immensely attractive and didn't know why so many women tried so hard to cover them up. They added character and uniqueness to a person's face. On Hayley, they were spellbinding.

Her lashes lowered, fanning her cheekbones before she raised her eyes again to meet his. "I'm sorry about springing this on you. I'd wanted to talk to you first about possibly opening the bookmobile for a few hours or even a whole day, if possible. But then I ran into Anna Leigh on my walk down the mountain, and she's never even been inside a library before, and my excitement got the better of me, and I invited her and her mom over. Then my mouth ran away with me again when I heard that man asking if I was willing to open the doors for everyone and . . . " She shrugged sheepishly. "I'm sorry."

Before he knew what he was doing, he reached out and squeezed her shoulder. She looked down, peering at his big paw on the delicate curve of her arm. Stupid of him. Of course she didn't want him touching her. Why would she?

He dropped his hand and curled his fingers into his palm. Not to keep the sensation of the touch away, he realized with surprise, but to savor the feel and warmth of her. Hold it close as long as possible.

Huh. He'd definitely never wanted to do that before.

"I totally understand if you don't want a bunch of people coming and going, interrupting your work. I stocked the books on the shelves in the bookmobile myself, so I have a decent recollection of what titles are available. I can make a list and let people choose from that, then pull titles people select. Or maybe there's a cart or something I can pile some books in and take around town that way."

Levi's cheek twitched under his beard. Why was he finding this exchange adorable and not annoying? With anyone else, he'd unquestionably be grinding his teeth so hard a headache would be starting to develop. With her, he found he wanted to smile.

"It's fine." His voice came out gruff—much gruffer than he intended or expected—and he frowned.

Hayley frowned too. A little wrinkle appeared between her eyes as she studied him. "It's fine that there may be a steady stream of people coming in and out of the service station? Are you sure?"

He nodded. He didn't blame her for questioning him. He hadn't exactly shown himself to be a man who anyone would call welcoming or friendly now, had he? But he could put up with a small, interspersed crowd for a few hours. The van could only hold a couple of people at a time inside anyway, and he figured the same rules of quietness in a library applied to the mobile ones as well.

"It's fine that they may talk and laugh and make a bunch of noise?"

So maybe the same rules didn't apply, but still, if it would make her happy, then he'd deal with the distractions. "I said it's fine."

The lines on her face softened. "If you're sure, okay, then."

106

Levi glanced around the room. There was work he could do in here. Some emails he needed to return and inventory to be ordered. He didn't have a buyer lined up for the Barracuda, so he could put out some feelers to see if anyone in the classic car world was interested in adding the Plymouth to their collection. It wasn't how he'd planned to spend the day, and he'd make zero progress on fixing the bookmobile, but he could tell her job was important to her and that the thought of getting to share books with others gave her joy.

He wanted to give her joy as well.

He reached behind him and found the knob, opening the door and gesturing to the garage. "Consider my shop as your library for the day. If you need me, I'll be in here, getting some work done."

She beamed up at him, the effect causing his heart to trip against one of his ribs. "You keep coming to my rescue, Levi. You really are a hero, you know that, right?" Without warning, she leapt forward and wrapped her arms around his middle, hugging him tight then skipping away before he'd even realized that her body was pressed snuggly to his, warm and firm and . . . comforting?

He stared after her retreating back. What had just happened? What had she said? Him, a hero? No one had ever called Levi a hero before. Uptight, neurotic—that, and more. A hero? Never in his life.

He wished it were true.

But then again . . .

If he were to do anything about the confusing swirl of uncharted feelings she stirred within him, well, he'd have to be the most selfish antihero to act upon them.

13

The blinds on the glass window separating the office and garage were open. Levi should have probably closed them so he could've gotten some actual work done over the past—he glanced over at the wall clock—three hours. Instead, he'd been peering through the horizontal slats, observing Little Creek's circulation librarian. Watching her over the span of the morning had solidified the first impressions formed in his mind about her.

She smiled easily and was friendly with all. Warmth exuded from her with every word and every glance, putting people at ease and making them feel welcomed and important. She thrived on interacting with each person who approached the bookmobile, seeming to glow brighter as she bid adieu to another new library patron with a stack of books tucked under their arm.

He understood why everyone seemed drawn to her. Why they lingered outside the van's side door to speak with her for just a few more minutes. What he didn't comprehend, however, was the pull *he* felt toward her.

Because he had never felt any sort of desire to spend time with another person before in his life.

Ever.

As a child, school had been torturous. Too many kids in too small of a classroom. Nobody followed the no talking rule, some whispering to seatmates while others would shout across the room to their friends on the other side. Which, of course, only made the teacher have to raise her own voice to be heard above the din.

Levi was slightly ashamed to admit, but he'd been a bit of a nightmare for his teachers. He'd learned that if he misbehaved, he'd be sent out to the hall or to the office—both places that were quiet and still enough that it didn't make his skin feel too tight, his heart race, or his head explode like someone had placed a stick of dynamite between his ears.

And church? Well, let's just say he had never experienced a peace that surpassed understanding beneath a steeple. The suit his mom made him wear itched, the PA system had a constant high-pitched hum, and the perfume the ladies wore gave him an instant headache.

Home wasn't much better. His sisters always bickered or had some sort of drama going on. They'd play music too loud or use too much body spray. There was no such thing as peace and definitely no such thing as quiet.

One day, he'd found some pieces of plywood in the garage and asked his dad if he could have them. Then he'd climbed a big oak tree in the backyard and nailed the plywood to a couple of thick branches. Not exactly a treehouse, but that platform in the treetop became his escape. Only his mom had ever been allowed up there with him. They would sit side by side, each reading their own book, neither saying a word. There, he could simply be. Guard down with no fear of being attacked by the world around him.

Why, then, did he have this unquenchable craving to simply be near Hayley?

After hours of watching her from a distance, the build-up inside him could no longer be denied. It was a need deep in his soul that he didn't understand. How could he, when he'd never felt this way about anyone ever before?

But so much in life didn't make sense. He'd given up trying to untangle the mysteries of existence a long time ago. All he knew was that he wanted to be near her, hear her voice, watch expressions waltz across her upturned face. Feel her smile. If only for a little while. Because a little while was probably all he could handle before things became too much for him. Everything always eventually became too much for him. Even the good things.

He glanced again at the clock. Lunchtime.

He hurried up to the house and threw together a few sandwiches, grabbing a bag of potato chips from the pantry and a couple of apples from the fruit bowl on the counter. He didn't have a picnic basket to carry everything in, but he did have a backpack he used while hiking, so he placed the food in that, then beat a path back down the hill again.

When he stepped into the garage portion of the service station, there weren't any other people around. Shuffling noises came from inside the bookmobile. Hayley straightening books and rearranging things, no doubt.

Levi would take advantage of the lull. He lifted his hand and knocked on the open door.

Hayley spun, a copy of *To Kill a Mockingbird* clutched to her chest. "Goodness gracious, Levi, you about gave me a heart attack. How can a man of your size make so little noise?"

"Sorry. Didn't mean to startle you."

She pushed back a strand of hair from her face. "That's all right. Did you want to come in and look around?"

Her voice was so inviting that Levi couldn't tell her no. Besides, he was actually a little curious. This van was another piece of her, and he was greedy enough to want to collect as many pieces of Hayley as he could.

He folded his body, ducking down and turning himself at

an angle so that he could fit through the doorway. It was a bit of a squeeze, but he managed to accordion himself in such a way that he made it through. Although now that he was in, the small, enclosed space seemed to shrink even more. His shoulders knocked into the shelves on both sides of him and he had to hunch down so as not to hit his head.

"Oh dear." Hayley covered her mouth, but her eyes belied her smile. "You're a bit like Alice after she eats the cake and grows so big that she doesn't fit inside the house anymore."

He gave her a wry look. "I'm glad my size amuses you."

"Not exactly the word I'd use," she said under her breath, but not so low that Levi couldn't hear.

Curiosity piqued, he wondered what word she *would* use to describe him.

Hero.

Yeah, he still wasn't believing that one.

Maybe he was a bit of a masochist after all. A good portion of his body was being touched by something—his arms by the shelves, his head and neck by the ceiling—and instead of squeezing back out the door so he could stand up straight, take in a deep breath, and shake off the sensations crawling along his skin, he lowered himself to his knees and pulled his elbows in tight to his ribs, making himself as small as possible to try and keep himself from rubbing against any parts of the bookmobile's insides.

"Cozy?" Hayley asked, amusement still written across her face.

On his knees, he and Hayley were about eye-level. She met his gaze, not breaking away to peer over his shoulder or even using the book in her hand as an excuse to look away to reshelve the title. She studied him much the same way he'd been studying her through the blinds all morning.

Whatever skittishness he'd caused her when they'd first met seemed to have vanished, even with the outrageous way he'd behaved toward her.

Speaking of behavior . . . "I'm sorry. For last night."

She shook her head lightly. "You don't have to apologize. I think I understand now."

Understood what? Him? There probably was something about him that needed *understanding*, and he hated that. Why couldn't he just be like every other guy in the world?

Case in point, every other guy would be reveling in this moment. Tight quarters with a beautiful woman who was paying them undivided attention? A perfect opportunity to flirt and be charming. Every other guy would be breathing in the scent of her. The scent of him *on* her. Of them. Mingled. That base, primitive, biological part of their brain triggered by the mixing of pheromones and the headiness of some sort of scented claim.

But the inside of Levi's head had begun to look like Chernobyl right before the nuclear reactors exploded. Warning bells blasting, pressure building. He needed to get out of the bookmobile. Quick.

"Not cozy," Hayley amended, sensing the change in him without him having to say a word. As if she could read him as easily as any one of the books on the shelves surrounding them. "Confining."

He wasn't sure how she did it, but one minute he was kneeling in front of her and the next she'd shoved him out the door.

He gulped in a couple deep pockets of air, his haywire nerves sparking less and less with each swallow of oxygen. "Thanks," he said. "And sorry again. About that." He waved his hand weakly at the open door.

He remembered when he was somewhere around the age of eight or nine, he'd asked his mom what was wrong with him. No one else seemed to have the same kind of trouble he did merely existing in the world around them, so obviously something must have been wrong with him. She'd gathered him on her lap and banded her arms around him like a boa constrictor—Mom gave the best kind of hugs, tight and heavy—and told him in a firm voice that there wasn't anything wrong. He was like a superhero—like Spiderman and his spidey senses. Levi had forced a smile to try and erase the worry he saw in her eyes, but in his heart, he knew she was just making that up to try to make him feel better.

He wasn't special. He was defective.

"Don't apologize about *that*." Hayley focused a stern look on him, appearing every inch a caricature of an exacting librarian, sans bifocals perched on her nose and hair tied back in a severe bun. Bossy. Authoritarian.

Levi kind of liked it. He kind of like it a lot.

"Never apologize for *that*," she stressed.

He nodded, wanting to change the subject, then lifted the backpack off the ground. "I brought lunch."

She brightened, and just like that, the embarrassment of his reaction was washed away as if it had never happened. "Thank you. I'm starving."

He looked around. There had to be something better than the oil-stained cement ground to offer her as a seat. He spotted the rolling mechanic creeper he used when he had to position himself under a vehicle's chassis. Not exactly a chair, but it was cushioned and would be more comfortable than the cold, hard ground. With a push of his foot, he sent the swivel wheels spinning toward Hayley.

She stopped the creeper's movement with her own foot, then lowered herself down on one side, patting the other.

Levi eyed where her hand made a tapping motion.

"There's enough room for both of us."

He hesitated. What if his body betrayed him again? What if the anomaly of her—or his reaction to her, rather—was just that? An aberration that was here for but a blessed moment but had already vanished? Right then, in the in-between, he still had the small sliver of hope that Hayley was different.

That he'd finally met someone who didn't make him feel . . . what? Too much? Wasn't that what most people searched for? Someone who made them feel more? More alive? More sparks? More of everything?

Yet another tally mark under the column that made him know something wasn't quite right with him. That he wasn't like other guys.

He wasn't standing there, hoping that if he sat next to Hayley that he'd feel more. That fireworks would shoot off or internal chemistry would ignite a fire between them. He wanted to sit next to her and feel, well, not less, exactly. Just . . .

He shook his head. He didn't know what. He just knew he didn't want and probably couldn't handle *more*.

Hayley's brow furrowed. "You're not going to sit?"

Levi moved to the side. The creeper was long enough for both of them, but barely. He didn't want to accidentally crush her, so he lowered himself slowly until he was perched in the padded bench, his knees almost up to his chin. He unfolded his legs and let them shoot out straight ahead of him, his heels digging into the cement floor.

"See? Plenty of room." Hayley smirked over the curve of her shoulder at him and then did a little shimmy to emphasize her point.

A shimmy he felt up and down his bicep as the sides of their bodies were lined up against each other, touching all the way from her shoulder against his arm, to her hip against his thigh, and her ankle against his calf.

He waited for the assault to come. For his skin to overreact, the hairs on his arms to rise like hackles on a dog, the snarling an uncomfortable sensation at each point where they touched.

It wasn't that he didn't like physical contact. He did, actually. It was just that he only liked certain types of touches. The other kinds . . . well, unfortunately, the other types were how most people touched one another. Lightly. Softly. Carefully. Caresses and gentle strokes. Touches like those made him want to crawl out of his body and flay off his skin.

Except with his family, Levi had never told anyone how he liked to be touched. One didn't go around commanding people to only touch him with firm, deep pressure; the harder the better. They'd have looked at Levi like he was some kind of twisted human with dark, depraved tastes.

Even though their bodies were pressed together, instead of scuttling away, Hayley scooted herself in his direction, pushing firmly into him and instantly settling his fired-up nerve endings.

"Sorry," she said. "I was about to fall off the edge."

"It's—" He cleared his throat. "It's fine."

More than fine. His body hummed with contentment instead of buzzing frantically. He sank farther into the seat. A satisfied calm came to rest between each one of his ribs, and he took in a deep, relaxed breath of air.

It hadn't been an anomaly. He'd never thought it would happen, but Levi had finally found someone he could stand to be around. Someone who quieted his spirit and calmed the chaos inside him.

He'd finally found her, and if the DOT timeline stayed the same, he was going to have to let her go in less than two weeks.

14

Word seemed to spread that the bookmobile was open for business, the influx of people streaming in the afternoon almost doubling what the morning had brought. Most of the people Levi had never seen before, which wasn't much of a surprise. Besides Jack MacDonald, who made a nuisance of himself to anyone within a drivable radius, and Deborah Smith, the retired doctor who Jack had dragged into Levi's house last winter when he'd been sick with COVID, Levi didn't really know many of his neighbors. He recognized a few faces here and there—the owner of the Chevy Silverado that he'd replaced brake pads on two weeks ago, for instance—but he couldn't put any names to those faces.

What he also couldn't do was fool himself into thinking he was going to get any work done. Not at the service station, anyway. Which meant he might as well go home and start chipping away at some of the things he needed to get done there.

He didn't exactly want to walk into the bay, not when there were—he peeked through the office blinds and counted—six people waiting to become new members of the Polk County library system, but he also didn't want to leave without letting Hayley know where he was in case she needed him for some reason.

Bracing himself, he opened the door and stepped out of his little sanctuary and into the fray. If he was lucky, he could catch Hayley for a quick word before anyone else stopped him to chitchat.

He'd only managed to take a few steps before Jack turned and noticed him. The other man's eye lit, and a smile bloomed on the lower half of his face like it had been planted in Miracle-Gro.

Levi frowned. Why was Jack even still here? How could the man stay in business if he wasn't behind the cash register of the General Store?

"It's good to see you come out of hiding, my friend." Jack grinned.

"I wasn't hiding," Levi grumbled.

"Sure, sure." Jack turned and moved so that he blocked Levi's path. "Hey, now that I have you here, I wanted to invite you to a meeting the other small business owners are hosting next week. We're getting together to discuss ways to bring in more revenue. I don't know how it is with your service station, but a lot of us are struggling to keep our doors open."

"Hmm," Levi replied noncommittally.

Jack chuckled. "As eloquent as ever, I see." He let some of his jovial attitude slip. "Look, I get that you like to be left alone and all, but we need to band together if we're going to survive in this economy. How do you stay afloat? There aren't exactly a lot of us who need your services very often."

Levi glanced at the vintage sports car up on the lift. "Supplemental income."

Jack scratched his chin. "That's not a bad idea." He clapped Levi on the shoulder. "See, we need your wisdom at that meeting."

"I'll think about it," Levi said. He had no inclination to give the gathering a second of consideration, but Jack would continue to hound him if he didn't at least promise to think about it.

"Good man." He wagged a finger at Levi, his grin firmly back in place. "You're a hard nut, but one of these days I'm going to crack you."

"Okay." Levi walked around Jack with a determined stride. The faster he got to Hayley, the sooner he could get out of there.

As if sensing him before he fully approached, Hayley turned from her spot at the open side door of the bookmobile, her soft smile in place. "Hey there, big guy."

Tension drained from Levi's shoulders. Just seeing her sweet smile and hearing the melodic cadence of her voice worked a small and immediate transformation in him. "Hi."

"Your ears must have been burning because I was just talking about you to Robin here." Hayley turned her attention to the woman in front of her.

Levi recognized her. She drove a Honda Odyssey that she brought in for regular maintenance. The engine was still running well with almost three hundred thousand miles on it.

Levi tipped his head. "Ma'am."

"Thank you for opening the service station in this capacity, Mr. Redding. I'm an avid reader and already access the library through their lending apps, but nothing beats a physical copy in your hands, am I right?"

"Like having a friend right beside you," Hayley concurred. "If you could see all the books on Levi's own shelves, Robin, you'd know that he agrees with you." She smirked at him as if they shared a secret.

"I thought I recognized a kindred spirit in you." Robin turned her open, welcoming face to him.

Levi cleared his throat as he split his attention between Robin and Hayley. He didn't want to be rude, but he was also itching to get away.

"Is there something you wanted to talk to me about?" Hayley asked, coming to his rescue.

Levi exhaled in relief. "I'm heading to the house. If you need me, that's where I'll be."

"Thanks for letting me know. Do you want me to lock up here when I'm done?"

He pulled out his keys and showed her which one would lock the office. "There's a padlock for the bay door as well." The alarm system he could turn on from the app on his phone.

He managed to make it out of the garage with a few dips of his head in acknowledgement to people but fortunately wasn't engaged in anymore conversation.

As much as he hated to admit it, his conscience pricked as he walked up the narrow trail to his house. Maybe he should put in a little more effort at being friendly. A smile wouldn't kill him. A few nice words here and there with people was well within the bounds of things he could handle. After he'd moved away from home, he was self-aware enough to realize he'd swung to the other extreme side of the social pendulum. Living the way he did, alone and shutting everyone out, made his life easier. But easier wasn't necessarily better. Maybe it was time to explore where a happy medium was. Where his true boundaries lay.

Once home, he beelined straight to his bedroom. The weather would hold for a little longer, but cooler nights were around the corner, and he needed to make headway on his winter supply of firewood. The house had central heat, but he used the fireplace for warmth and to cut down the cost of his electric bill. He'd already downed a few trees on his property and used the chainsaw to cut them, but the wooden stumps were still waiting to be chopped with an ax and stacked inside the woodshed. Which meant he needed to get out of his coveralls and into his well-worn pair of denim jeans and a breathable T-shirt.

119

He opened the door to his bedroom and walked in, stopping when his shoe made a weird crinkle sound that didn't belong to the wood floors. Looking down, he spotted a folded piece of paper peeking out from under his sole. He bent down and picked it up, his pulse doing a little skip before settling again. Papers didn't grow legs and walk to their destinations, and there hadn't been any memos or notes he'd left lying around that would have fallen on the floor. Which meant Hayley must have slipped a letter under his door this morning before she'd left the house.

He unfolded the paper, the looping cursive handwriting causing him to smile. Her handwriting was a bit like her personality, unreserved and cheerful. Sitting heavily on the edge of his bed, he settled in to read, a bubble of hopeful anticipation inside his chest.

Dear Levi,
  Do you know that your letter is the first I've ever received? I mean, I get the ones addressed to Ms. Holt that go on to congratulate me on being preapproved for their credit card, but those don't count.

Levi chuckled even as his heart swelled. Illogical pride pumped in his bloodstream at being a first in Hayley's life. A first for anything—even something as simple as a personally penned letter—felt intimate somehow. Like it connected them in a way that was unique. She could never have that with another human being. It was something that now belonged only to him.

It probably sounds silly, but I always wanted a pen pal. My obsession with the idea of writing letters more than likely started after I read Daddy-Long-Legs *by Jean Webster during one of my hospital stays. I wish I could say it was only the thought of having a special friendship at the other end of a postage stamp that intrigued me, but I refuse to be embarrassed to admit that I spent quite a bit of time daydreaming about my nonexistent pen pal falling hopelessly in love with me through our letter exchange.*

Levi looked up from her hypnotizing handwriting and focused on the blank white wall in front of him, processing what he'd just read. His brain tripped over a phrase she'd so easily written, as if something so defining were as effortlessly communicated as sharing a favorite color or admitting you'd never tried guacamole.

One of my hospital stays. Just how many times had Hayley been admitted to the hospital in her life? What had caused her to be admitted? Was the medical condition no longer an issue, or was it something she still struggled with in adulthood?

His gaze whipped to the window as if he could see down to the garage and Hayley there. A protective surge rose within him, but he forced himself to stay where he was. His barreling in and acting like a brute wouldn't serve any purpose besides assuaging his own concerns. Hayley certainly wouldn't thank him for it.

You just saw her and she was fine, he reminded himself instead.

But what if she needs a hospital again? With the roads closed, there's no way to get her to a doctor, his unhelpful brain picked at him.

He clenched his teeth. If it came to that, he'd move every single one of those boulders with his own bare hands.

He unlocked his jaw and forced his gaze back to the letter. She'd had a girlish fantasy about falling in love through written words exchanged with a stranger. He wasn't a wealthy philanthropist fourteen years her senior paying for her college education, nor was she an orphan whose name had been chosen for her from a gravestone, but they were near-strangers and he was more than capable of fulfilling a long-held desire of receiving letters.

He shouldn't do it, try to make her fall in love with him. It would be like catching a butterfly and keeping it in a glass jar when it was made to fly and share its beauty with the rest of the world. It would be selfish of him, wanting to keep her all to himself.

But how could he let her go when she was the only one who had ever silenced the noise in his head? When she seemed to be able to read him as easily as her favorite book while everyone else had only ever looked at him like he'd been written in a language they couldn't decipher? It would be selfish, but he was okay with a little villainy if it meant he wouldn't have to say good-bye.

Levi read the rest of Hayley's letter. She went on to talk about how her love of books sparked in her the desire to become a librarian, especially once her parents had told her they could no longer afford to constantly buy her new books. After that, she'd walk to the library at least once a week on her way home from school, collecting book boyfriends like Jesse Tuck, Gilbert Blythe, and Prince Kai.

Levi wasn't sure how he could compete with those fictional heroes, but he could find pen and paper and craft letters that he hoped would start to make the earth beneath her feet crumble until she found herself falling as hard and as fast as he was.

15

I hate to admit it, but Mayor Breckenbridge had done good. Maybe I should take back my curse on him.

Mrs. Fieldman looks behind her when she reaches the bay doors and gives me a little wave with the hand not clutching the first two books of the LUNAR CHRONICLES series. I smile and wave back, dropping my hand once she's rounded the corner and is out of sight. The diner owner is the last patron on a rather successful series of days.

I don't know if it's the novelty—the bookmobile's maiden voyage and all—or the fact that everyone is stuck in Turkey Grove at the moment, or if the residents here have been waiting for library services to be a possibility in their lives all this time.

Whatever the reason, I'd call the last week a triumph. Not only have I been able to help people sign up for library cards, check out books for them, and show the new patrons how to work the library's webpage in order to put holds on other titles they'd like me to bring next time, but I was also able to lend a hand to Jack's nephew in filling out his FAFSA application, then point him to an ACT study guide. I'd also overheard Jack talking to Levi about a small business meeting they were planning to have. I'd then been able to pull Jack aside and show him the research tool that allowed patrons access to databases with industry-specific information curated for businesses and entrepreneurs.

All in all, I couldn't imagine things having gone any better. Levi had been gracious to allow me to use his garage in the afternoons to open up the bookmobile. We'd developed a sort of rhythm that seemed to work well. He never stuck around too long after his neighbors started showing up, but he didn't act put out either. Assured me he was staying busy getting ready for winter. I still felt a little bad, but seeing all the good the bookmobile was doing for the people of Turkey Grove assuaged most of my guilt.

I dig my thumbs into the muscles on either side of my spine, then arch my back. Even though this week has been good, it's also been long. I'm ready to lock up and call it quits for the evening.

I finish putting everything in the bookmobile away and turn off the tablet, though I plan to bring the device with me. Signal is spotty, but Jack was right that the General Store parking lot is one of the more consistent places with a strong signal. Because of that, I've been setting up there in the mornings, creating a Wi-Fi hotspot for anyone needing to use the internet. One thing I'll talk to Mayor Breckenridge about when I get back is investing in satellite internet for Cletus. Leveling the playing field, bridging the gap, and building community hubs are all values that libraries stand for, and we can't do that successfully without connectivity.

Double-checking that I have everything, I shut Cletus up for the night, then engage the deadlock on the office door. My shoes make soft slapping noises on the hard concrete beneath my feet, echoing in the large space. The sun has dipped behind the tops of the trees, casting long shadows across the parking area. I push the button on the wall to lower the sectional garage door, the gears and moving metal clattering in the otherwise quiet country air. With a thud, the door finishes its descent and I secure the padlock.

"Meow."

The pathetic cry comes from somewhere behind me. I think of Anna Leigh traipsing all over the woods looking for Jolene. What's with everyone's pets running away lately? I look up the mountain to Levi's house longingly but turn on my heel with a sigh. Someone is probably worried about their lost kitty right now. No matter how much I want to get up that mountain, I can't let a pet spend the night out in the cold.

"Here, kitty kitty kitty," I call.

Another plaintiff meow rips into the air, followed by two more. Three missing cats? Oh dear. I hunch down and search the bushes alongside Levi's building.

"Meow."

There, among the brambles, is a small cardboard box. I reach in, careful not to get scratched by the branches, and gingerly pull the box out. Inside lay three tiny newborn kittens, one gray, one brown, and one a creamy blond color. Their eyes are closed, and they wobble on their legs anytime they try to stand.

"You poor little dears!" I pick the box up and cradle it to my chest.

These aren't lost pets. These kittens have been purposefully dumped here. Who would do such a thing?

I hold the box tighter. "No one is going to hurt you now." My gaze returns to the top of the mountain, and I nibble on the inside of my cheek. Newborn animals are a lot of work. Feedings every few hours, constant attention. But I'm basically a stray and Levi took me in. He wouldn't turn his back on these helpless creatures either, would he?

I look down at the mewling triplets. "You guys are going to have to be extra cute and win him over."

On the off chance that I'm wrong and the bundle in my arms aren't outcasts but have simply been misplaced by an irresponsible person who had been by for the bookmobile, I head across the street to the General Store. If there's one thing I've learned, it's that Jack MacDonald knows everyone and everything that goes on in Turkey Grove.

A little bell over the door jingles as I step in.

Jack is standing behind the counter and grins when he sees me. "Hey there. What can I do you for?"

I walk over to him and tilt the box toward him. "I found these kittens outside the garage. Any idea if they belong to someone and were accidentally left behind?"

Jack reaches up and adjusts the brim of his stained ball cap. "Left, you say?"

I nod.

His gaze lifts and meets mine. "Let me make a few calls real quick, but my guess is that whoever left them doesn't want them back."

My heart squeezes. These kittens are too young to be away from their mother. If I hadn't found them, they probably wouldn't have lasted through the night.

I mosey away from the counter to give Jack a little privacy as he makes his calls. The store is smaller than it appears from the outside, only five aisles cutting straight paths down the middle of the space. I weave between two shelves and peruse the items he has stocked. Sarsaparilla candy in the shape of tiny wooden barrels, Slim Jims, and individual bags of potato chips on one side. Fishing tackle, small garden tools, and mosquito repellant on the other. Farther down are a few nonperishable food items next to household cleaning supplies.

I peek over and see that Jack is still on the phone. The dog treats remind me that I'm going to need something to feed the kittens, but they're too young for solid food and I don't think straight cow's milk is going to do it. I doubt Turkey Grove has a feed store or pet store, which are the only two places I can think of that would have a kitten-specific formula.

a blanket. My stomach flips over on itself as I lift my hand to cover my smile. Levi the lumberjack and Levi the human kitten pillow are two sides of the same coin, and both are making me feel some kind of way.

Levi opens his eyes, the tips of his ears turning a cute shade of pink. There's a nest of blankets and fluffy towels beside his shoulder, obviously where the kittens were *supposed* to go.

I lean my shoulder against the doorjamb and grin at him. "What happened here?" I whisper.

"Would you believe me if I said they overpowered me?" he whispers back.

My grin widens. "I saw you wield that ax, mountain man. I ain't buying it."

The pink travels to his cheeks. "I guess adorable things are my weakness." But he's not looking at the kittens asleep in a row down the core of his body. He's looking at me. As if implying that I am an adorable thing that makes him weak.

Is Levi Redding, self-proclaimed grump and recluse, *flirting* with me? My mind scrambles to catch up. Sure, I've moved past my initial assumption that I annoy him and he can't wait to be rid of me, but it's a huge leap from *that* to flirting. Flirting implies liking. More than liking. Or, as the middle schoolers are oft to say, *like* liking. I've been under the impression that the attraction here is entirely one-sided. Have I been wrong yet again?

And what, exactly, am I going to do with this information?

Dumpurrdore uncurls and stretches, making Levi wince.

"Claws?" I ask with a smirk.

He nods while trying to disentangle said claws from his light gray T-shirt.

"I came in to ask if you have anything to feed them with. The formula is made, but they aren't old enough to eat without being hand-fed."

He gently lifts the other two kittens and settles them into

the soft, warm bed he'd made for them on the ground. "I have a couple medicine syringes that should work."

I follow him back to the kitchen where he opens a drawer and pulls out two small oral syringes with black lines along the sides to indicate milliliter measurements. We take them and the bowl of formula and head back to the laundry room. I set the bowl on the floor, then lower myself to the tile and sit crisscross. Levi joins me on the floor, his knee and shoulder pressed against mine because of the tight space. He hands over a syringe, then scoops Hermeowne up and places the brown kitten in my lap before gathering Meowfoy against his chest. It's hard to get the formula in the syringe with just one hand, so I fill Levi's so he doesn't have to set Meowfoy down.

"Thanks," he says. He moves the tip of the syringe to the kitten's mouth and puts the slightest bit of pressure on the plunger to let out a small drop of milk. "Should we name them, do you think?"

"Oh, I, uh, already kind of named them." I duck my head, only slightly embarrassed that I hadn't waited on him to offer suggestions.

He stops feeding to lift his eyes, a question in them.

I point to the kitten in his arms with my chin. "That one you're holding is Meowfoy. This one"—I puff out my chest to indicate the one cradled there—"is Hermeowne. And that one"—I flick my gaze to the gray kitten attempting to walk across the blankets but falling down every other step—"is Dumpurrdore."

The skin around his eyes crinkles in amusement. "I'm sensing a theme."

"You're very astute."

"So that one's the only girl, then?"

My face flushes. "Checking the gender first would have been a good idea, huh?"

There's no sound coming from his lips, but his eyes are laughing at me. "Maybe." He sets the empty syringe down, then gently places Meowfoy on his feet, head facing away, and scratches the kitten on his back right above his tail. The tail raises as if on reflex, and Levi lowers his head to study the kitten's backside. "This one is a boy." He checks the other two. "They're all boys."

"Oh." Oops. "I guess Hermeowne needs a new name then."

"What about Harry Pawter?"

I blink at Levi. "Brilliant."

A soft smile plays at his lips. He looks relaxed. Maybe the most relaxed I've ever seen him.

"I got your letter," he says out of the blue.

I'd forgotten all about the letter. It feels ages ago since I slipped it under his door. At the mention of it, though, anticipation thrums through me. I'd written things that I probably wouldn't have said out loud. Amazing how the written word does that, makes you braver and more vulnerable at the same time. With Levi's initial letter, I'd felt like I understood him in a way that I haven't with anyone else simply because of that openness on the printed page.

A strange sort of disappointment sinks in my belly. I was kind of hoping that he'd write me back, but if he's bringing the letter up in conversation, I guess he'd rather talk about it than pen me another note. But of course he would. Across-the-hall pen pals is a silly notion. Letters are for long-distance, not for people who are practically living together.

"I wrote you back. Sorry it took so long."

My breath catches as my eyes snap up and pin on his. "You did?"

He nods. "I slipped it under your door, like you did."

My bottom lip is pulled between my teeth. I look at him, look at the door, then make my decision and stand. "I'm not even going to pretend to come up with some excuse about

133

needing something from my room right now that neither one of us would believe, so I'm just going to come right out and say it. I'm leaving to go read that letter now. I'll see you later."

I set the fed kitten down on the pile of blankets and retreat to my room, Levi's delighted laugh ringing in my ears.

16

Dear Hayley,

Books have a way of shaping us that is unexplainable. Our thinking, our worldview, our sympathies and desires can all be influenced by a creative pen and an open mind. While you were secretly wishing to be wooed in an epistolary fashion, I was holding on to the hope of an epic adventure filled with clues and riddles to be solved that would lead me to a great treasure. I have Treasure Island *to thank for those hours of imagining buccaneers and buried gold. Who knows, maybe it's not too late for either of our childhood bookish fantasies to come to fruition.*

My heart leaps into my throat, but I mentally tell it to slow its roll. It would be easy to jump to conclusions here. Just because Levi hints at the possibility of me finding love through letters and he's writing me letters doesn't mean he intends to be the man wooing me in epistolary fashion, as he put it. His statement is infuriatingly benign, actually. More of an off-handed comment than anything else. Was it a hint of sorts, or am I still operating under a lumberjack, kitten-pillow, hormone-induced haze?

Were your many hospital stays the beginning of your love of books? I imagine you probably had a lot of time where your movements were restricted and you escaped the drab and depressing hospital through stories. Will you tell me about it sometime? Why you needed medical attention (are you still at risk?) and the impact that had on you?

I nibble on the inside of my cheek. I don't have a problem telling people about my organ transplant. It's a fact that happened in the past, end of story. Except that it really isn't the end of the story. I still have to be vigilant and careful every day; eat right, exercise, take immunosuppressant medication daily so my body doesn't reject the transplant. Anytime I get a cough or a fever, everyone worries it's a warning sign of an infection. Even a common cold can be extremely dangerous, and I see the doctor more than the average person.

Not only that, but organ transplants have an expiration date. My new liver added years to my life that I wouldn't have without it, but the new-to-me organ won't last forever either. I'm living on borrowed time. That's something that doesn't come up in conversation naturally and can be a major mood killer, as I'm sure anyone can imagine. But Levi has specifically asked, and there isn't any reason not to tell him. Except that he'll probably look at me with pity . . .

I square my shoulders. Well, I'll just have to put it all in a letter, then, that way I won't have to watch his expression change, and I can warn him not to treat or look at me any differently or I'll curse him with perpetually damp socks for the rest of his life. The threat of blisters and fungal infections should scare him straight.

For me, books have always been a comfort, an escape. As you can imagine, living in a house with six other people was loud and often overwhelming. We lived in a typical suburban community, so there weren't any woods to escape to, but we

*did have a large, old oak tree in the backyard. I'd climb up
there, as high as I could, until my sisters bickering faded to a
decibel that didn't make my ears bleed. I needed something
to block out the world around me and found that if I focused
on a book, immersed myself in a story world, then everything around me sort of dimmed and waned. For most of
my childhood years, I had a hard time figuring life out. But
getting inside a character's head and seeing things through
their eyes and how they dealt with whatever life threw at
them helped me to sort out my own thoughts and feelings.* ·

First lumberjack Levi, then kitten-pillow Levi, and now
vulnerable-about-his-childhood Levi? How is a girl supposed
to withstand this type of swoony onslaught?

Wait. Why *am* I trying to withstand?

I'm an emotionally secure woman attracted to an unattached
man and the reason I haven't expressed to him said attraction
is . . .

I chew on the inside of my cheek again. Oh look. There's
more letter to read.

I finish reading more about Levi's family and how he learned
he liked working on cars after he and his dad restored a 1970
Pontiac GTO during his freshman and sophomore years of
high school. Levi signed his name without any type of formal
closing like *Your Friend* or *Warm Regards*. Just his name in his
nearly illegible but endearing handwriting. I go to refold the
letter but stop when I notice a postscript.

*P. S. Maybe you're like me and also wished for clues and
riddles to lead you to a hidden treasure (when you weren't
dreaming about your very own Jervis Pendleton, that is). If
that is the case, then here is your first clue:*

ORAL, p. 286, l. 12

ORAL? Like, relating to the mouth? That cannot be right. I refuse to believe his clue has anything to do with tongues, teeth, or saliva.

P. 286? Wait, does that *p* stand for page? Page 286? Which would mean the *l* stands for line. Line 12 of page 286 of a book with the acronym ORAL. What book has a title that could be shortened to those four letters?

I rack my mind trying to come up with a title, but without even a genre to narrow things down, there could be millions of options. Funny enough, my brain can't think up a single one.

I grab my phone. Time for reinforcements.

> **Me:**
> Do either of you know a book with the title acronym of ORAL?

As I wait for Martha and Evangeline to answer, I retrieve the library's tablet and power it on. While the handheld device boots up, I mentally flip through options. Once the library's logo loads, I type in my employee username and password and log on to the library's database.

Our Rogues and Ladies? The closest hit is *Lady Rogue* by Suzanne Enoch. That's not it.

One Royal Announcement Later? My screen tells me *We couldn't find any titles matching your search terms. Try another search.*

Over Rivers and Lakes? A children's book for aquatic adventures pops up.

My phone vibrates where it lays on top of my thigh, and I snatch it up.

> **Evangeline:**
> Do you know who the author is?

Me:

If I knew the author, I'd just look up all of his/her titles until I found one that matches ORAL as a title acronym.

Evangeline:

Fair point. Is this for a patron? A search like this will be almost as hard as when all they know about a book is that it has a blue cover.

Martha:

Could it be *Of Roses and Lilies*? It's the first book in a popular YA fantasy trilogy.

I have no idea if that's the clue Levi left, but I quickly type the title into the search bar. A cover appears in dark colors. Blood-red roses and snow-white lilies intertwine with thorny vines that add an element of danger to the mood, especially when one thorn seems to pierce a rose, its color bleeding onto a single lily in an ominous way. A shiver runs up my spine. I think this is it.

My gaze moves to the right of the cover image, and my heart falls to my stomach. The library has two copies, but they're both currently checked out. I could buy a digital copy and send it to the Kindle app on my phone, but ebooks show locations, not page numbers, so I wouldn't know when I reached page 286, much less be able to figure out which was line 12.

I groan but place a hold on the book and tell myself a little patience never hurt anyone.

Me:

Thanks! I think that's the one I was looking for.

Evangeline:

YOU were looking for? For yourself and not someone else?

Me:

Evangeline:

Ok, now you definitely have to spill.

Me:

It's nothing. Levi just left me a little clue to something that is on a specific page of that book.

Martha:

How very Dash and Lily-esque of him.

Evangeline:

I love that Netflix miniseries!

Martha:

The books are better.

Evangeline:

Is this some sort of romantic scavenger hunt involving book quotes that the hunky mechanic has sent you on? 😌

Me:

Who said anything about him being hunky?

Martha:

She's hung up her official matchmaking hat, but the woman is still a hopeless romantic.

Evangeline:

> And unless you send a pic to prove otherwise, I'm imagining that man as Hayley hero material.

Evangeline doesn't know how close to nail-on-the-head she is with her assessment. Levi is the kind of man who can stop a woman's heart in her chest and then send a bolt of electricity to get it started again with a single brooding look.

Could Evangeline also be right about Levi's postscript clue being of a romantic nature? He said it led to a hidden treasure, but what kind of treasure is he talking about? What does line 12 on page 286 say?

I could ask him. Straight out. Just march right up to him and ask him what it says. But that would spoil the game.

I refold his letter and place it back in the envelope, a thrill of possibility buzzing through my body and overriding any caution. I think maybe it's time I make my own move on this little gameboard between us.

17

I wish I could say that I have a plan as I make my way out of my room, but I've never been good at chess or other strategy-type games that require thinking multiple steps ahead, so I'm just going to wing it and hope that I stumble into a checkmate. The king I'm trying to capture being Levi, obviously, and a confession that I'm not the only one feeling this attraction between us.

Intuition, don't fail me now.

I make my way down the hall, pausing at the closed laundry room door. Tiny little meows sound from the other side of the pressed particle board, and I crack the door open and peek my head inside. No Levi. I close the door with a quiet snick and pad the rest of the way into the living room on socked feet.

Levi's not here either, but my gaze zeroes in on the bookcases lining the far wall. My heart makes a sudden shove against my ribs. Why hadn't I thought of this before? Of course Levi would have a copy of *Of Roses and Lilies.* Even if he'd had a specific quote memorized, he'd have had to look up the passage to see what page and line it was on to mark it in the postscript of his letter.

I hurry to one end of the bookcase and start scanning every

title written along every spine. I'm halfway through the second bookcase when a throat clears behind me.

"Needing a good book to borrow?"

I tug on the last book I've looked at and pull it out an inch to mark my place before pivoting on my heel. "I might be in the market. Do you have any recommendations?"

One corner of his lips hitches up a fraction. "What are you in the mood for?"

I tilt my chin up so I can meet his gaze. "Hmm. Let me think." I tap my lips dramatically as if deep in thought. "Know any good YA fantasy titles?"

His golden eyes flash, the only outward show of any inward reaction. "I might."

"I hear *Of Roses and Lilies* is good. Have you read it?" My tone is saucy and flirtatious. I don't want him to have to guess about my interest like he's making me do.

"I might have." His half smile ticks up another fraction of an inch.

"Any particular parts that are your favorite?"

He pauses as if considering my question carefully. "Yes, actually."

"Care to share?"

He shakes his head as he presses his lips into a thin line.

I want to pump my fist in victory because, if I'm not mistaken, he's actively trying to hide an honest-to-goodness smile.

"I wouldn't want to spoil anything for you."

"I love spoilers," I press. "I'm one of those weirdos who reads reviews and searches for the spoiler warnings."

"Next you'll tell me you skip to the last chapter and read it first."

"Is that a bad thing?"

"Yes."

"Why?"

He stares at me with an unreadable expression until I break and laugh.

"Fine. I promise not to jump to the end. Just to page 286. Can I have the book now?" I hold out my hand.

"You asked if I've read the book, not if I own the book."

I huff an exaggerated sigh but don't bother suppressing my grin. "Levi, do you own a copy of *Of Roses and Lilies*, and if you do, may I borrow it, please?"

He shrugs and indicates the shelves behind me, an invitation to look for myself.

Hold up. Are we or are we not having a tête-à-tête right now? Was that whole exchange *not* playful banter but his usual reticence to say more than a few words at a time?

A deep, low chuckle rumbles in his chest, and I feel the vibration travel down each of my vertebra, locking my spine into place.

The arms he had folded over his chest fall to his sides. "While you're looking, I'll start on dinner. How do burgers sound?"

I'm still pulsating with the percussion of his laughter to care much about food. "Burgers are fine," I say as a reflex.

Levi nods and walks away. I watch his retreating back.

My rigid spine slumps. That had not gone at all how I was expecting. What happened to being a mature, emotionally healthy woman and putting all my feeling cards on the table? *Show your cards, Hayley.*

I will. I will!

After I find *Of Roses and Lilies* and read the passage he left as a clue.

There's a chance the line could be romantic in nature, like Evangeline said. Although there's an equal chance it could be directions to an actual hidden treasure, since his inspiration was taken from a childhood love of *Treasure Island*.

Either way, maybe finding out what is written there will help me decipher Levi as well. I'm not necessarily worried about putting myself out there and confessing that I'm developing feelings for him only for him to let me down gently. I'll be disappointed, and yeah, the rejection won't feel good, but I'll get over it. The real tragedy would be for both of us to be harboring this desire for each other and neither of us being willing to open up to the other. Maybe it's knowing that my time in this world could run out at any moment, but I don't want to waste a single second entertaining undue fear when I could be filling my days experiencing love and laughter.

None of the books on the shelves I can reach is the one I'm looking for. I take a step back and look up. There are still two rows of books that are above my head. Of course Levi wouldn't make this easy on me. For anyone but a giant, those books aren't accessible without a ladder, and because this isn't a fairy tale but a home collection, there isn't a built-in rolling ladder in sight. There are, however, two wooden boxes near the fireplace with a few logs in one and remnants of old newspapers for kindling in the other. I empty the boxes and carry them over to the bookcases, stacking them on top of each other. Carefully, I climb on top of my makeshift stool and run my finger along the spines of the books on the top shelves.

"Do you like cheese on your—"

Levi's voice startles me, and I jolt with a squeak. My quick movements send the precarious tower beneath me rocking like shifting tectonic plates. I wobble to stay upright, wishing for the first time in my life that I'd taken ballet classes for longer than two weeks, then maybe the probability of me not face-planting right onto Levi's hardwood floors would be higher right now.

Levi's grunt-curse rips through the room, and I feel myself tipping right before his large hands circle my waist and steady me.

"I got you." His warm breath fans across my cheek, sending the baby-fine hairs that have slipped the elastic band of my ponytail to dance in my peripheral vision.

I grip his shoulders, the adrenaline spike of almost falling emptying from my system as quickly as it had flooded my veins. Levi's fingers flex above my hips, instantly grounding me and drawing my attention to him. The room is silent except for the pounding of my heart against my breastbone and the whooshing of my quick breaths in my ears.

We're nearly eye-to-eye with me perched on the boxes like I am. Except he's not looking into my eyes. His gaze is transfixed a couple of inches lower, all his focus narrowed onto my now-parted lips, his long eyelashes curved over the apple of his cheeks. There's the faint white line of a scar that disappears beneath the coarse stubble of his beard, and I wonder what other details about Levi I've missed.

His fingers flex again, the tiniest amount, but enough that my system is flooded once more. This time it's with awareness and not adrenaline, and it's another type of falling altogether that I'm in danger of. The way he's looking at my mouth, with raw longing and unbridled desire, erases any question from my mind that I'm alone in feeling the pull between us.

I lick my lips, his gaze so heavy I can feel it like a physical touch. Tension coils through my body, my muscles tightening around my bones like boa constrictors, my heart thump, thump, thumping. Every part of me is poised. Ready. Waiting for Levi to lean forward and press his lips against mine.

He doesn't move. Not even a flinch. If not for the fire in his eyes and the ragged sound of his shallow inhales, he could have been made of granite.

My thumbs press into the slope of skin at the base of his neck. "Levi." His name comes out so breathy that I wouldn't have even recognized I said it if I hadn't felt my vocal cords form the word.

Levi hums but otherwise remains unmoved. What is he thinking right now? Or maybe his thoughts have been completely hijacked by the overwhelming need to *feel* like mine have.

But if that's the case, why isn't he kissing me at this very moment? Because the thought of his lips on mine, the wonder of if his beard will scratch the sensitive flesh of my lips and if I'll like it, is the only thing I can think about.

"Levi," I try again. If he doesn't kiss me soon, I might combust on the spot. "Levi, do you want to kiss me?"

His gaze tears from my mouth and tackles mine, pinning me to the spot.

"Because," I push out, "I would really like for you to kiss me."

His grip on my waist tightens almost painfully. If he were to remove his hands, there would probably be red marks where his fingers had been. A thrill shoots through me. I shouldn't love how almost punishing his hands on me are, but I do. I've been treated with kid gloves like I was fragile and breakable more than half my life. But Levi isn't holding me like he's afraid I might break. He's holding me like he would fight anyone to the death if they tried to drag me away from him.

"How?" His gravelly voice is clipped as he forces the single word past his lips.

It's hard to make room for any other thoughts in my head, but I manage to accommodate one single question in answer to his. "What do you mean, how?"

He emits the low grunt that sounds like it could be a four-letter word as he closes his eyes and leans forward. He rests his forehead against mine and takes in a long breath. "This is probably the worst time in the world to be confessing this, but I've never kissed a woman before." He leans back, and his eyes pop open again, searching mine, a determined set to his jaw. "But even if I had, I've never kissed *you*. So, I'm asking how. How do you like to be kissed, Hayley? Because, yes, I very much would like to kiss you right now, but only if I can do it right. Only if I can touch you in a way that feels good for you."

My brain, my heart, my breath all stutter at Levi's words. How has a man with as much raw masculinity as him never been kissed before? How have I, who have kissed plenty of men, never once been asked about my own preference or even realized the impact such a question would have on me?

Everything clicks into place, and I know. I *know*.

My hands move from his shoulders, and I thread my fingers into his hair, tugging at the ends. "I've never been kissed by *you*, so why don't we find out together, hmm?"

He searches my gaze for a half second more before his arms band around me and he crushes me to his chest. But while his hold is tight and firm, his lips find mine in a featherlight kiss, tentative and unsure. He pulls back slightly, his brows thunderclouds of warning on his face. His arms tighten even further before his head surges forward and he captures my lips with a confident seal of his own.

His mouth is a soft island surrounded by the coarse scruff of his facial hair. The opposing textures and the assertive pressure of his lips elicits an unconscious moan in the back of my throat. "If you're taking notes," I say between kisses, "I like this."

He chuckles. "Duly noted."

He kisses me softly, reverently, hungrily, frantically. He kisses me a million different ways, and I let him know that I like every one.

Beep, beep, beep, beep.

Levi yanks himself away at the sound of the smoke detector, leaving me blinking, lips swollen, and chin slightly burning from the friction of his beard. He lifts me off the towering boxes like I weigh nothing at all and sets me back down on my feet.

"I forgot about the burgers," he says sheepishly, his chin dipping down toward his chest.

Which I, of course, find utterly adorable.

He walks to the kitchen, and a few seconds later I hear the stove click off even though the smoke detector is still blaring.

"Well, these are inedible now."

I rouse myself enough to follow him and find him scraping charred and blackened beef patties into the trash can. I grab a dish towel and search the ceiling for the source of the obnoxious beeping. The detector is mounted in the center of the kitchen, so I move to stand under it and use the dish towel as a fan. It takes a good while, but the beeping finally stops.

"How does cereal sound?" Levi's still wearing that sheepish expression as he fills the skillet with water to soak in the sink.

I grin. "I love cereal for dinner. And maybe while we eat, we can talk?"

He opens his mouth to respond but is cut off by the doorbell. His mouth closes, and his brow furrows. "Who can that be?" He moves around me toward the front door.

I guess talking—and any more kissing—will have to wait.

18

He'd kissed her.

Levi's feet moved on autopilot toward the front door as his mind continued to replay what had just happened in his living room. He hadn't planned to do it, but he'd kissed her. That euphoric thought was replaced by the one that still had him shaking his head in disbelief and in complete and utter exhilaration. Against all odds and logic, she'd *wanted* him to kiss her.

He could still feel the press of her soft mouth across his lips. They continued to tingle in the echo of her touch. Whatever nerve receptors he had there were dancing a happy little jig. He licked his lips, not even a little surprised to find the aftertaste of her still heady on his tongue. The sensory inputs of her kiss had not ceased the moment they broke apart. She'd imbedded herself under his skin, taken up residency in the space of his mind, and set up a direct line to his heart.

He gripped the knob and ripped open the door. "What do you want?"

Levi winced at the harshness of his own words as soon as they left his mouth. Man, he really had become a grouchy old man, hadn't he? Besides, the woman and little girl in front of him had no idea that they'd shown up at such an inopportune time.

"Sorry." He rubbed at the back of his neck, his conscience pricking. It was time to start making an intentional effort to be a bit more friendly to those around him. "What I meant to say was, hello, how can I help you?"

The woman in a lightweight flannel blinked in surprise, while the little girl in uneven pigtails beamed up at him. She held a cardboard box in her arms, and she seemed to be nearly humming in excitement. "You're funny," she laughed.

He hadn't thought he'd said anything particularly humorous, but he remembered thinking farts were the most hilarious thing in the world when he was about her age, so obviously the bar for jokes was low for kids.

The girl's mom cleared her throat. "We heard Hayley found some orphaned kittens that the two of you are taking care of. We brought over some supplies that might come in handy if you need them."

"A coyote got Mittens in the spring. I had to be a step-mama to her babies, but I was a nice step-mama, not a mean one like Cinderella's." The girl readjusted the box in her arms. She tilted her head as she peered up at him. "Are you gonna let us in, or are you gonna just stand there like a bump on a log?"

"Anna Leigh!" the woman cried in horror, her eyes wide as dinner plates as an embarrassed red hue tinged her cheeks. "That's not the way we speak to our elders." She moved her gaze to Levi with contrition written in every line of her face. "I am so sorry. We can just leave the supplies and get out of your hair."

"But Mama!" Anna Leigh whined in protest. "I want to see the kittens! Plus, we need to show him how to make the kittens go to the bathroom." She pursed her lips at Levi like she'd sized him up and wasn't impressed with what she saw. "Bet you don't know that mama cats lick their baby's behind to make

151

them go potty, did you? And you probably didn't know that as a step-daddy, it's your responsbability to do it now, did you?"

Levi rolled his lips between his teeth to keep from smiling. Something told him this little munchkin expected him to take his new responsbabilities very seriously and wouldn't find anything she'd just said a laughing matter. He opened the front door wider and took a step to the side in a silent invitation to come in. "You're right. You better show me how to be a good kitty step-daddy. I don't want to get anything wrong."

Anna Leigh didn't need any further encouragement. She bolted through the open door and into the house, disappearing down the hall.

"Sorry about her," her mother said. "She doesn't have a filter, though Lord knows I've tried to install one in her brain."

Wouldn't that be a crying shame. "Don't worry about it."

"I'm Shelby, by the way. I don't think we've ever been formally introduced." She held out her hand.

Levi shook it, motioning her into the house.

"Oh my gosh, they're so cute!" Anna Leigh's excited voice pierced through the walls, and Levi let himself grin this time. He took a step toward the laundry room to join her, and he assumed Hayley as well, when Shelby stopped him with a touch on his arm.

"We brought supplies for the kittens, but I also stopped by to let you know that Trisha Donolly has an extra room in her house that Hayley can stay in until the road clears. I know you're a private person and playing bed-and-breakfast host isn't something you'd normally sign up for, so"—she shrugged—"now you don't have to anymore."

Hayley leave? His chest constricted, and black spots danced in his vision. He knew she wouldn't stay forever. That she'd eventually leave when one of the roads was cleared and the bookmobile was safe to drive again. She'd go home. Back to her life in Little Creek. But leave now? Today?

No. Absolutely not.

He ground his molars, his jaw aching at the pressure. Hayley wasn't going anywhere. Especially not now. Especially not after that kiss.

"I can let her know—"

"No," he growled.

Shelby recoiled at his harsh tone.

He uncurled his fingers from the fists he'd unconsciously formed and tried again with a more patient and kinder tone. "It's fine. She's already settled here, and the road should be cleared soon anyway. There's no reason for her to have to move again."

Shelby frowned. "Are you sure?"

"Yes." More certain than he'd been about anything before in his life.

She shrugged, appearing unconvinced but not having a reason to press the matter. "If you're sure. I'll let Trish know not to expect Hayley, then."

"Thank you," Levi managed to say.

She nodded, then looked toward the other side of the house. "Well, we better head on in there and let Anna Leigh show you how to be a proper cat daddy so you can get back to your evening."

Back to his evening, sure, but more importantly, back to Hayley.

The door to the laundry room was wide open, Hayley and Anna Leigh sitting side by side and cooing over the kittens. Anna Leigh had Harry Pawter cupped in both of her hands as she rubbed her cheek along the kitten's soft fur.

"What are you going to do with them?" Anna Leigh asked.

"I'm not sure yet," Hayley replied softly.

"Can I have one, if my Mama lets me?"

"Absolutely not." Shelby's elbow bumped Levi as she crossed her arms over her chest and gave her daughter a firm look. "No more pets. We practically live in a zoo as it is."

Anna Leigh rolled her eyes. "It's not a zoo, Mama. It's a farm, and farms are supposed to have lots of animals."

Shelby's gaze became pinpricks. "No."

Hayley turned to look over her shoulder at where Shelby and Levi stood. Her eyes twinkled with mischievous delight. "Better watch out, Levi. She's stealing your favorite word."

Levi gave her a deadpan look, which just made her cackle in laughter.

"I don't get it. What's so funny?" Anna Leigh looked between them.

Shelby unfolded her arms and took a step forward. She squatted down beside her daughter. "Never mind, baby. Why don't you show Miss Hayley and Mr. Levi what we brought and how to use it. We need to get back home so I can start dinner."

"Yes, ma'am." Anna Leigh set Harry Pawter back down on the bed of blankets with his brothers, then reached for the box and opened the flaps. She pulled out a heating pad. "Kitties can't regu . . . regu . . ." She scrunched up her face. "Shoot. I can't ever get that word right."

"Regulate," her mom helped.

Her face brightened. "Right. Regulate. Kitties can't regulate their body temperature, and the mama cat is the one that keeps them warm. But since there isn't a mama cat, you use a heating pad."

"Make sure you put it on the lowest setting and wrap it in a few towels," Shelby supplied.

Anna Leigh looked back in the box, then pulled out a bag without looking at it as she set it on the floor. "Here's some leftover formula mix. You just mix it with water." She pulled out a few bottles and then gave a demonstration on the proper way to hold the kittens while feeding them.

"You know a lot about taking care of baby animals," Hayley said with obvious pride in her voice.

Anna Leigh looked at her blankly. "Like I told Mr. Levi,

being a kitty parent is a big responsbability." She narrowed her eyes at Hayley. "Can you handle it?"

Hayley straightened her spine and adopted the most serious expression Levi had ever seen on her face. "I will do my best."

Anna Leigh nodded, appeased. "Good." She reached in the box once more, this time retrieving a shallow plastic pan and a half-filled bag of cat litter. She wrinkled her nose but looked Hayley and Levi directly in the eyes. "This part is kind of disgusting, but you just have to do it anyway." She showed them how to rub the kitten's abdomen and stimulate the back end with a warm moistened tissue after feeding to get the kitten to go potty in the litter box.

Shelby had to nearly drag Anna Leigh away from the kittens after all her explanations until Levi promised she could come back the next day to check on them.

"Call me if you need help!" the little girl shouted right before her mom shut the car door and drove away.

As soon as the car's rear lights disappeared from view, a low rumble rippled through the sky overhead, pulling both Levi and Hayley's attention up to the ominous gray thundercloud rolling into view.

"That doesn't look good," Hayley said.

Levi grunted, his body going rigid as if preparing for a back-alley brawl. He gritted his teeth and curled his fingers around his thumbs. Without a word, he turned on his heel and stormed inside.

19

Why now? Why, out of any time in all eternity, did a thunderstorm have to strike tonight of all nights?

Levi paced the length of his bedroom, turned on his heel, and ground a path into the carpet in the other direction. His heart drummed a wild beat against his ribs, his breath coming in short bursts. His brain had switched to fight-or-flight mode, but he was caged in this sixteen-by-sixteen room, so he couldn't flee. On top of that, his adversary was an unwelcome weather pattern, which he couldn't very well duke out. Instead, he pressed the backs of his knuckles into the sockets of his eyes, his jaw clenched tight. A humorless laugh escaped his thinly pressed lips. If he believed in such things, he'd say the universe itself was conspiring against him.

All he wanted to do was march up to Hayley, hold her in his arms, and spend the rest of the night getting to know her better. Catalogue every nuance of flavor her mouth held. Memorize every expression that flashed through her decadent eyes. Imprint her touch to his skin so he'd always have her with him.

A distant clap of thunder shattered the night sky, causing every muscle within his body to seize without his permission. Anger, with embarrassment following quicky on its heels, raced through his bloodstream, leaving him more agitated and keyed up than he'd already been. He banged his closed fist against his temple, his fight against himself just as much as anything else.

There was a gorgeous woman in his home who, against all odds, actually seemed to like him and didn't find him entirely off-putting, and he was trapped in his room, barricaded away. He couldn't let her see him like this, see what storms did to him. What woman would want a man who became an impotent, cowering thing because of a little thunder?

Levi didn't think he could hate himself more than he did in that moment.

A flash of lightning illuminated the night sky through his window. He jerked his hands up, pressing his palms over his ears. He wanted to punch a wall instead. Thunder rumbled outside, loud and long and ominous. A crash of a cymbal followed by the roll of a drum.

Forget punching the wall. He wanted to put on his headphones, turn the volume up to help drown out any unpredictable loud bangs, and binge-watch an entire season of *Parks and Rec* until he could quote every Leslie Knope line.

He'd have to come up with some excuse to tell Hayley. She was probably out in the living room, wondering where he'd gone and when he'd come back. They were supposed to be talking over a dinner of Frosted Flakes, and instead he was acting like a cornflake himself. He really hoped his absence wasn't making her second-guess their kiss. Or worse, that he was hurting her feelings by staying away, seeing his absence as some sort of rejection.

He hung his head and squeezed his eyes shut. He really didn't want to hurt her feelings.

The window rattled with the next shout of thunder, and he jumped, his heart galloping away from him. A whimper escaped his lips. A cowardly, unmanly whimper.

He could *not* let her see him like this. If he was ever going to get a real shot with Hayley—a shot at a real relationship—he had to hide this side of himself. Resigned and ashamed, he grabbed his headphones from the drawer of his bedside table. He was just about to slip them on over his head when a tentative knock sounded on his door.

"Levi?" Hayley's voice came out soft and small.

Levi froze. He couldn't open the door, but ignoring her altogether would only make the situation worse.

A dull thunk echoed from the wooden slab separating them. A sound not of knuckles rapping but something heavier. Like a forehead coming down to rest upon the wood.

"Levi," Hayley said again, a bit plaintive and slightly desperate, "this is embarrassing to admit, but I'm just going to come out and say it. I'm afraid of storms. I . . . I don't want to be alone right now. Do you think . . ." She cleared her throat. "Would you please come out? Please."

Her voice broke on her plea, ripping through his pride. Without a second thought to his own preservation or what she'd think of him or if the night and storm would bring the end to something that had only just begun, he marched across the room and flung open the door. She stumbled forward and landed right at the center of his chest. He lifted his arms and wrapped them around her, drawing her closer by pressing his palms against her spine.

She tilted her head back and looked up at him through glassy eyes. "Thank you," she breathed.

He deserved accusations like *Where did you go?* or *Why were you hiding?* but instead he received a thank-you. He did not deserve this woman.

He looked down at her and noticed the deep hue of fear ringing her irises. It was receding, but the evidence of her mounting terror was still visible. What a cad he'd been, thinking only of himself and leaving her all alone to face something that obviously caused her distress.

Guilt weighed heavy and unpleasant in the pit of his stomach. "I'm sorry." Maybe it was her own bravery at admitting a fear only accepted among children still sporting a one-digit age or maybe he wanted to make her feel better in any way that he could, but he found his own confession slipping forth. "I don't like storms either."

Like a bully cornering its victims, lightning flashed in a blinding streak, thunder laughing with the force of a villain. Hayley and Levi both flinched, their hold on each other tightening.

"You don't happen to have a weighted blanket, do you?" Hayley asked through shallow breaths. "I learned a long time ago that it helps with my anxiety any time a storm blows through."

Trinity had suggested the same thing to him, but he hadn't bothered to follow through on her recommendation. Now he wished he had. "No, sorry."

The sky above them roared like a lion on the prowl in the savannah. Levi's body tensed, but at least he'd been able to keep himself from jumping or clapping his hands over his ears.

Hayley pulled back enough to study him. Her lips quirked to the side, but then she blinked. "I think I have an idea, if you want to try it."

What did he have to lose? His pride was already shattered. "Sure."

She took his hand and led him to his bed. "Lie down on your back."

"Excuse me?" Levi gaped at her, not sure he'd heard her right.

She rolled her eyes. "Don't worry, Mr. Redding. I'm not attempting to steal your virtue. This isn't the Regency period. If it were, you'd already have to marry me to save my reputation."

He'd never expected to smile during a storm, but he found his lips tilting up. "Should I be worried about your brother challenging me to a duel for your honor?"

Hayley snorted. "Hardly."

He eyed her, then the mattress. "I think the rules of post-feminism construct say you're going to owe me at least a dinner after getting me in bed with you."

She laughed, her face losing some of the strain it had been holding. "Deal."

Boom!

Hayley let out a mewling noise that belonged more to one of the kittens in the laundry room than a grown woman. The time for joking had passed. He didn't know what she had planned, but Levi was willing to do anything if it would wash away the panic starting to rise in her eyes.

He propped a couple of pillows up against the headboard and stretched out on the mattress. "Now what?"

She placed a knee on the bed. "Now I'm going to be your weighted blanket."

"I don't think—"

But Hayley didn't wait to hear what he thought. She draped herself over him like a human blanket. The top of her head nestled under his chin against his chest. He sucked in a breath and held it, afraid to move. Her chest expanded against his stomach as she breathed, her legs moving until they found a comfortable position on top of his.

The weight of her pressed him firmly into the mattress, compressing against him in a solid mass unlike anything he'd ever experienced before. Honestly, it should've been too much. An invasion into his personal space that his body should've instantly objected to with alarm bells ringing and defensive measures rising.

But the weight of her, the feel of her, the shape of her . . . everything about her wasn't too much. It was just right. It—*she*—was what he'd needed. What he'd always needed.

"Your pulse is racing," Hayley murmured, her head to the side so that her ear lay right over where his heart pumped in his chest. "Is this not helping? Should I get up?" She moved her hands to the mattress to push herself up.

Levi banded his arms around her back, hugging her to him and trapping her where she was. "My pulse isn't racing because of the weather," he whispered, hoping she'd understand the deeper meaning behind his words.

"Oh," she said, then curled her arms loosely against his sides, all poise to retreat gone.

He hugged her just a bit tighter. "Is this helping you?"

"Yes. I feel safe here in your arms. And I like to listen to your heartbeat and feel your chest rise and fall. The steady rhythm is comforting, and I can focus on it instead of what's happening outside."

As if someone had taken a knife and sliced open the cloud above them, rain pelted the roof, pouring down in sheets. Hayley tightened her arms against his sides, and Levi tightened his hold on her in return.

He licked his dry lips. He was in uncharted territory and didn't quite know how to proceed. A great conversationalist he was not, but he wanted to make the effort. Both for her benefit as well as his own. "Do you want to talk about it?"

She hesitated. "Why I'm afraid of storms?"

"Yes." The ends of her hair tickled his fingers. He reached up and stroked the strands at her head, following the length all the way down to her shoulders. Again. Long, languid strokes. Rhythmic. Soothing. For the both of them, he hoped.

She hadn't said anything for so long he'd figured whatever was the cause of her fear, she didn't want to talk about it.

But then she spoke. "During one of my hospital stays, a big storm hit. The kind where the sky goes nearly black even though it's only two o'clock in the afternoon. A tornado warning was issued, and I lay in the hospital bed watching nurses take turns at the window, peeking through the blinds and assessing the storm's progression. The sound of the rain alone was what I imagined a machine gun on a tin can to sound like, and that's saying nothing of the reverberating booms caused by the thunder. I was a little nervous but not too scared. Storms like that happen all the time around here, right? I'd already lived through some, and nothing bad had ever happened before."

He kept stoking her hair. "But this one was different."

"The power went out, but again, I didn't really think anything of it. I knew hospitals had backup generators, so I just waited for the generator to kick in and the lights and machines to come back on and start working again."

An ominous foreboding ballooned in Levi's chest.

"It took too long. For whatever reason, the generator didn't kick in right away, and by the time maintenance got them running, it was almost too late. The little boy in the hospital bed next to me had to be resuscitated. He very nearly died."

Levi hugged her tight and kissed the top of her head. What should he say? Anything he could think of would only sound trite or platitudinous. He had to try, though. To give her some sort of comfort.

"I'm so sorry you had to experience that." He gave her head another kiss. "Anyone would be scared of storms after a trauma like that. Your feelings are valid."

Hayley pulled in a deep lungful of air. She lifted so she could look into his eyes. "I don't like to think about it, so I need you to distract me from those memories. Tell me why don't you like storms."

Levi stiffened, and not because of any thunder.

Hayley's brows drew low. Concerned. "I'm sorry. You don't have to tell me if you don't want to. But I hope you know that you can." She paused as if deciding if she should say more. She must have chosen not to because she became quiet. Simply rested her head against his shoulder and looked up at him.

Their faces were so close that it would be easy to lean down and kiss her. Wipe away her bad memories and questions and hopefully every thought with the press of his lips to hers. It was tempting. *She* was tempting. But it also didn't feel right.

Even after Hayley had shared something painful and personal, Levi still wrestled within himself. It was a hard thing, admitting to struggling with everyday things that no one else seemed to think twice about or even notice. No one seemed to understand why he had such a low tolerance to certain textures or found a combination of noises an assault on his ears or why certain smells could trigger immediate headaches. Why sometimes as a child he'd engaged in what he'd heard some adults describe as abnormal behavior like spinning or hanging upside down for long periods of time. He'd lost friends because he'd always decline invitations to things like concerts or trips to the movies or parties. He'd been dubbed the weird kid and had grown up to be the grumpy guy.

But Hayley had already seen his quirks. She'd already experienced his temper when he'd reached his limit and it became more than he could handle. And she was still there, literally closer to him than anyone had ever been as she loaned him her weight to manage his anxiety.

He swallowed hard, then pushed the words out. "It's the thunder."

She didn't seem surprised at all at his admission. "Because it's so loud?"

"Partly. More so because it's unpredictable. I never know when thunder will crash, and so it's like fighting blind. I can't protect myself."

"Have you ever tried using noise-canceling headphones?"

He readjusted his hold on her, supporting her shoulder more since she'd shifted off center. "Now you sound like my sister Trinity."

"And?"

He shook his head, weighing his words and deciding whether to let the conversation end there or go further.

She peered up at him. Her eyes were deep pools of liquid chocolate, inviting him to dive in. To *be* all in. They held a promise that he was beginning to let himself believe. The way she looked at him, the weight of her pressing down on him with comforting, steady pressure—it made him feel safe. He'd spent so much of his life trying to protect himself from everything outside of himself, but he didn't have to do that with Hayley. In fact, he was beginning to think that maybe he'd finally met someone willing to make room for him in their life.

"Trinity is studying at Clemson to be an occupational therapist." He was so proud of her, but he had somewhat mixed feelings on things she'd said to him since starting the program. "She thinks . . ." He looked at the ceiling, not wanting to face the embarrassment that always came with the admission. "She thinks I have a sensory processing disorder."

Hayley didn't say anything.

In fact, she didn't say anything for so long that he peeked down to gauge her reaction, a little afraid at what he'd find.

She blinked at him innocuously. "And?"

"And what?" He wasn't sure how he'd expected her to react, but it hadn't been like this.

She rolled her eyes and pushed herself back up so her weight was center over his body. She crossed her arms over his chest, then rested her chin on top of her arms and peered up at him through her lashes. She swiped at her bangs that had fallen into her eyes and settled back into position again. "You're acting like an SPD diagnosis would be a death sentence. Like having problems processing the information your senses send to your brain somehow makes you defective or something. That's just not true." She looked at him, her smile slowly turning flirtatious. "I happen to think you're a pretty amazing guy, Levi Redding."

He couldn't wait another minute; he needed the pressure of her lips on his more than he needed his next breath. In one strong move, he gripped her elbows and hauled her body up his own, capturing her mouth in much the same way she was capturing his heart.

20

Levi braced his hands against the bookmobile's body as he leaned under the hood and inspected his work. The new alternator gleamed in its place, the colorful insulation housing to the new wires he'd installed leading to their respective locations. Now that the issue of the vehicle starting and providing the electricity it needed to run and recharge the battery was fixed, he planned to make sure everything else was in good shape so Hayley wouldn't ever find herself stranded again while on the job.

He checked each of the spark plugs, replacing one that had a blister on the insulator tip. He was surprised to find the timing belt still in good condition, but the radiator hose had a two-inch crack in it and definitely needed to be replaced before it got any worse.

The alarm on his phone dinged just as he finished tightening the last nut. He reached for the rag draped over the side of the van and wiped at the grease on his fingers before sliding his phone out of the pocket of his coveralls and silencing the alarm.

Time to head back up to the house to feed the kittens. He locked the garage and trekked up the mountain, wishing that Hayley would be there instead of providing what library services she could from the General Store parking lot. After the storm a few days ago, they'd created a schedule. It made more sense for them to take turns feeding the kittens every few hours so they'd both have longer stretches getting work done. Admittedly, the plan had worked out well on a productivity level. He'd managed to get a lot done on the bookmobile and only needed the rest of the day and maybe a few hours of the next to finish getting it up to snuff.

What a bittersweet thought that was.

Hungry meows greeted him as soon as he opened the door, rising in volume and urgency as he padded into the kitchen and started preparing the formula that Shelby and Anna Leigh had provided. Bottle in one hand, he made his way into the laundry room. The kittens wobbled as they stood and tried to walk toward him on their unsteady feet. It wouldn't be too long before they learned to use their tails for balance and started stalking and pouncing, playing with one another and with him.

He picked up Dumpurrdore, the gray cat almost in danger of tumbling off the side of the blanket and onto the hard tile floor beneath. "Woah there, little fella."

Dumpurrdore meowed, his lips stretching wide, showing his razor-sharp baby teeth and scratchy pink tongue. Levi held him the way Anna Leigh had insisted and brought the formula up to his mouth. He repeated the process with Harry Pawter and Meowfoy, shaking his head at the names that Hayley had chosen, both charmed and amused.

Once all the kittens had eaten their fill, sleeping in a milk-drunk state, with their little bellies bloated, Levi gathered the mealtime supplies, stood, and turned toward the open door. His gaze snagged on an envelope that had been taped to the wall above the light switch, his name written across the front in Hayley's familiar loopy script. A flush of pleasure washed through his body from head to toe. He deposited the bottle on top of the washing machine and reached for the envelope, clawing out the letter within.

Levi,

I hope you don't mind that I'm writing to you again. I know it probably seems silly, but I like our letters and don't want to give them up. Is that okay?

More than okay. He'd never held any particular desire for a pen pal, but now that he'd started these letters with Hayley, he didn't want to stop. He still wanted to keep talking and spending time together, but these penned notes back and forth were almost like a secret portal into another world—direct access to Hayley's innermost thoughts and emotions. He wouldn't give them up for anything.

In your last letter, you asked me why I was in the hospital when I was a child. I could tell you wanted to ask again when I told you about why I was scared of storms, but you didn't. Thank you for that. I didn't have it in me to explain further then, but I'll share more with you now.

When I was young, I went into acute liver failure. The doctors didn't really know why. It's just one of those things that happens without rhyme or reason sometimes, I guess. Anyway, it was touch-and-go for a little while. As you can imagine, my parents were really scared. I was really scared. The doctors were ultimately able to stabilize me, and the search for an organ donor began. I won't burden you with all of the details of the in-between, but I did receive a liver transplant right before my twelfth birthday.

Levi looked up from the paper, stunned. Hayley had almost died as a child? There could have been a reality in which he never would have met her? Where she would no longer have made the world a brighter, better place to live in?

A keen sense of loss sliced through him, the injustice that some lives were cut short arbitrarily leaving him reeling. In that now-wide space that had been cut open, protectiveness rose up. He knew he didn't have the power or authority to control things such as medical emergencies or who lived or died, but that didn't stop the desire from growing within him.

He wanted to keep her safe, far away from harm.

Wait. Was she safe now? Did having a transplant mean that she wasn't in danger anymore?

His fingers itched to pull out his phone and read everything the internet had published about acute liver failure and organ transplants. Life expectancy, risks, prolonged treatments, prognosis. He had a million questions burning him from the inside out and an urgency that he made himself tamp down. Nothing had changed for Hayley in the few seconds it had taken for him to read the last two paragraphs. If she wasn't currently worried about her health, he needed to take her lead and not worry too.

How many times would he have to repeat that to himself to start to believe it?

Forcing his eyes back to the paper in his hand, he made himself finish reading Hayley's letter before jumping down an internet rabbit hole of medical journals, WebMD, and Reddit threads.

I know we haven't talked about us or had a define-the-relationship conversation yet. Is there even an "us" or a re-lationship to define? Are we two strangers who've become friends who sometimes kiss and comfort each other during thunderstorms, or are we more than that?

A growl crawled its way up his throat. Was she serious with this? He didn't go around kissing random women. He didn't go around kissing *any* women. He thought he'd made that perfectly clear. Hayley had been the first woman he'd ever kissed, and if it were up to him, she'd be the *only* woman he ever kissed. His nostrils flared as he considered her not knowing where he stood when it came to her.

I don't know what you're thinking right now, if you've read those questions and had an instant reaction one way or the other. But . . . and hear me out . . . take a moment. Breathe. Things aren't as simple as I wish they were.

Levi's gut twisted. For him, it was that simple. For him, she was a walking, breathing miracle. A gift from God. If she didn't think things were simple, then the complication tangled only in her mind.

Whatever the hurdle, he'd remove it. If she wanted him like he wanted her, nothing—absolutely *nothing*—would stand in his way.

You have to understand, receiving a new liver was a gift. One that I can never fully express my gratitude for or ever pay back. But living with an organ transplant—there's a big question mark over my head that isn't over everyone else's. The transplant has given me more time, but how much time? I've already exceeded the statistical benchmarks of one year and five years. I count my blessings that I've even surpassed the ten-year mark. I'm closing in on twenty years. How much longer can this borrowed organ last? Not forever. They never last forever, Levi. I'll either eventually need another transplant or . . .

She didn't say what that *or* was. She didn't have to. The edge of the paper crinkled in Levi's fist, and he had to make a conscious effort to loosen his grip before he ripped the thing in half.

He already knew the world wasn't a fair place. He only had to step outside to be proven right on that accord. But for Hayley to have experienced all she had, for her to live under the shadow of an unstable future when she should be standing on the precipice of a million possibilities and a lifetime to explore each one, to talk like she'd already given up without a fight . . .

He shook his head. Sometimes reality was too hard to believe.

I've always tried to live in the moment. None of us are promised tomorrow, but my tomorrows seem even more uncertain, and because of that, I've attempted to make every day that I do have count. The here, the now. Living every day to the fullest. I don't look too far into the future. I don't really plan ahead. I just . . . am.

But you, Levi. You aren't built that way. You are steady and true. Methodical and routine. You have structure and stability and longevity. Your life is a straight path ahead of you, and I think that's one of the most beautiful things I've ever seen.

Levi's throat thickened. He didn't like the tone Hayley's words were taking. As if in writing this down, she was coming to a decision all on her own. That whatever path she saw him on was one that she couldn't walk along beside him.

I've learned that the key to happiness is gratitude. I have to be grateful for what I've been given, especially when I've been given so much. Literal life! If I lose sight of that, if I turn my eyes from the things I do have and start wishing for things that just aren't in the cards for me—things like growing old with someone I love and who loves me in return—then I'm robbing myself of a contented heart during the time I have left.

You deserve forever, Levi, but I just don't have forever to give.

She'd signed her name at the bottom, but the last two letters were smudged. Evidence of a tear that had fallen onto the paper and dried. Evidence that essentially ending things between them before they'd ever truly gotten started was hurting her as much as reading those words had hurt him.

It was all the evidence he needed.

21

I really appreciate all of your help this morning," Jack lifts his ball cap off his head, then runs his fingers through his dark curls before resetting the cap back in its place. "I would've had to close up the store if you hadn't watched the place for me."

I smile. "It wasn't any problem at all. Is everything okay with Shelby and Anna Leigh?"

"Oh, everything is hunky-dory now. Their toilet was overflowing like the banks of the Ocoee after that storm, but I was able to get everything fixed right up."

That's some imagery I could have done without. "Well, I'm glad you were able to lend a hand. They're lucky to have such a helpful neighbor like you."

Jack shrugs. "Shelby's my sister, and Tom—that's her husband—is my best friend. He's up in Alaska right now, working on a seasonal fishing boat. It's a tough situation, but the money is good."

"I'm sure it's a relief to both of them to know that you're close by."

"Even if I wasn't, Shelby has the support of the community. Turkey Grove is tight-knit. We take care of one another here."

He eyes me, a gleam entering his gaze. "You know, there might be something else you could help me out with."

"Oh yeah?" I ask warily, not quite sure I care for that particular look on his face.

"We have a town small business meeting coming up here shortly and would really love it if Levi joined us. Think you could do a little persuading on that front?"

My cheeks heat to think of the display I must have made of myself for Jack to have picked up on my feelings for Levi. The slight warmth turns to a scolding burn in an instant as I remember the letter I'd left him to find in the laundry room when he went to feed the kittens. Whatever sway or connection I might have held, I've severed it with that letter.

Has Levi seen it yet? Read it?

Maybe I should've told him my history sooner. There's never really a good or organic time to blurt out you're not sure if you're going to wake up one morning in organ failure and die. I've never told any of the guys I've gone on dates with because there's never been a need. We both knew that we were only together to have a good time. We enjoyed each other's company and had fun, but neither of us was in danger of losing our hearts to the other and therefore there wasn't any risk, only reward.

But Levi isn't like that. *I'm* not like that *with* him. It's way too easy to think about what could be. To picture myself beside him ten, twenty, forty years down the road, kids and grandkids surrounding us with laughter and love. To forget the realities that are my life. That if I were to get pregnant, it would be one with high risks and the danger of something going wrong with either my health, the baby's, or both. That there isn't any guarantee that my donor liver will continue to function the way I need it to, or that if it does stop working properly, a new liver can be found and a second transplant performed. Or if I'd accept it.

I hadn't sat down with a pen and paper with the intention

of slamming on the brakes between us. I'd only thought to answer his questions about why I'd spent time in the hospital. Open myself up a little more and share about my past, hoping that he'd do the same and I'd get even more vignettes into what experiences had formed Levi Redding into the man I know. But as I wrote, my mind kept turning. Things I'd refused to entertain before kept resurfacing, refusing to be pushed back down any longer. My mind kept forming that picture decades down the road, and I realized the heaviness in my chest was grief over something I don't have and possibly can never have.

"Hayley?" Jack's voice shakes me out of my introspection. "What do you think? Can you talk Levi into joining us?"

I paste on a smile even though my insides are now a puddle of emotional mush in the pit of my stomach. "We'll see," I say noncommittally.

Jack bobs his head in acknowledgment, then says he's going to be in the back working on inventory if I need him. I wave him off, moving in the opposite direction to return to the little setup I have outside under an elm tree. It's slightly secluded, but I've been in this spot every day for well over a week, so people know I'm here. So far today, I haven't had even a single patron stop by, but the morning is still young.

Sitting down, I pull out my little notebook and a pen, thumbing through the pages until I find the next empty space. The pen scratches the paper as I write the day's date at the top and *Filled in at the General Store for Jack MacDonald so he could handle a plumbing emergency at his sister's house.*

It doesn't feel like enough.

It will never, can never *be* enough.

The hard slap of boots crunching on loose gravel makes me lift my head. I freeze, eyes widening as Levi's long stride eats up the distance between us, and then slip my journal into my bag. His face is a thundercloud, shoulders bunched almost to his ears, his body a tight coil of contained tension under his faded blue mechanic coveralls. He jerks to a halt in front of me, his jaw flexing in determination as he slaps a hand against the top of the game table, a copy of Matthew Perry's memoir that had been standing up now falling on its face.

"What is this?" Levi asks in a controlled tone that makes my skin tingle.

My gaze darts down to his hand, the envelope holding my letter pressed between his palm and the tabletop. I lift my eyes and swallow.

"What is this, Hayley?" he asks again. Quieter this time, though each word seems to have been sharpened on a whetstone of pain.

Tiny pinpricks stab behind my eyelids as a lump forms and lodges in my throat. I knew this would be hard. For both of us. I knew it, but the knowing didn't leave me any more prepared.

"I'll tell you what I think this is." He places his other hand on the table and leans forward, invading my space until our noses are only inches apart.

The faint smell of mint on his breath mingles with the sharp hints of engine oil and sweat. The combination is so distinctly him that I'm hit with a fresh wave of grief. After this, I won't be able to take my car to get an oil change without being reminded of Levi and experiencing this sense of loss all over again.

"I think this is you attempting to think you know what's best for me and giving me a way out." He's searching my eyes now, the hard lines of his face softening the longer he looks at me, as if he sees and recognizes how much it cost me to write each one of those words on that piece of paper.

I swallow the emotions thick in my throat and slowly nod just once. What else can I do? We both know that he's right.

He raises his hands and brackets his callused palms on either side of my face, gripping my head in a firm hold that's sending the message that neither of us are going anywhere. "I don't want a way out, Hayley. I'm all in, you hear me? I am

176

all in." His voice breaks in a strangled cry as he pulls my head forward and presses his lips to mine.

We kiss like it's an argument. Every feeling of frustration, despair, and unfairness is spoken in nips of lips and clashing of mouths. I can hear him accusing me of playing the martyr and not allowing him to make his own decision in the flex of his fingers on my scalp and the way he grazes his teeth along my bottom lip. His silent plea to give him a chance and not push him away is spoken in the gentle caress of his thumbs along my cheeks.

I kiss him back with the same urgency, grabbing at him and clutching his shoulders in such a way that I know I'm holding on to him physically in this moment the way I wish I had the possibility of holding him close forever.

I argue back, meeting his lips in rebuttals. *I'm trying to do the noble thing*, I say as I trail small, closed-mouth kisses from one corner of his mouth to the other. *I wish things were different.* The message is sent in a guttural moan that vibrates through my chest. He swallows the sound, taking it into himself, and then pours more of his own conviction back into me through his embrace.

A tear slips past my closed lids, and all of a sudden anger I didn't even know was inside of me boils in my gut.

It's not fair. Nothing about my life has been fair. It isn't fair that someone had to die so that I could live. It isn't fair that other people my age are getting married, having kids, and buying their first home while I'm lying to myself that I'm content without those things. It isn't fair that Levi removed the rose-colored glasses of disillusionment from my eyes and makes me yearn for something that would be selfish of me to pursue.

A sob breaks from my lips, pouring out from a place deep and hidden inside. So hidden, I hadn't even been aware it was there. I'm heaving now, my shoulders shaking and tears spilling from my eyes like a broken dam.

These thoughts and feelings are coming at me like a stalker I didn't know I had. They must have been there all this time, lurking in the shadows, and now they've sprung out and struck me with the force of a mean right hook. I can't ignore them any longer. Can't hold them back. Writing that letter . . . facing Levi . . . it's brought things I didn't even know I felt to the surface. Desires. Dreams. Guilt. Regret. Anger. Sadness. I'm overwhelmed by it all.

Seemingly unperturbed by my choking sobs and loud sniffles even though I know the unearthly cries I'm making must be akin to an icepick stabbing at his cerebellum, Levi gently kisses away my tears and strokes my bangs away from my face.

He moves around the table, his arms long enough to keep his hold on my face while he does so. He scoops me up and takes my seat, resettling me on his lap. My legs drape across his, and my head tucks against his chest. He rocks me gently back and forth, making calming shushing noises and squeezing me in a tight hug.

I don't know how long I cry, but eventually my tears start to dry. I wipe my eyes and place a hand on Levi's chest to dislodge myself enough to sit up. His arms loosen but don't fall away. My mouth opens to apologize, but he shakes his head before I can say a single word.

His jaw is tight again, and I feel bad because I know that I've caused this man both emotional and physical pain today. That martyr voice in my head tries to tell me *See, you're already hurting him. That's only going to get worse, not better. The right thing to do is walk away before you cause even more damage.* But I try to quiet the unwanted accusation before it takes too much of a stronghold in my thoughts.

Levi's gaze bores into mine, grappling hooks shot into my very soul to seek purchase. The man is waging an invasion on my heart. "Before we kissed the first time, do you remember what I asked you?"

As if I could ever forget. "You wanted to know how I liked being touched," I say in a whisper.

He traces the shell of my ear with his finger. When we first met, he flinched at any physical contact between us. Now, he can't seem to stop himself from touching me any chance he gets.

"It was more than just touching. I wanted to know what your needs were, Hayley. I know what it's like for people to not be considerate—to assume we all think or feel or process the same way. But we don't. And if what you need is someone who lives in the moment with you without thought of the future, then carpe diem is my new life motto."

His Adam's apple bobs as he swallows. "Look, I know I'm not the poster child for good communication. I tend to retreat and shut the world out when things get to be too much." He pushes back my bangs, tucking my hair behind my ear. "I don't want to do that with you, and I don't want you to do that with me. We have to communicate—talking, letters, carrier pigeons—anything. I know it's not going to be easy. None of it will be easy."

He pauses and looks into my eyes, letting me know he understands everything I tried to tell him in the letter and all the implications that knowledge brings. He knows, and he's still right here. "But good things are worth fighting for, and you, Miss Hayley Holt, are the very best thing that has ever happened to me. So, I'll say it again. I'm all in. For however many days you have on this earth. For however long you will have me. I'm not going anywhere."

22

Wouldn't it be nice if one conversation was all that it took to make things better?

Worried about something that could have huge ramifications and cause colossal heartache? Have a little chat. Bam. Everything is peachy keen again, and all parties can smile and go on with their lives as if they no longer have a care in the world.

If only it were that simple.

Levi may have said all the right words, but I can't help but still feel uneasy. The man had never even kissed a woman before me! Obviously, he isn't someone who dates casually for fun since he's reserved himself for so long. Probably until he was ready for commitment. And here I am, Miss Have-No-Future, robbing both him and the woman who should have been given that gift and privilege like a wanton little seductress.

Okay, maybe I need to lay off the historical romances for a bit.

The point remains, however, that even though Levi says he's okay taking things between us one day at a time, I'm not sure he's being truthful with himself. Also, there's still the issue of whether I can be content with that anymore. I have in the past, true, but I've also never been with Levi before now.

And since he's made me start thinking about all the things I realize I want and can't have, I'm not sure I can push myself back into the carefully contained box I resided in previously.

"Mail delivery for a Miss Hayley Holt." Jack grins at me, holding out an envelope.

I reach for it, realizing I'd been so wrapped up in my thoughts that I hadn't even been aware that he'd walked over. I squint against the brightness of the sun behind his shoulder. "General Store owner and postal worker? I didn't know you were such a renaissance man."

"I only do special deliveries." He laughs and throws me a wink.

I look down at the addressed envelope. Beneath my name, the direction reads *Under the Elm, General Store Parking Lot, TN*. I laugh and look back up. "What's this?"

He points to the return address.

You're Not-So-Secret-Admirer, You Know Where to Find Me, Anywhere You Are, TN.

"I can see why someone would need to use you to deliver this. The United States Postal Service wouldn't know what to do with this thing."

Jack grins. "Probably the same thing they do with letters to Santa." He gives me a two-finger salute. "Enjoy your letter." With that, he turns and marches back into his store.

My lips curl in a smile as I flip the envelope over so I can slide my finger under the sealed flap. When did Levi even have time to write a letter and get it to Jack? It hasn't been that long since he left me sitting here, lips swollen from his convincing kisses and mind trying to rediscover its equilibrium after he'd left it and all my thoughts spinning off their axis.

My phone rings, startling me. I set the envelope down, disappointed, and dig my phone out of my purse. Evangeline's name is on the screen, and I tap on the green accept button, holding the phone up to my ear. "Hey, aren't you at work?"

Evangeline will sneak texts here and there when the library is slow, but she doesn't usually make personal calls during work hours unless there's an emergency.

I try not worry, but it feels like this perfect little bubble I've been living in has suddenly popped. Had I really forgotten, even momentarily, about the rockslide? If something is wrong, if one of my parents are hurt or Tai's had an episode with his asthma, I can't rush over there.

"Yes, but Martha and I snuck away for a minute to call you. *Of Roses and Lilies* was just returned." Her voice is pitched high with her excitement, and it takes me a second to realize this isn't an emergency call.

"What?" I ask, a bit dazed, needing to hear a second time she's not calling because someone is in mortal danger but because . . . a book was returned? I'd care about this why again?

"*Of Roses and Lilies*," Evangeline squeals. "Did you find the page yet?"

I realize she's talking to Martha, who must have been turning to a specific page while Evangeline called me. Then I remember.

ORAL, p. 286, l. 12. Levi's clue to a hidden treasure.

My heart pounds against my ribs, and I clutch my phone tighter, holding my breath in anticipation.

"Got it," Martha says. "What line was it again?"

"Twelve!" Evangeline and I both yell at the same time.

"Okay, okay, calm down. Sheesh." I can picture Martha rolling her eyes at us. "Let's see here." She draws the words out absently as she searches for the right passage. "Ten, Eleven, Twelve. Here it is."

"Let me see," Evangeline says.

"Ouch!"

"What happened?" I ask as sounds of fumbling and a muffled apology comes over the line.

"Evangeline has a very hard skull, that's what happened," Martha grumbles.

"We may have knocked heads when I leaned in to look at the book," Evangeline explains sheepishly.

"I love you both, but will one of you please tell me what the passage says?"

"Right, sorry." Evangeline clears her throat. "It says, 'I'd never fully understood what people meant when they talked about defining moments. How could a single blink in time change the trajectory of an entire existence? It didn't make sense. And then you walked into my life, and all of a sudden, I knew. They were right, and I'll never be the same again. All of my tomorrows are now and will forever be shaped by that single pinprick in time when you walked through that door and changed my world.'"

A vacuum sucks all the sound out of the atmosphere. No one says anything. It's complete silence, and when little spots start to dance in my vision, I realize that I've even stopped breathing. Slowly I exhale, then refill my lungs. A songbird titters from a branch above me.

"Wow." Evangeline manages to breathe out the single syllable, the first of us to even be able to coherently assemble a reaction into a word.

"Yeah," I respond. *Wow* is right. There's so much more to think and say, but my brain is stalled on *wow*, not able to move forward.

"I think it's safe to say this guy is smitten with you," Martha chimes in. "In this instance, Evangeline was right."

"In this instance?" Evangeline sounds affronted. "I've been right more than once, I'll have you know."

Martha doesn't respond verbally, but I imagine she's giving Evangeline a very pointed look.

"So the hidden treasure Levi alluded to . . ." My mind is finally crawling forward toward deeper implications.

"I'm pretty sure he's saying that treasure is you, sweetie," Martha says gently.

Levi had given me that clue even before we'd kissed. *"All of my tomorrows are now and will forever be shaped by that single pinprick in time when you walked through that door and changed my world."*

Liquid pools along the bottom of my eyelids, and a strangled sound that's half cry and half laugh tears from my throat. I shake my head and raise a clenched fist to my mouth, biting down on my knuckles.

That man is not fighting fair. How can I attempt to convince either of us of the logical course of action when he goes and says things like this? Claiming his world was changed simply by my walking into it?

Yeah, well, how much worse will it change when I'm forced to walk out forever? When I inevitably Nicholas Sparks him?

A tear slides down my cheek. The truth is, he's changed my world as well. And as much as I hate to admit it, I know my tomorrows are also shaped by his influence in my life—whether that be for only a few days or an undetermined amount of time.

I sniff and wipe at my dripping nose. I'm happy, I swear it. I know the evidence is proof to the contrary, but what girl wouldn't feel happy to be wooed by such words? Except, along with the happiness, there's that pit of concern. That sense of loss that wasn't invited to the party but crashed the scene anyway.

I really wish it would let me just have this moment without trying to ruin it for me.

"Has he left you any other clues?" Evangeline asks.

I'd forgotten that she and Martha were still on the phone. I sniff again and blink rapidly to dry my eyes and rein my thoughts back in. "Umm." Seeing the envelope Jack handed me minutes ago lying on the table, I snatch it up and rip the letter out, scanning the handwriting at the bottom for another postscript.

My heart stills, then beats wildly against my sternum at the sight of the curves of the *P* and *S*.

"Umm, yeah. Yeah, he did. Just now, in fact."

Evangeline makes some sort of indiscriminate sound, like she's choking back a shriek of excitement. "Well, don't keep us in suspense. What does it say?"

My vision is still a little watery, so I have to squint to be able to read Levi's horrible handwriting. "I think it says *AK, pd. 1878, p. 25.*"

"AK," Evangeline muses. "So a book with only a two-word title."

"But what is pd?" Martha asks. "That wasn't in the first clue."

What *was* pd? 1878 . . .

My body stills. "Could pd stand for publication date? A book published in 1878?"

"I think you're right," Martha agrees.

"AK 1878? It's *Anna Karenina*!" Evangeline practically shouts.

Martha groans. "If that's the case, how can we know which printing he used to find the quote? The page numbers are likely to be somewhat off in each, don't you think?"

"Here, hold this," Evangeline says, and since I'm miles away, she must have shoved something into Martha hands.

"What are you doing?" Martha asks, and I'm wondering the same thing.

"I'm doing a search for every romantic quote in *Anna Karenina*. Obviously."

"It might not be a quote of a romantic nature this time," I say.

Evangeline snorts.

Yeah, even I didn't buy my lame attempt.

"'I think,'" Evangeline reads, "'if it is true that there are as many minds as there are heads, then there are as many kinds of love as there are hearts.' Aww, that's sweet. Do you think that's it?" But she doesn't wait for either of us to respond. "I'm going to keep searching."

"Let me look," Martha says, then there's shuffling again and they must have traded phones. "'I've always loved you, and when you love someone, you love the whole person, just as he or she is, and not as you would like them to be.'"

It's way too early to be talking about love, isn't it? Sure, our time together has in some ways seemed like I've stepped outside the space-time continuum. The calendar may not have even flipped to the next month, but I feel like I've lived an entire lifetime in that span. I can't remember a time when Levi wasn't in my life. When he didn't hold me during thunderstorms or make my heart melt watching him cuddle kittens. I've enjoyed learning the nuances of his facial expressions and take way too much pleasure in knowing I'm probably the only person on the planet who knows that when the muscle in his jaw bulges, he's bracing himself for something he perceives is a threat, but when that same muscle ticks, it's because he's reaching his threshold of stimulation and needs some space to decompress.

But love? That's not what's going on here.

"'He knew she was there by the joy and terror that took possession of his heart. Everything was lit up by her. She was the smile that brightened everything around,'" Martha reads.

"That's you, Hayley." Evangeline's voice comes quick and soft. "You bring light into the lives of everyone you come in contact with. I'd bet anything this is your clue quote."

"I think she's right," Martha agrees. "And the page number it's on definitely suggests it could be."

I don't say anything. Mostly because I don't know what *to* say. Not to Martha and Evangeline, and not to Levi.

Not even, I think, to myself.

"Oh! I think I see someone at the front desk. Looks like it's time to get back to work. Bye, Hayley," Evangeline sing-songs before the call is disconnected.

I sigh and return my phone to my purse. Levi's letter weighs heavy in my hand, and there's a sense of trepidation weaving its way around my ribs as I stare at the piece of paper. I'm almost afraid to read what he's written. For a man of few words, he's been sure to make every single one of them count. I feel like I'm standing on a stone wall with cracks in its foundation. One more sweet word from Levi, one more soft look, and I'll topple and fall right over.

Truthfully, I'm already more than halfway to falling.

"Hayley!" Jack yells my name as he barrels out of the General Store's entrance, his lips cracked open in a wide grin.

I look up from the letter in my hands and force a semblance of a smile. "What's up, Jack?"

"I'm glad I caught you before you packed up." He stops in front of the table and hooks his thumbs through his belt loops, still grinning. "The Department of Transportation just called. They said they should have the road back open by tomorrow afternoon. Isn't that great news?"

23

The news of the road getting cleared and reopened spreads about as fast as you'd expect in a tiny little speck of a town. If put to a race, I swear a good old-fashioned small-town phone tree would beat out even the viral tendencies of social media in getting the word out about something.

That's why when I walk through Levi's front door and see him standing on the other side waiting for me, a knowing expression on his face, I'm not surprised. I am relieved, however, that I don't have to be the one to tell him our little intermission from everyday life is coming to an end.

That's kind of how my stay here is starting to feel. An intermission. Like there was a Before, a Pause, and now . . .

Now, I don't know. I can't go back to the Before. Meeting Levi has changed me too much to fit in the same role that I played in the Before. But what does the After look like? Who am I now? Do I try to find the same level of contentment I had, living each day as wholly as possible, intentionally trying to bless someone else with a random act of kindness?

And where does Levi fit in? If the whole goal of my journal is to keep myself accountable to paying the gift I was given forward, shouldn't I apply those same principles where he's concerned? How is that being kind when it's so incredibly selfish on my end? Shouldn't I—

"I can practically hear your thoughts from here, you know." Levi's lips tilt just slightly.

The small uptick is hard to see under his facial hair, but I'm beginning to suspect it would be impossible for me not to notice the different subtleties of his movements. For a man of his stature, you'd think it would be hard to miss a single one of his muscles shifting beneath his clothing, but you'd be surprised.

I jut my chin and cross my arms. "You think you know me, huh?" I challenge, desperately trying to hold on to this intermission for as long as I can.

His amber eyes catch flame as his minuscule smile drops, all seriousness snapping into place. "Darlin', I'd love nothing more than to study you for the rest of my life until there's nothing about you I don't know."

I lick my lips, my pulse stuttering. "Th-that's not very one-day-at-a-time of you," I say breathlessly, a desperate reminder. Although I'm not quite sure which one of us I'm reminding.

"I disagree." He stalks toward me slowly. "It's the very definition of one day at a time. One day and then the next and then the next. Every day. All the days, Hayley. Every single one of them." His giant palms cup my cheeks, and he tilts my head up, preventing me from tearing my gaze away so I don't have to witness his heart in his eyes.

"You're not fighting fair," I accuse weakly.

His face softens, and he gives me another imperceptible grin. "All's fair."

My mind fills in the rest of the saying—*in love and war*. Because that's what we're in, isn't it? A war—a battle of our hearts—for the chance at love?

My eyes close. I can't bear to look at him a second longer. It's too much. It makes me *feel* too much. Too much hope. Too much despair. Desire, dreams, loss, regret. I'm overwhelmed again. My heart feels too big for my chest and my skin too tight for my body.

Is this how Levi feels when he reaches his limit?

The thought barely has time to run through my head before Levi's hands are falling away from my face. His palms pass over my shoulders until they press between my shoulder blades, pulling me into him. My cheek nuzzles the soft fabric of his shirt, and I breathe in the clean scent of him mixed with stringent overtones of engine oil. His arms squeeze, holding me firm and secure against him.

"A little too tight, big guy," I squeak out like a strangled mouse.

His hold immediately loosens so it's no longer a vise. "Sorry." Embarrassment tinges his voice since he obviously doesn't quite know his own strength.

He keeps me safe in his embrace until I finally start to relax and my mind isn't being attacked by a thousand thoughts and feelings all at once.

"It's going to be all right," Levi tries to assure me.

I lean my head back so I can look up at him. "You can't know that." No one can know that. Except God. And unless I'm mistaken, He hasn't bestowed on either of us the gift of prophecy and shown us our futures.

Levi presses a soft kiss to the top of my head. "I can and I do." He looks between my eyes, his forehead wrinkling. "You haven't read my letter yet, have you." He says this not as a question, so certain he is of the answer.

"I was interrupted before I could."

Levi nods, then lets go of me with one arm, his opposite hand tightening his hold on my hip to make sure I don't get any ideas of stepping away.

Never crossed my mind, big guy.

He reaches into my bag and pulls out his letter. He meets my gaze for a split-second before bending at the knees, shov-

ing his shoulder into my middle, then lifting me up in a fire-
man's carry.

I squawk in surprise, my fists reflexively grabbing on to the
fabric of his shirt on either side of his waist and holding on
for dear life. All the blood rushes to my head, my hair spilling around my ears and curtaining my peripheral vision. All I
can see is the slope of his backside and the long length of his
strong legs beneath me.

"Levi! What are you doing? Put me down!"

His muscles flex as he walks, my own derrière pointed up at
the ceiling and the heat of his palms searing through the thin
layer of material of the borrowed leggings I'm wearing. I can
feel the imprint of every one of his five fingers along the back
of my thighs as he carries me into the living room.

"Faster this way," he says calmly, like he's not hauling me
around his house like a sack of potatoes.

"Put me down!" I demand again.

My body tilts forward, and before I know it, I'm sliding
down the front of him. Because of his height and the fact he's
taking his sweet time returning my feet to the ground, I'm
hyper aware of each dip and curve and plane of his body. All
the blood previously trapped in my head rushes through me,
igniting me in an inferno.

I want to hide my face so he can't see my reaction, but it
would be futile, seeing as a pleased smirk is starting to curve
behind his beard.

"Your blush makes your freckles stand out even more." He
bends down and kisses my nose, where I know freckles splatter
my skin as if a drunken painter had been whipping around a
brush filled with brown paint willy-nilly. "It's adorable."

I resume the same position that worked so well for me the
first time (Yes, that's sarcasm. No, I don't know why I think
it will be more effective the second time around) and jut my
chin out, attempting to glare at him. "That was uncalled for."

"Was it?" He looks down at me with a faux innocent expression. "Again, I think we're going to have to agree to disagree. In fact, I think I might find it extremely called-for to carry you around with me everywhere."

I gasp. "You wouldn't."

"Is that a challenge?" He dips his head until we're eye to eye. I purse my lips at him. "Since when did you go from grump to flirt?"

"You know exactly when." He kisses the tip of my nose again, then pulls me down on the couch, his arm around my shoulder as he snuggles me into his side. He unfurls his letter with a flick of his wrist and hands it to me. "Read."

I give him one more fake glare before snuggling deeper into his side. "*Dear Hayley,*" I read out loud. "*Let me tell you a story.*

"*Once upon a time there was a boy who had superpowers that didn't seem all that super to him. Super hearing. Super smelling. Super touch. All his senses cranked up to super-level. But instead of other superheroes whose powers could be used for good and to help other people and even save the world, these abilities only seemed to overwhelm the boy and cause him discomfort. Like Goldilocks and the three little bears, everything was either too hot or too cold. Too hard or too soft. Nothing was ever just right.*'

"Levi." I stop reading and wrap my arm around Levi's middle, squeezing and wishing I could give a hug to him as a child.

"Keep reading," he grunts as he pokes the letter with his finger.

"*The boy hid himself away, trying to cope with powers he never asked for, alone because it was just easier that way. He had given up on the idea that there was a place where he fit, much less the hope of finding a person who didn't seem too hot or too cold, too hard or too soft, but someone who was just right just for him.*'"

I can't help myself. I stop reading again, and I look up at the same time his Adam's apple bobs in his throat. He licks his lips and points to the letter, silently telling me to keep going.

"'You are just right, Hayley. You are the calm in the storm, the light at the end of the tunnel, a deep inhale when I can't catch my breath. In a world where everything else seems so very wrong, you are my just right.'"

Levi pushes the piece of paper into my lap, then turns so he can look into my eyes. "I know you're still trying to figure things out, but please, I promise you we can figure them out together," he pleads in a whisper that pierces my soul. He lifts a hand and runs his fingers through the hair at my temple, cupping the back of my head as if desperate to keep me in place.

What can I say to that? I am undone. I can't fight anymore. Not him, not myself. Is it the right choice or one we'll later both regret? I don't know. But there's nothing left I can do but give in to sweet surrender. "Okay."

"Okay?" he asks, like he has to make sure he heard me right. "No third-act breakup?"

I bark out a laugh I didn't even know I was capable of in this emotionally charged moment because, come on, who expects this burly man to know what in the world a third-act break up even is?

I shake my head, a soft smile still on my lips. "No one likes third-act breakups."

Levi hauls me into his lap. "No, they do not," he breathes against my mouth before capturing my lips with his own.

The kiss he gives me is the very definition of oh so very *just right*.

24

"Well, this is it, Cletus. Just you and me and an open road once again." I pat the side of the bookmobile.

Levi raises his brow at me. "Cletus?"

"I told you already. You don't know everything about me." I smirk sassily up at Levi.

He slides his hands into his pockets and leans a shoulder against Cletus, grinning down at me. "Never said I did. Only that I wanted to. One day at a time."

"Hmm. Well, today's lesson on Hayley Holt is that she tends to name inanimate objects."

He nods, nonplussed, like my doling out monikers to non-living things isn't something that surprises him in the least. "Noted."

"Are you sure?" I narrow my eyes to little squints and tilt my head playfully. "I don't see you writing anything down."

He taps his temple. "I've got it all right here."

"Good, because you never know when there'll be a pop quiz." I wiggle my eyebrows.

"I'm not worried." He lets his gaze travel the length of my body. "I plan to study the subject matter very thoroughly."

Wow. Okay. He just went from zero to sixty on the flirting meter, and I am here for it. "Very good," I croak.

194

Shoot. Croaking like a toad isn't the least bit sexy. I clear my throat to try again.

Levi pushes off Cletus and takes a few steps toward me, looking around the shop. "Now I'm curious, though. Did you name anything else besides the kittens while you were here?"

Wait. What happened to flirting? Did I miss my opportunity? "That depends," I draw out the last word so it sounds more like *deep ends*, trying to come up with a way to get back on the playful-banter train.

He stops his aimless stroll and turns to look at me. "Depends on what?"

"On whether your tow truck already had a name or not." Yeah, I think I need to work on my flirting game.

His gaze moves to where his big tow truck is parked on the other side of the asphalt pad. "You named my truck?"

The funny thing is, his voice doesn't sound at all incredulous. In fact, if I had to place an emotion to it, I would almost say he sounds slightly giddy by the prospect.

I nod, turning to look at his big hulking truck as well. "Considering I was a damsel in distress and he came to my rescue, I dubbed him Sir Galahad."

Levi's face splits into a grin. "One could argue that it was I who came to your rescue."

I nudge his side with my shoulder. "Sure, one could argue that, I suppose."

"But the 4x4 is the one that gets the title of a chivalrous knight?"

I sigh deeply and shake my head as if saying *what can ya do?* "I do not make the rules, sir."

Levi laughs, deep and rumbly, and I want to punch my fist in the air and do a little happy dance. While he's been freer with his smiles and laughter, each one still feels like sweet victory.

"By definition, I believe you are exactly the one who makes the rules."

I hold my hands palms-up and shrug in a maybe gesture.

He shakes his head, mirth still present in the crescent shape of his mouth.

"Speaking of the kittens . . ." I've been putting this conversation off, but there isn't any more time left to delay talking about our triplets.

His brow quirks. "Were we speaking of the kittens?"

"You asked if I had named anything besides them," I point out helpfully.

"Ah yes."

"Anyway, the kittens." I nibble on my bottom lip. "I know they were my idea—to rescue them, I mean—and take care of them, and I kind of foisted them on you."

He grunts, and I've become such an expert on what each of his unintelligible guttural throat sounds are that it's basically my second language now. Which means I know that this particular grunt, short and clipped and more of a deep rumble, means he disagrees with everything I just said.

Which, sure, to watch him interact with the kittens, no one would believe that I in any way twisted his arm or that he wishes they weren't disturbing his sleep every few hours for feedings and bathroom massages, but still. The truth remains, I was the one who brought them into his perfectly private life and now I'm peacing out. Guilt, anyone?

"Now that I'm leaving, we should probably talk about custody. Three baby kittens are a lot of responsibility. Do you think we should separa—"

"We're not splitting up a family," he growls.

I bite back my smile at his vehemence at keeping baby animals together when litters are separated and adopted out all the time. I mean, I feel the same way—I don't want to split the brothers up either—but I didn't really expect Levi to feel so strongly on the matter.

Just when I think I can't possibly get any more attracted to this man, he does or says something so incredibly teddy-bear-sweet like this, and I melt like butter on a hot biscuit.

"Okay, so they stay together. I'll have a hard time getting away from the library for their scheduled feedings, but I'm sure Evangeline and Martha can—"

"Hayley." Levi's palms land heavy on my shoulders. "Harry Pawter, Meowfoy, and Dumpurrdore can all stay here."

"Are you sure?" I can't help but feel a little relieved.

I wasn't quite sure how I was going to make it work, honestly. I'd begun to come up with a rudimentary plan to smuggle the kittens into the library, but it required a pair of cargo pants and lasers, and I'd let my mom borrow my cargo pants the last time her and Dad went camping. Considering she still hasn't given them back to me yet, it's a good thing we have a plan B.

Levi's face goes soft. "I think I was always meant to be a cat dad."

"Aww."

"Besides, Anna Leigh might do me bodily harm if she drops by to check on the triplets and they aren't here anymore."

"Don't tell me you're scared of a nine-year-old girl who has a tutu-wearing pig for a pet."

Levi shudders comically. "Terrified."

"Don't worry, big guy." I laugh and pat his coarse cheek. "I'll keep you safe."

"Thank you."

I look around the garage, stalling. I rack my brain, trying to think of any other excuse to prolong this good-bye, but there's nothing left. The time's finally here, and all I can wish for is a few more minutes.

"Are you sure you won't let me follow you back to Little Creek? Just to be safe?" Levi asks. He looks like a dog who's been commanded to sit and stay.

"You've got Cletus running again, right? No reason to worry that he's going to give up the ghost on the way back?"

Reluctantly, he shakes his head. "I've given him a thorough going-over, and he's got a clean bill of health now." He strokes his chin. "Although I can always disconnect the battery terminals if it means you'll stay longer."

"Thank you, Dr. Redding." I wink. "And as much as I'd like to take up your offer of sabotage, I probably should get back to my responsibilities in Little Creek."

"Can't blame me for trying."

"But to answer your original question, following me isn't necessary. You're busy, and I've already monopolized enough of your time since being here."

"Hayley—"

I hold up a hand. The way he growled my name, I know he was about to contradict me.

"It's true, and we both know it." I walk over to him and slide my arms around his waist. "I'm not saying either one of us would change anything or that we regret the time we've had together, but I also know you probably have a lot of work to catch up on."

He bends down until his forehead rests on mine. "I'd rather make sure you get home safely. Everything else can wait."

I look up so our eyes meet, so close I can make out every gold fleck like sunbursts in his irises. "I promise to call as soon as I park Cletus at the library, not a second later. If you don't hear from me in an appropriate amount of time, then you have my permission to mount Sir Galahad and gallop to my rescue."

He sighs, capitulating. "When can I see you again?"

"Not tired of me yet?" I grin.

"Never."

"We'll see about that."

"I'm serious." Any sense of humor fades from his face. "I want to take you out on a real date."

Apprehension prickles along the backs of my arms. Not from the idea of dating Levi. I mean, I'm still wrestling with everything that a real relationship means, but the thought of spending time with him only brings me joy. It's the word *date* that is causing alarm bells to ring in the back of my mind.

"And where would we go?" I ask with as little hesitation as possible.

He thinks a moment. "Pop culture has taught me that dinner and a movie are the standard destinations when two people go out with the intent of romance. We could do that."

I try to hold back a grimace. This is what I was afraid of.

"What?" He blinks down at me. "Why'd you make that face?"

My eyes are squeezed shut, so I open one slightly to peek at him. "It's just . . ." I open both eyes and sigh. "The movies? Can you honestly see yourself enjoying going to a theater? Or a crowded restaurant for that matter?"

Levi looks away, and the muscle in his jaw begins to tick. Restaurants and theaters are hotbeds of unceasing stimulation on multiple fronts. He knows I'm right, and he hates it. The self-loathing is practically writing itself along the tightening lines around his eyes.

I lift my hand, place my four fingers behind his ear, and press my thumb into his pulsing jaw muscle. It takes a minute, but he finally sighs, unclenches his teeth, and meets my gaze again.

This beautiful, *not* broken man. I hate that past experiences have caused him to see himself the way he does. That it somehow defines him in an unfavorable way because considerations and accommodations need to be made. But, hello! Who among us doesn't need some sort of accommodation for something—whether because of a physical trait, a past trauma, or . . . *something*! That need doesn't make any one of us weak or broken or less than anyone else. It makes us human.

"There isn't a law written down anywhere that dictates a

couple *has* to go to dinner and the movies on a date. Actually, if you think about it, it's pretty cliché, don't you think? No originality involved whatsoever."

A look crosses his face that I don't like. Resignation, I think it is. "You don't have to do that."

"Do what?"

He looks away again. "Make excuses for me."

"No one is making excuses for anyone here," I scoff, outraged. "I'm just stating facts. If a guy takes me to dinner and a movie, then I don't think that he's put much thought or effort into our date. He could be taking any woman on the planet to those places; it's nothing special. Honestly, it says a lot about him even before the date begins, and I usually don't have high expectations for more than a way to kill a night."

I want more than that with Levi. And I want us both to be comfortable and enjoy ourselves when we spend time together. "Besides, there's something that sounds better than going out on a date anyway."

His forehead scrunches. He doesn't believe me but he's curious. "What's that?"

"Staying *in* on a date." I wiggle my brows at him, then add a little shoulder shimmy action.

He smiles slightly but shakes his head. "Okay, I may be a novice at this whole dating thing, but that just sounds like hanging out to me."

"Oh, grasshopper, you have much to learn. Soft music playing in the background, a delicious home-cooked meal, candlelight. Just the two of us. And our brood of kittens, of course. Because, while you may have sole custody now, I demand visitation rights, which means you have to bring our babies along. What do you say?"

"I say—" he leans in and kisses my lips—"I can't wait." He kisses me again. "And also, if eating together in the privacy of one of our homes, just the two of us, constitutes a date, then maybe we're a lot farther along in this relationship than either of us thought, seeing as we've technically been dating since we met. According to your definition, that is."

I grin against his lips as he kisses me again. "What an interesting observation."

25

With Hayley gone, the quiet crescendoed to deafening levels. Usually too much noise—whether volume or from too many competing sources—was what gave Levi issues. Now the tension in his shoulders and the pressure building inside him were directly linked to the absence of the sound of Hayley's voice and laughter.

Levi needed a distraction. Something to get his mind off the fact that she'd only been gone a little while and he was already missing her like crazy. Who would have thought the guy who craved time and space to himself would have such a yawning pit in his middle when he was given just that?

Levi marched into his office and toggled the mouse to wake up the computer. Hayley had been right; he had some work that he needed to catch up on. Finishing the order on a few parts he still needed for the Plymouth, for starters. After that, he could check for any new listings of cars for sale. See if anything looked good and could be his next potential flip project. The engine he'd found at the salvage yard needed to be cleaned up still, then he could sink it under the Barracuda's hood and see how she purred. He hadn't lined up a buyer yet, so he could work on that too.

Bringing up his supplier's website, he logged on and checked the otherwise quiet country air. With a thud, the door finishes its descent and I secure the padlock.

"Meow."

The pathetic cry comes from somewhere behind me. I think of Anna Leigh traipsing all over the woods looking for Jolene. What's with everyone's pets running away lately? I look up the mountain to Levi's house longingly but turn on my heel with a sigh. Someone is probably worried about their lost kitty right now. No matter how much I want to get up that mountain, I can't let a pet spend the night out in the cold.

"Here, kitty kitty kitty," I call.

Another plaintiff meow rips into the air, followed by two more. Three missing cats? Oh dear. I hunch down and search the bushes alongside Levi's building.

"Meow."

There, among the brambles, is a small cardboard box. I reach in, careful not to get scratched by the branches, and gingerly pull the box out. Inside lay three tiny newborn kittens, one gray, one brown, and one a creamy blond color. Their eyes are closed, and they wobble on their legs anytime they try to stand.

"You poor little dears!" I pick the box up and cradle it to my chest.

These aren't lost pets. These kittens have been purposefully dumped here. Who would do such a thing?

I hold the box tighter. "No one is going to hurt you now." My gaze returns to the top of the mountain, and I nibble on the inside of my cheek. Newborn animals are a lot of work. Feedings every few hours, constant attention. But I'm basically a stray and Levi took me in. He wouldn't turn his back on these helpless creatures either, would he?

I look down at the mewling triplets. "You guys are going to have to be extra cute and win him over."

On the off chance that I'm wrong and the bundle in my arms aren't outcasts but have simply been misplaced by an irresponsible person who had been by for the bookmobile, I head across the street to the General Store. If there's one thing I've learned, it's that Jack MacDonald knows everyone and everything that goes on in Turkey Grove.

A little bell over the door jingles as I step in.

Jack is standing behind the counter and grins when he sees me. "Hey there. What can I do you for?"

I walk over to him and tilt the box toward him. "I found these kittens outside the garage. Any idea if they belong to someone and were accidentally left behind?"

Jack reaches up and adjusts the brim of his stained ball cap. "Left, you say?"

I nod.

His gaze lifts and meets mine. "Let me make a few calls real quick, but my guess is that whoever left them doesn't want them back."

My heart squeezes. These kittens are too young to be away from their mother. If I hadn't found them, they probably wouldn't have lasted through the night.

I mosey away from the counter to give Jack a little privacy as he makes his calls. The store is smaller than it appears from the outside, only five aisles cutting straight paths down the middle of the space. I weave between two shelves and peruse the items he has stocked. Sarsaparilla candy in the shape of tiny wooden barrels, Slim Jims, and individual bags of potato chips on one side. Fishing tackle, small garden tools, and mosquito repellant on the other. Farther down are a few nonperishable food items next to household cleaning supplies.

I peek over and see that Jack is still on the phone. The dog treats remind me that I'm going to need something to feed the kittens, but they're too young for solid food and I don't think straight cow's milk is going to do it. I doubt Turkey Grove has a feed store or pet store, which are the only two places I can think of that would have a kitten-specific formula.

Pulling up a new web browser tab on my phone, I search for what I can feed the kittens and find a formula recipe consisting of condensed milk, water, plain yogurt, and egg yolks.

Jack steps into the aisle, hands in his pockets. "If anyone knows anything, no one is saying."

I look down at the bundle in my arms. The kittens are sleeping, their little bellies rising and falling peacefully. I look back up at Jack. "What about you? Will you take them?"

He holds his hands up, palms out like I've just told him this is a stickup. "I can't. Allergic." As if to prove his point, he sneezes.

My conscience pricks at forcing three helpless kittens onto Levi, but what else am I supposed to do? I can't just let them die. I find a dusty can of condensed milk on a shelf and grab it and a carton of farm-fresh brown eggs. Hopefully Levi will have yogurt in his refrigerator.

I peer down again at my precious bundle. These little angels need names. Something special and cute. Evangeline has Kitty Purry, and Anna Leigh has Fancy. Maybe something along the same lines, punny but bookish. I run a finger lightly over the gray kitten's back, then eye the other two. My lips quirk.

"You're going to be Dumpurrdore," I tell the gray cat, thinking of the Hogwarts headmaster's long gray beard. "And you"—I tickle the pale blond one under the chin—"I'm going to name Meowfoy, but no funny business, you hear?" I turn my attention to the brown kitten. "Which makes you—" I tap my chin, thinking. "Hermeowne."

I pay Jack and thank him, then readjust my grip on the box and bags, practicing a speech in my head that sounds similar to that of a child trying to convince her parents to let her keep the pretty kitties. I know Levi likes his solitude, and he's already been more than hospitable, but how could he resist the cuteness of these little squishy bean toes?

Thwump, crack.

My gaze peels from the kittens in my arms and up the hill-side, searching for the source of the loud sound that puts me in mind of a lumberjack. My eyes widen as they land on Levi. His back is turned toward me, his feet spread about shoulder-width apart, with a pair of faded jeans slung low on his hips and showing off a pair of muscular legs. An ax hangs from the grip of his right hand, and in a smooth, powerful motion, he swings the tool in a wide arc behind him, up over his head where his other hand meets to grip the handle. Then he brings the sharpened head down with a crack on the log in front of him.

My pulse picks up speed, and my stomach muscles tense against the fluttering sensation happening in my middle. A voice in my head that sounds suspiciously like my own breaks past any filter set in place, the *hubba hubba* ringing in my ears and making me squirm at my own indecency. I'd never really gotten before why romance writers like to add a scene of the hero splitting wood to their manuscripts. I've maybe even rolled my eyes in the past. But I get it now. Toootally get it.

Levi's arm arcs as he swings the ax again, muscles along his back rippling while those corded ropes in his arms are taut and hard. One of the kittens meows, which makes Levi twist at the waist to investigate the sound. His pale amber eyes catch mine, and I clear my throat of the physical response watching him chop wood has given me before answering his silent question. "Someone abandoned a trio of kittens."

His thick eyebrows slant downward in displeasure, and he stomps his way toward me.

My heart thrashes inside my chest. I really need to get a grip on myself and my runaway hormones. I'm not sure if the fierce expression on Levi's face is over the idea of a person throwing away a living thing like a piece of trash or if he's upset that I've upended his solitude even more with three mewling, needy newborns. But my racing pulse at his intense look, coupled with his recent display of strength and the untamed wildness about him, needs to get back in check before I do something spontaneous and potentially disastrous. Like press my lips against his.

He stops in front of me, his gaze darting between my eyes and the kittens before he reaches in and scoops up Meowfoy in one of his giant hands. The little furball is dwarfed by his palm and lets out a plaintiff cry.

"They're so small," Levi whispers almost reverently.

It's a juxtaposition, seeing this mountain of a man with such a tiny kitten. He's keeping his movements slow and careful, exuding a gentleness and dexterity that one would think impossible because of his size.

His tenderness with the kitten is doing absolutely nothing helpful in turning off these intense feelings coalescing inside me. Quite the opposite, in fact. The picture before me of Levi cradling the kitten, bringing the ball of fluff up to his face, is almost enough to make me lose my tentative restraint.

Meowfoy lifts one of his bean-toe paws and sets the pad on Levi's nose. Levi's brows raise in surprise, and he stills as if afraid to make any sudden movements. In a blink, a tiny pink tongue darts out and licks Levi right between his nostrils.

Levi blinks in amazement. "It's rough."

I realize he means the kitten's tongue and let out a soft puff of air encased in a chuckle. "Have you never been licked by a cat before?"

He shakes his head while he moves Meowfoy over to the side a few inches to nuzzle the kitten against his cheek. The kitten licks Levi again, this time along the patch of skin right above his thick beard. Levi smiles wide, pure delight written on his face. "My family always had dogs while I was growing up. They still have two Pomeranians. Yappy little things that shed like crazy." The tone of his voice leaves no doubt as to his opinion on the dogs.

Meowfoy licks him a third time. Levi's eyes widen even further in wonder. "It feels like sandpaper."

"Yeah, a lot of people don't like when cats lick them."

Levi lifts Meowfoy even higher, resting the broad expanse of his forehead against the kitten's itty-bitty one. "It's perfect."

I guess I had nothing to worry about, bringing the kittens back to Levi's with me. Turns out he's one-hundred-percent a cat guy. I clear my throat again. "So you're not mad that I've saddled you with even more houseguests?"

He looks away from Meowfoy to meet my eyes, returning the kitten to the others, then taking the box from my arms to carry it himself. "Let's go get them settled in their new home."

He moves aside to let me head up the trail first. Once we're inside, he busies himself in the laundry room, saying he's going to make a warm, cozy place for the kittens in there while I get to work making the formula so the kittens can have full bellies.

I mix all the ingredients in a bowl, then remember the kittens probably aren't old enough to lap up the milk mixture on their own. Or are they? I've never taken care of a baby animal before, so I really don't know. I pull out my phone and look up the question, not feeling all that vindicated when it turns out I'm right and kittens need to be bottle-fed until they're three or four weeks old. Something tells me Levi doesn't have a bottle lying around in his house anywhere. Unless one of his sisters has kids who come to visit? Then again, if they did, there'd probably be a crib in the room I'm sleeping in because Levi's consideration for his family is unmatched.

I head to the laundry room, prepared to ask him what he thinks we should use to get the formula into the kittens' tummies. As soon as I open the laundry room door, I freeze, unprepared for the sight before me. Levi is lying on the cold, hard tile floor, Dumpurrdore curled up asleep in a ball on Levi's stomach, Hermeowne in the same position on Levi's chest, and Meowfoy tucked up under Levi's chin, using his beard as his virtual shopping cart, then compared that to the list of the parts he didn't have on hand. It was important to use as many of the original parts as possible in restorations. Collectors could easily spot when something was off.

The trill of the desk phone to the right of his keyboard broke through the stillness around him. He picked up the receiver and brought it to his ear. "Hello?"

"Hey, little brother. It's your favorite sister."

He leaned back in his office chair and twined the phone cord around his finger. "Hello, Aliyah." Because of the spotty reception, his family always called his landline instead of his cell when they wanted to get ahold of him.

An outraged gasp sounded through the speaker. "Rude. Wait, I said little brother. You're just messing with me."

"So sorry, Nova," Levi said another of his sisters' names, though not the one on the phone.

"No one thinks you're funny," she grumbled.

Not true. He'd made Hayley laugh plenty of times. Not that he was ready to tell his sisters about her and get bombarded with a million different questions, so he'd continue to let them think that he lacked a sense of humor. "You're right, Constance. My apologies."

"Just for that I should wear my most floral-scented body mist later," Constance threatened, even though she never would do such a thing.

He sat up straighter. "Wait, you're coming over? Today?"

"Don't tell me you forgot."

Levi racked his mind, trying to remember when they'd talked about her visiting, but he came up with nothing.

"Dad's birthday party? Ring a bell?"

Levi let his head drop. How in the world had he not remembered his offer to host a family dinner to celebrate Dad's birthday? The offer had exploded out of his mouth in desperation after his sisters had told him their not-so-amazing idea of having

203

a huge get-together that included a DJ and a guestlist of over a hundred people. Of course it was only after they'd looked at one another with sly grins that he began to suspect he'd been played. They'd wanted an intimate family gathering all along, and he'd walked right into their trap of the easiest way of getting him to agree. In their defense, however, they knew that he'd be more comfortable in his own home, so in a way, they were also being considerate. A very roundabout, manipulative way, but still.

"With the road being blocked, we thought we might have to postpone, but Aliyah just told us the rockslide was cleared and the road is open again. By the way, prepare yourself for a mini rant from Mom. She's a bit miffed you didn't call to tell her about the situation, although we all reassured her you're fine. Anyway, everyone had already cleared their schedules for today, so we're still planning to head your way. I just wanted to double-check that you didn't need us to bring anything, especially since you've been stranded there the last two weeks. I know you have that tiny little general store, but I wasn't sure what supplies were looking like."

He'd bought a large portion of frozen chicken breasts the last time he went to the wholesale store, so he could defrost those in cold water over the next few hours. There were plenty of zucchini in his garden that would grill up nicely. A salad would be easy to throw together, and he was pretty sure there were a few canisters of dinner rolls in his fridge. "I'm good as long as you're still bringing the cake."

"You sure?" She sounded skeptical.

"Yep."

"If you say so. Hey, hold on. Trinity wants to talk to you."

There was some fumbling noises that caused static, then the line cleared again. "Levi?"

"Yeah, I'm here."

Trinity didn't say anything for a bit, and Levi started to wonder if the call got disconnected.

"Look," she finally said. "Don't be mad, but I was just wondering if you still have those noise-reducing earplugs I got you."

He rubbed at his temple. "Yeah, I have them."

"Okay. That's . . . that's all I wanted to know."

She wouldn't ask if he'd used them. Not with the way he'd reacted when she'd given them to him in the first place. But her asking if he still had them was her gentle way of reminding him they were there and they could be helpful. Letting him know she supported him too. Even if he'd been a stubborn, prideful bull in the past.

He sighed and let his hand drop. "Thanks, sis."

Maybe it was time to dig those earplugs out of his bedside table and try them out. They were small and hardly visible once in, so his family shouldn't have any reason to think he was being rude by trying to ignore or mute them. Not that they would jump to that conclusion even if the ear protectors were big and bulky, but still. The thought was in the back of his mind, nevertheless. Besides, they weren't supposed to cancel out all noise, just reduce the decibels to a more manageable level. Couldn't hurt to try, right?

Levi hung up the phone and covered his eyes with his palms. He had four hours before utter chaos descended upon him. Groaning, he stood and walked out of the office and up to his house. It would take that entire time for him to both mentally and physically prepare for his entire family to be in his home at the same time.

Guess he shouldn't have complained about the silence earlier.

The kittens greeted him with hungry meows as soon as he entered the front door. "I'm coming, little guys." Preparing the formula had become such a routine that it didn't take much brain power, just muscle memory.

With a bottle in one hand, he opened the laundry room door with the other. "Here you go. Lunchtime."

The kittens increased their cries as he neared. He lowered himself cross-legged onto the floor, then scooped up all three felines at once, depositing Meowfoy and Dumpurrdore in the small space between his thighs and lifting up Harry Pawter to feed first.

"You know," he said as Harry Pawter sucked the milky white formula hungrily. "Now that the road is open, I need to make you three an appointment to get checked out by a vet." Maybe one in Little Creek since he already planned to be heading that direction. It wasn't an excuse to see Hayley—he didn't feel like he needed one of those—but you could be sure that he'd create as many opportunities as possible to be in her company.

After the kittens were fed and settled back in their blanket nest for a milk-induced nap, he set about getting things ready for his family. First, he started thawing the chicken. Then, he pulled his sister's clothes that Hayley had borrowed from the dryer and returned them to the laundry basket. He'd have to thank Constance for being so forgetful. For once, her absent-mindedness had been beneficial to him. He lifted the laundry basket and carried it into the guest room, where he'd be a nice brother and fold everything for her.

The essence of Hayley still lingered in the room. He looked around, taking in the gold gilded mirror, the plethora of throw pillows, the frilly duvet. Would he ever think of this room as his sisters' again, or would it always now be associated with his temporary roommate?

His gaze snagged on a small, field-notes-sized journal lying on the bedside table, half hidden by the antique stained-glass lamp. It looked familiar, but he couldn't remember ever seeing one of his sisters writing in a notebook of that size. Trinity, maybe? Notes from one of her classes?

He overturned the laundry basket onto the bed so the clean clothes lay in a heap, then pivoted to the nightstand. Picking up the journal, he opened the book and stilled.

Dates marked the top of the two open pages. Like a diary. But not a diary, because instead of flowy sentences of innermost thoughts, bullet points—a single one on the left page and three on the right—marked the lined white paper.

He remembered where he'd seen this notebook before. In Hayley's hands. He'd seen her jotting something down and then hiding it away just as quickly.

His brows pulled together. Why would she be embarrassed for someone to read . . .

He scanned the left page's bullet point. *Cook dinner for Mrs. Perkins and take it over to her house since she's not feeling well.* He tilted his head to read the right page.

Donated 3 bags of dog food to the animal shelter

Volunteered 2 hours at the animal shelter

Fostered Genie for the weekend (should this one even count? She paid me in doggie kisses)

He flipped the page. Scanned. Flipped the page. Scanned. It was a daily recording of good deeds. He looked at the date at the top of the open page. The day of the rockslide.

This wasn't right. He shouldn't be breaching Hayley's privacy by reading her journal without her permission. He went to close the book, but against his will and intent, his gaze catalogued every word, even though there was a giant *X* mark across the page. They imprinted on his brain before the cover could shut.

Put Levi at ease. Make him comfortable by filling in all the uncomfortable silences—carry the conversation on my own, if necessary.

Levi chuckled, remembering the disaster that night had turned out to be because of her incessant chatter. Then, his smile faded as the inference of the inscription settled around him. An uncomfortable spasm radiated from behind his sternum, locking his joints into place.

Was that what he'd been to her? A charity case she could write down in her book and complete with a checkmark?

He dropped the book like it was a burning coal, and it landed with a thud on the floor. He pressed the heels of his palms to his temples and squeezed.

No. He shook his head violently. That wasn't right. His insecurities were just trying to hijack his thoughts and distort what was real. Despite what was written there, he knew without a shadow of a doubt that he wasn't just a bullet point in a journal. Hayley couldn't have looked at him the way she did or kissed him with such feeling out of simple kindness or to check off a good deed.

The fingers on both of his hands formed fists around his tucked thumbs. Even if Hayley were standing in front of him and he heard her say those words, watched them form on her lips and tongue, he still wouldn't believe that he meant nothing more to her than a journal entry or two. His heart knew better. It knew the truth.

Levi closed his eyes again, searching his mind. Why would she so diligently keep a record like this? It was almost as if . . .

His chin lowered to his chest, the answer becoming clear. *Oh, Hayley, darlin'.*

He looked at his watch and swallowed down a curse. There wasn't enough time. He wouldn't be able to drive to Little Creek and back—not to mention have a conversation with a certain beautifully kind and *deserving* woman who needed a tiny bit of sense knocked into her—and get everything ready for his dad's birthday dinner before his family showed up. As much as it pained him, returning Hayley's notebook and holding her in his arms until she saw reason would have to wait.

26

our hours later on the dot, the crunch of tires coming up his dirt drive alerted Levi to his family's arrival. He lowered the cover on the gas grill to let the chicken breasts cook a little longer, then made his way from his back deck, through the house, and opened the front door just as his mom climbed the last step of the front porch.

She opened her arms wide as she smiled at him in her full and infectious way. "Levi, I'm so happy to see you're well." She wrapped her arms around his waist and gave him a firm squeeze before stepping back and patting his chest a few times. "Even if I'm a little upset at you for not calling to let us know about the rockslide. Not something a mother wants to learn about from the news, hmm?"

Not expecting a response, she walked around him and into the house, leaving room for his dad to follow in her wake. Levi's father was a tall man, but even still, the top of his head only came to his son's chin. They gave each other side hugs, and his dad squeezed his shoulder.

"Happy birthday, Dad."

"Good to see you, son."

Dad walked into the house, and Levi turned to take in his sisters. They had varying degrees of smiles on their faces, and

Levi was unsure what they had planned. Sometimes they'd remember they were adults and act accordingly, but other times they'd pull some sort of sibling shenanigan—especially when they were all together like this.

Yet another reason why he preferred when they visited one at a time.

Constance smirked at him. "We're going to give you a choice this time, bro. Draw out the torture, or group hug and get the greetings out of the way all at once."

Levi waved a hand at them. "Let's get this over with."

His four sisters grinned, then circled him like a pack of hyenas coming in for the kill. He rolled his eyes while he held out his arms. Aliyah and Trinity hugged him from the front while Nova and Constance wrapped their arms around him from behind. He let his arms fall on top of his oldest and youngest sisters' shoulders, squeezed, then let go.

None of his sisters moved away from him. He squeezed again, then let go. They still held on.

"Okay. That's enough." He patted their heads and shifted his weight a little to the side, hoping they'd get the message.

Aliyah raised her face and gave him a look of mock innocence. "Oh, is it now?"

"Yes," he ground out.

Constance poked him between the ribs before stepping back, the other three following her lead. "Still full of charm, I see."

"And you're still a pain in my side." He dramatically rubbed where she'd poked him.

She shook her head and grinned.

"Do you need any help with dinner?" Aliyah asked.

"I've got the grill going out on the deck."

"I'll go check it." She walked past him into the house.

Trinity held up a bag he hadn't noticed before. "And I'll go put some decorations up because I'm going to assume you didn't think of that detail."

At Levi's guilty look, she laughed.

"Don't worry about it. I got you covered." She patted his arm as she strode past him.

Nova and Constance stared up at him, strange expressions on their faces.

"What?" he asked.

Nova narrowed her eyes. "Something's different about you."

"Yeah. What's going on?" Constance took a step closer, peering at him like she was trying to solve a puzzle.

Levi wasn't sure what to say to that. Thankfully, Trinity saved him by exclaiming loudly, "You got kittens?!"

Nova blinked. "Since when did you become a pet guy?" But curiosity of little balls of fluff overrode whatever interrogation had been about to commence as she darted inside.

Constance pointed a finger in his face. "Don't think you're off the hook. Something's different, and as your big sister, I want to know what it is."

Levi ignored her and followed her into the house.

Trinity stepped out of the laundry room with Dumpurrdore snuggled up in her arms. "Look how adorable he is." She tore her gaze away from the kitten and gazed at Levi with eyes so round a Disney princess would be jealous. "When did you get kittens? And where's their mama? They look too young to be away from her."

Nova popped out of the room with Harry Pawter smooshed to her cheek. "They're so cute."

"Someone dumped them outside the garage a few days ago," Levi explained.

"And you've been taking care of them?" Constance asked incredulously. His sisters shared a look.

"We can take them back with us if you need us to," Trinity offered.

"Why would I want you to do that?" Levi shoved his hands in his pockets to keep from reaching out and snatching

211

the kittens away from them. Those were his cats. His and Hayley's.

Nova stared at him, mouth slightly agape as if she couldn't believe she'd heard him ask that question. "Because three kittens make a lot of noise meowing at all hours of the day and night. Not to mention the smell of them and their litter box. And you're . . . you."

Levi bit his tongue. Could he really blame his sisters for thinking he couldn't handle the kittens? Or even want to? He'd been complaining about his Mom's Pomeranians all his life. Yappy little devils.

"Yes, I'm me. Your powers of observation are astounding," he told Nova with the blandness of dry toast. He met each of his sisters' gazes in turn. "No consorting and conjuring up plans to smuggle my cats out of here, you hear me? A rescue mission is not needed. Not for them, and not for me."

Aliyah scrunched her face. "So, you're telling me you're a cat dad now? I'm having a hard time processing this new information."

Wordlessly, Levi took the kittens from his sisters and cradled all three of them along the bed of his forearm, stroking the fur between their ears.

Nova blinked. "I'm not sure I would've believed it if I wasn't seeing it with my own eyes. Our brother is evolving, guys."

Levi brushed past the quartet to return the kittens to their blanket nest. "And yet somehow you're still as dramatic as ever."

Nova laughed, and when he stepped out of the laundry room, closing the door behind him, it was to his four sisters' smiling faces.

"Oh yeah." Constance tapped her upturned lips. "I definitely see a change."

Levi willed his expression to stone. He'd already endured the third degree because of the kittens. He needed a little break before another round. "Excuse me. I need to check on dinner."

Blessedly, his sisters let him escape to the back deck without following him. Both the chicken breasts and zucchini spears were finished cooking when he checked. With a pair of metal tongs, he moved the golden meat to a plate, happy with the uniformed char marks and the smell of rosemary, thyme, and garlic that he'd seasoned the chicken with.

Trinity had just finished setting up his outdoor picnic table with a birthday-inspired tablecloth and festive paper plates and cutlery. Aliyah and his mom were tacking up a *Happy Birthday* sign to the railing of the deck. Levi put the plate of chicken on the table. Once he retrieved the salad he'd made earlier from the refrigerator, along with a pitcher of lemonade, they could eat.

"Oh! We forgot the balloons." Trinity rushed back through the house toward the minivan. When she came back, a half dozen balloons floated around her head. She tied the string to a folding chair Levi had placed at the head of the table. "There."

"Need any help with anything?" Mom offered as she walked into the kitchen with Levi.

He closed the refrigerator with his hip. "No, this is the last of it."

"I'll tell the girls and your father to wash up."

Levi carried the rest of the food to the table, then surveyed the buffet, making sure he hadn't forgotten anything. Chicken, salad, zucchini . . . oh! He'd baked some pre-made dinner rolls and left them warming in a bowl under a tea towel. He turned to head back into the kitchen, then stopped in his tracks before he barreled into his mom, who'd planted herself in the doorway.

"Levi, why are there two toothbrushes in your bathroom?" Her voice didn't sound accusatory as much as it did confused.

Constance and Nova eyed each other, then dashed back into the house. To look for more clues, no doubt.

Levi rubbed at the back of his neck. "Someone was stranded in Turkey Grove because of the rockslide. They stayed with me until the road opened back up."

His mom's eyes softened as she looked at him, her smile approving. "That was real sweet of you, hon."

"It was a woman!" Nova's voice cried with glee from the direction of the bedrooms. Constance marched down the hall, carrying the laundry basket full of folded clothes in her hands as evidence.

Levi groaned and rolled his eyes. "Constance, those are *your* clothes," he tried to deflect. But Pandora's box had opened, and there was no closing the lid on it again.

Dad took a seat at the table. "You girls leave the poor man alone." He gave Levi a sympathetic look before stabbing a zucchini spear with his fork and setting it on his plate. "Sorry, kid. You being the only boy . . . well . . ." He shrugged. But didn't that say it all anyway?

"Why do you think it was a woman?" Trinity asked.

Constance had set the laundry basket down in the living room, and now every female in his family gathered around it like it was the queen's jewels on display.

Levi sighed and took a seat across from his dad. "Should we just go ahead and eat without them? The food's going to get cold."

His dad snorted. "And incur your mother's wrath? I don't think so. No, what you need to do is go ahead and surrender now and promise to answer all their questions if they just come to the table. You can call it my birthday gift." He winked at him.

"I know those are my clothes," Constance replied, "but these have been rewashed. They smell like they just came out of the dryer, and they've been here almost a month."

"Oh, so you think this mystery woman had to borrow your clothes while she was here, then did laundry before she left?" Aliyah asked. "And Levi didn't call first to ask your permission?"

"He knows I wouldn't have cared," Constance said dismissively. "Especially if the woman didn't have anything else to wear."

Levi hung his head. The muscles in his neck were starting to tense.

"I'm still trying to wrap my head around the fact he let a stranger stay with him in his fortress of solitude instead of foisting them off on someone else in town." That was Nova's disbelieving insight.

"Is it more or less surprising if the stranger was a woman?" Trinity posed the question.

No one spoke for the beat of three whole seconds.

"Do you think . . . ?"

"No, it can't be."

"Personally, I'd given up thinking it would ever happen."

"He's never even gone on a single date, has he?"

Everyone talked over the other, and even though his sisters and mom were inside, their voices carried, swirling like a swarm of hornets around Levi's head. He rubbed at his temples.

His dad leaned across the table. "Sur-ren-der." He pronounced each syllable slowly and distinctly before straightening back up. "A woman's mind is a confusing place for a man, and you've got five women in there who love you to pieces and have been speculating about your love life for so long that they aren't going to let this go so easily. Me?" He shrugged. "You're an adult and it's your life, and I think we should leave you alone to live it, but those women in there"—he hooked his thumb over his shoulder—"their love is a whole lot more hands-on. Take it from someone who's been under the microscope of their undivided attention before."

Levi took in a deep breath, then let it out on a sigh. Even though he hated doing it, he raised his voice so he could be heard over the others in the house. "Come out and eat, and I'll tell you what happened. And if you promise to take turns, I'll answer your questions the best that I can."

"Really?" Nova poked her head out of the doorway first. "Because I have a million questions."

"I'm sure you do," Levi grumbled.

Mom walked out next, beaming. She looked happier than when Dad had surprised her with a week at an all-inclusive resort in the Maldives for their twenty-fifth wedding anniversary.

Had they really been that worried about him? Levi kind of wanted to remind them that the key to happiness and feeling fulfilled wasn't in a romantic relationship or marriage, but with the way they were staring at him with barely concealed glee, he knew he'd only be wasting his breath. His older sisters had both fallen in love and married service members who were currently deployed, and while his younger sisters were single, they had both been in committed relationships before. He was the only one of them who hadn't ever been on a single date.

His dad said a blessing over the food, and as soon as his tongue hit the roof of his mouth to pronounce *amen*, Constance jumped. "Well? We're waiting."

Levi put a chicken breast on his plate and passed the serving dish down the line to Trinity beside him. "Is everyone forgetting that the reason we're all together is to celebrate Dad's birthday?"

That seemed to take the wind out of their sails. Until his dad piped up and said, "When you get to be my age, birthdays tend to be just another day. Having my whole family around me, well, there's no better way to celebrate than this." He took a bite and chewed. "Although, since it *is* my birthday, I find I'm curious to hear this story of yours as well."

"The birthday boy has spoken," Aliyah crowed.

Levi would've loved to have pointed out to his father that he'd just said he thought the family should leave Levi's love life alone, but he saved his breath. He knew when he was beat. "The town of Little Creek recently acquired a bookmobile."

"What does that have to do with the mystery woman who stayed with you?"

Aliyah pierced Nova with a knife-tipped look. "Don't interrupt and maybe we'll find out."

"Girls," Mom scolded. She nodded encouragingly to Levi. "Go ahead, Levi. A bookmobile, you said?"

He opened his mouth to continue, but a knock at the door interrupted him. His sisters groaned.

"Who could that be?" Trinity turned at the waist to look toward the front entrance.

Levi wondered the same thing as he stood to answer the door. The only person besides his family who had ever come up the mountain to his house was Jack. Levi twisted the knob, expecting to see Jack's sweat-stained ball cap and grinning face on the other side. But it wasn't Jack.

"Hayley. What are you doing here?"

27

Hayley smiled sweetly up at him. "We really need to work on your delivery, big guy, or I might get the impression that you're not happy to see me."

"No, sorry. Of course I'm happy to see you. Just surprised." Levi shifted his weight and cast a quick glance behind him. As expected, every member of his family was straining their necks to try and get a peek at who was at the door.

He held back his groan. The timing of this couldn't have been worse. His family was boiling over with more questions than a Jesuit priest during the Spanish Inquisition, and that curiosity was going to naturally bleed over to Hayley when they saw her. He wished he could be confident that his sisters and mom would be cool and not overwhelm Hayley with their interest, but they were more likely to jump all over her like a puppy recently released from the pound.

It wasn't like he hadn't planned to introduce his family to Hayley and Hayley to them, but he'd always thought that would be *after* they'd gone out on a few official dates. *After* he felt assured that Hayley was as committed to pursuing their relationship as he was and not entertaining any thoughts that he'd somehow be better off without her or that ending things before they got started would somehow spare him a measure of future pain.

But, as they said, it appeared that time waited for no man and had literally come knocking on his door that very moment.

Levi felt the presence of others at his back before he saw or heard them.

"I apologize in advance for anything that's about to happen or be said," he rushed to say.

Hayley stared at him quizzically right before the door opened wider and Constance appeared on one side of him and Nova on the other.

"Hello there," Nova greeted brightly.

Hayley's gaze flicked between Levi and his sisters. "Um, hello?"

Constance slapped him on the chest with the back of her hand while she smiled at Hayley. "Pardon our brother's rude manners. I'd say he was raised by a pack of wolves, but then that would make us the wolves, wouldn't it? I'm his sister, Constance."

Hayley's eyes cleared, and she smiled in return. "Oh! Hello! I think I owe you a big thanks." She lifted her chin to look up at Levi. "Right?"

He nodded, resigned. The cat was about to jump right out of the bag in three, two, one . . .

"I hope you don't mind that I had to borrow your clothes recently. You really helped me out."

Levi could feel the vibrating energy bouncing off both of his sisters. Between the two of them, he'd probably set off a Geiger counter if someone pointed one his direction.

"I don't mind at all," Constance crowed. "In fact, I'm *extremely* happy that you were able to make use of them."

Her words were perfectly normal, but the unhinged grin on her face and the barely contained excitement were enough to make anyone feel hesitant. For some reason, however, Hayley didn't seem to pick up on the undercurrent of nosiness as she stood there relaxed instead of on guard, as she should be. Maybe he could still rescue her from a ruthless though well-meaning cross-examination.

"What are you doing here?" He winced as his tone came out gruffer than he intended.

Hayley's brows collapsed over her eyes as she looked at him. *Why are you acting like this?* her expression seemed to say. Her mouth, however, said, "I left something that I need, so I came back to get it. I didn't realize this was a bad time, though."

Her journal. She'd come back for her journal.

Nova stepped forward and wrapped an arm across the back of Hayley's shoulders. "This isn't a bad time at all." She looked at Levi with narrowed eyes. "Is it, brother?"

"It's our dad's birthday, and we were just starting dinner. Why don't you join us?" Constance held out her arm in invitation while also turning to stare Levi down and dare him to revoke the invitation.

Hayley looked to Levi, a silent question in her eyes.

He gripped the back of his neck before nodding once.

Constance and Nova gave each other quick glances of triumph before leading Hayley to the back deck, Levi on their heels. The rest of his family seemed on high alert, like a pack of prairie dogs popping out of their underground burrows to give unblinking focus to the newcomer. He suppressed a sigh and prayed the attention about to be poured on Hayley wouldn't scare her away.

"Everyone, I'd like you to meet Hayley Holt, the circulation librarian from Little Creek." Levi went around the table introducing all the members of his family to Hayley.

His mom quickly put the beginning of his story of Little Creek obtaining a bookmobile together with Hayley's sudden appearance. "So this is who stayed with you while the road was closed? It's so nice to meet you, my dear."

Levi retrieved another plate and some silverware from the kitchen and set them down on the table beside his own. The bench seat was snug with one more person, but he wasn't going to complain about having Hayley pressed up against him.

His dad elbowed him and winked. "Cozy."

Levi refrained from rolling his eyes. No matter what he claimed, Dad was just as bad as his mom and sisters were.

"Levi was about to tell us about the rockslide and his mystery guest, but now that you're here, why don't you tell us about you yourself?" Mom smiled warmly before bringing a bite of salad to her mouth.

"Well, what would you like to know?" Hayley leaned further into Levi's side, even though the action wasn't necessary since they were glued together like two pieces of paper in a kindergartener's art project, and whispered to him, "Can you pass the zucchini, please?"

Six pairs of eyes darted around the table, connecting with someone before shooting off and connecting with another member of the family. Everyone had one burning question that they were dying to know, but no one wanted to come right out and ask it.

Levi scowled at his family as he handed over the dish. "Really?"

Hayley laughed, the melodic trill that never ceased to take the edge off his fraying nerves. She patted his leg under the table. "It's all right. A girl gets trapped with a guy and everyone wonders if the forced proximity is the environment needed to kindle a romance. Considering they're your family and love you, Levi, it only stands to reason that they'd want to know if something happened or not." She took a bite and chewed, her face showing surprise. "This is really good. What did you season it with? Lemon?"

He nodded absently. She wasn't upset or overwhelmed or

feeling awkward about his family's invasiveness? Did that mean he had room to hope that she felt as sure about the rightness of them being together as he did?

"So . . ." Aliyah drew out. "*Did* something happen?"

Hayley nodded without contest. "Oh, something definitely happened."

Every person around the table except Levi and Hayley erupted, all talking over one another in an effort to get their question answered first. Levi's ears burned.

"You need to spell this out for us. We require details."

"I hope he was a complete gentleman and didn't take advantage of the situation."

"Are you guys, like, together, then?"

"Was it love at first sight?"

Hayley's hand on Levi's leg squeezed, bringing his attention to her. His nerves were rumbling under his skin like the engine of an F1 race car, and he was afraid they'd take off with his sense of control if everyone kept talking all at once.

Hayley winced. *Sorry*, she mouthed. She reached into her pocket, held out her hand, and uncurled her fingers. A pair of noise-reducing ear defenders lay in her palm. "I had them in my jacket from a concert I went to recently. Trust me, they help," she whispered.

Levi looked down at the small earplugs. He caught Trinity watching him with bated breath out of his peripheral vision. With slow movements, he took the earplugs from Hayley's palm and pushed them into his ear canals. He could still hear the cacophony and chaos around him, but the noise was muted to a more manageable level.

Hayley tipped her chin up and leaned closer so her mouth was by his ear. "Now cover your ears real quick."

He did as he was told, and as soon as his hands pressed to the sides of his head, Hayley let out a piercing whistle.

Everyone ceased talking and gaped at her.

"Phew, now. That's better." She picked up her fork like nothing at all had happened and took a bite.

Levi's dad elbowed him again. "I like this girl."

Levi stared at Hayley in disbelief. His appreciation for her was only growing as well. Soon it would overtake his whole being.

Hayley helped herself to the platter of chicken, ignoring the wide-eyed stares directed at her.

Levi couldn't help himself. He busted out laughing, deep belly laughs that shook his whole body and made his sides start to ache. Had he ever seen anyone shut his whole family up that way? Especially when they were on a roll like that? The moment and the looks on their faces had been priceless.

Hayley's grin took on a twist of pride while everyone else peered at him like he'd grown a second head.

"I don't think I've ever heard him laugh like that before, have you?" Aliyah stage-whispered out of the side of her mouth to Trinity.

Trinity simply shook her head, still staring at him dumbfoundedly.

His chortles slowly died, and Hayley flipped her hand on his leg palm up in invitation. He twined his fingers through hers.

"I hope you'll forgive our bad manners, Hayley." His mom cleared her throat. "I think we all lost our heads there for a second."

"I probably should have worded what I said a little differently," Hayley offered magnanimously. "But to put your mind at ease and answer at least some of your questions, your son was a complete gentleman, and, in twenty-first-century standards, nothing happened." Her cheeks took on a becoming rosy hue. "You know, like—" she gave a delicate little cough— "*that.*"

Levi swallowed the second round of laughter threatening to bubble out of him. His little sprite was adorable with her flushed cheeks, but he didn't want to embarrass her further by making her think he was laughing at her discomfort.

"Was anyone really worried on that account? He's never even liked a woman enough to get over his issues and kiss her," Aliyah said. A second later, her eyes rounded, and she covered her mouth with her hand. "I'm so sorry. That was inappropriate and uncalled for. Ignore me." Her face turned scarlet from either shame, embarrassment, or both. "I'm the sister who too often puts her foot in her mouth."

Hayley's grip on Levi's hand tightened.

Levi hung his head. Aliyah may not have meant to say that out loud, but they were probably all thinking it. What woman would be okay with all his rules? For his sisters, he'd asked them not to wear scented skincare products, to use headphones when listening to music, to eat any of their favorite crunchy snacks in their room so he wouldn't have to hear them chew. They'd all agreed because they were his sisters and loved him, but they obviously didn't think any other woman would be willing to restrict their lives in such a manner.

Hayley shifted in her seat so she faced him. Her nostrils flared, and the pink flush to her skin had darkened with the rise of her emotions. He realized with a start that she was angry.

He opened his mouth to reassure her. Aliyah hadn't meant to be hurtful. She just sometimes spoke without thinking it through first.

"Levi, your sister seems to think you couldn't possibly be keen on me." While her gaze remained gripped on his, her features softened. Her eyes still sparked, but with mischief and playfulness taking over the ire of before.

Everyone else around the table faded away. He could ignore them all, their boisterous well-meaning invasion of his private life. He could ignore anything as long as he was tethered to the lifeline of her unwavering gaze.

"I think we should prove her wrong." Her gaze dipped to his lips meaningfully for a second before rising again in question.

His eyes widened in surprise. If he'd had a million guesses, he still wouldn't have been able to predict that this was the direction the evening would have taken. He registered some sort of noise coming from the other side of the table but blocked out the intrusion. He dipped his chin and gave Hayley an *are you sure* look.

In response, she lifted both of her hands and threaded her fingers through his beard to bracket his head and pull his mouth down to hers, sealing their lips together in a kiss.

Hoots and hollers echoed around them, and Hayley pulled back with a satisfied smirk on her face.

"Instead of birthday cake, y'all are eating humble pie for dessert," his dad laughed.

Levi's neck heated as Hayley ran her thumb over his lips.

"Lipstick," she said by way of explanation, then picked up her fork again to resume her meal.

Levi stared at the side of her face as everyone began talking around him. He could hear them asking questions and sharing anecdotes, but he wasn't paying all that much attention to the conversation. He had his own questions burning in his mind. Ones he couldn't ask until he could finally get Hayley alone again.

28

That will be $12.72," the barista at Cotton-Eyed Cup of Joe says from the open drive-through window.

I smile at her and squint against the morning sun that's shining through my windshield. "I'd like to pay for the car behind me as well."

"Well, isn't that sweet of you." She beams her approval.

She adds the totals together, and I hand her my debit card to pay, glancing at my notebook that's lying in the passenger seat as she processes the order. The rectangle of bound pages has been giving me judgy eyes ever since I drove away with it from Levi's house yesterday evening. He'd seemed a little off in his behavior, but I'd pinned that on having to deal with his whole family all at once. From things he'd said to me in the past, I knew they could overwhelm him pretty quickly. Personally, I think they're great and can tell they love Levi a lot, but I can also see how they could be a bit much concentrated in one room like that.

Even with my self-assurances, however, a niggle of doubt won't leave me alone, a continuous finger poke to the brain. It was obvious that Levi had stumbled across my notebook before I'd arrived since he'd had it on hand instead of me having to go and look for it. He'd given it to me without a single question, but there was something akin to hesitancy in his eyes. Had he peeked inside? If so, had he seen his own name written within?

My stomach churns as possible reactions roll through my thoughts. I mean, if it had been me who'd stumbled upon my name in a book like that, I'm sure I'd have questions. Possibly even some pretty negative inferences, if I'm honest. Even so, I hope he didn't jump to any erroneous conclusions. I worry my bottom lip. Just what exactly *is* marinating in his mind right now?

"Here you go, hon." The barista hands me my debit card back, and I return it to the holding slot in my wallet. Once my hands are free, she extends a traveling container with three cups—a London fog for Evangeline, a Mexican hot chocolate for Martha, and the first pumpkin spice latte of the season for me.

"Thank you so much." I smile once more at the employee. My gaze falls again on the blasted notebook that's become more damning evidence than proof of well-being. Shame climbs like vines along the walls on my insides as the faux leather cover stares back mockingly. I put the coffees down on top of the notebook hoping to silence the nonverbal accusations, roll up my window, and shift into drive.

I've never wanted to inspect my motivation for keeping that notebook or any of the previous ones I've filled over the years. In fact, I've been pretty firmly rooted in the comfortable state of denial. Any time my thoughts started to prime the wells of reason, I'd turn on the flashing bright lights of *it's good to be intentional about making someone else's day brighter, of making the world a better place*, and I'd focus on that truth alone until the desire to probe deeper passed. Because, seriously, who can argue that doing at least one good deed a day is a bad thing?

But now it's like a mirror is being held up to my face, forcing me to look at my distorted reflection. Or, more accurately, now that someone else is aware of the Band-Aid I've been using to cover what is more than likely a case of survivor's guilt—among other things—and has ripped the bandage off, I'm forced to look at a wound I haven't allowed to properly heal.

I turn into the library's parking lot, my gaze snagging on a giant blue tarp covering the left corner of the roof that I hadn't noticed yesterday when I'd dropped Cletus off, having parked him in the upper lot on the other side of the building.

What in the world happened? My heart sinks as I press down on the brake pedal and duck my head to get a better view.

I realize I'm experiencing some of what the Pevensie children did when they walked through the wardrobe and into Narnia and back—that time didn't work the same between the two worlds. I'd been gone but had expected it to be like no time had passed here in Little Creek. Obviously, that wasn't the case, and a lot has happened in my absence. Like the library roof looking like a half-frosted cupcake for a Smurf-themed party.

I pull into a parking space and turn off my car, gathering my belongings and the tray of coffees. As I walk toward the building, I can't help but try to get a glimpse of what the damage is under the tarp.

I store my belongings in the back room and make my way to the front, drinks in hand. Evangeline is turning on the computers at the huddle of desks set up for patrons' use while Martha is riffling through some papers in the children's section.

"Good morning," I call out.

They both stop what they're doing and immediately turn to me, smiles overtaking their expressions.

"I brought fuel for the day," I say as I lift the cupholder in the air.

"I'd say you shouldn't have, but I have a feeling this is going to be the most Monday-est Wednesday in the history of time," Martha says as she pulls out her hot chocolate and takes a long sip.

"The reason for that have anything to do with the tarp on the roof?" I ask, fishing for the story of what happened.

Evangeline collects her London fog and takes an appreciative sip. "The storm that blew through decided to blow off half the shingles on the roof. There are a couple of roofing companies that are supposed to drop by today to check out the extent of the damage and then give the board of trustees a bid on repairs."

Martha's face clouds. "Hopefully the powers-that-be can apply for and be awarded a federal grant for the renovation. The last I heard, private donations are at an all-time low right now and revenue from city and county taxes are barely enough to cover our current expenses."

"What about insurance? Won't they cover the cost of a new roof?" I ask.

Evangeline winces. "According to Ryan, the property insurance policy the library holds is an actual cash value one instead of replacement cost value. Which means the payout will only be what the insurance adjuster deems the roof was valued at before the storm damage. Which will probably be significantly lower than the money required to replace the roof."

Martha and I share a concerned look. That doesn't sound good. If budget cuts are on the horizon, what will go? The bookmobile was a donation, but it still requires money for fuel and maintenance. Martha's been growing the children's department with crafternoons, STEM-focused activities, and focused presentations by special guests like the wildlife rescue facility and the power company. Some of those don't cost the library anything because they're considered community outreach within their own company, but for others the library pays an honorarium.

A more pressing thought stabs at my temple. Should we be worried about our jobs?

Evangeline blows out a hard breath as if ridding herself of the negativity, then paints on a bright face. The woman has a strong belief in faking it until you make it.

"I'm sure it will all work out." She turns to me, her grin becoming more pointed. "Besides, now that Hayley is back, I think we can agree that the more pressing question is when we can meet this new man of hers."

I tap my chin as if deep in thought, trying to keep the tone light and playful. If it were up to Evangeline, I'm sure she'd have Levi and I married in a Gatlinburg chapel by nightfall. Me, on the other hand . . .

Well, things just aren't that simple.

"Can we really call him *my* man?"

"Yes!" both women respond. Evangeline's is a shout of exclamation while Martha's is a more subdued agreement, along with a small shake of her head like she can't believe I'm being so dense.

"The man writes love letters to you," Evangeline points out.

"They're regular letters, not love letters," I correct.

She rolls her eyes. "Letters with secret love messages in them." Her gaze narrows. "Why are you being intentionally obtuse? Oh my gosh, you didn't pull a too-dumb-to-live heroine card or fall into a miscommunication trope, did you?"

I turn the Martha. "Is she the pot or the kettle, do you think?"

Evangeline taps her toe. "I learned from my mistake, and you can learn from it too instead of making the same one yourself."

"Why do you think I've made some sort of mistake?"

She throws her hands up. "Because you're skirting around claiming him as your man and downplaying how utterly romantic the fact he writes you letters is. I've seen you go out with a string of men. You keep things surface-level and fun. This time things are different, and most people tend to get just a little bit scared when things are different, especially when something big is on the line. Like your heart."

So much for keeping things light. I glance to Martha for help, but she only shakes her head at me, unwilling to get in the middle of Evangeline and her pursuit of romance all around her.

Evangeline takes a step closer and picks up my hands to cradle in her palms. "Is that it, Hayley? Are you scared? Because it's okay if you are. Vulnerability is terrifying."

This has gotten too real too quickly. I'm already dealing with the crumbling walls of my *possible* disillusionment from my notebooks as well as my own unsurety about the rightness of continuing things with Levi. I can't deal with Evangeline's probing questions right now on top of that.

I laugh like the whole exchange has been a joke from the start. "You need to simmer down, Cupid. Levi's coming over to my place later this week, and I'm going to cook him dinner." I hold up my hand. "And before you ask, no, you can't crash our date so you can swoon over the idea of another happily-ever-after in real life. Go enjoy your own with Tai."

She wrinkles her nose at me. "Spoilsport."

The sound of the deadbolt hitting the strike plate at the front entrance thunks through the room and draws our attention. Mrs. Kittle stands on the other side of the glass with her canvas library bag slung over her shoulder. The library has a thirty-item limit for checking out media, and Mrs. Kittle comes every twenty-one days on the dot to exchange her thirty items for another thirty.

Martha glances at the clock on the wall. "We were supposed to open three minutes ago." Her gaze sweeps the library. Half the computers still need to be turned on, including the one we use behind the circulation desk as well as the self-checkout scanner. Toddler story time will start in an hour, and she probably still needs to gather whatever props she plans on using for the day.

I flush, knowing I'm the reason we're so behind already this morning. "I'll get the door."

I walk to the front with a welcoming smile on my face for Mrs. Kittle. There's a lot in my life I need to sort through, but that's going to have to wait. For the next eight hours, I plan on escaping into the literary worlds around me.

29

The animal shelter left a voicemail requesting help with a group of dogs they were getting from another shelter over its capacity limit. That's code for *Hayley, we need help wrestling dogs in the shower.* My least favorite volunteer task at the shelter, hands down.

After the day I've had at work, I just want to go home, channel my inner Garfield, and stuff my face with a big plate of lasagna while watching a period drama on PBS. The grim expressions of the roofers who were in and out all day making assessments and coming up with repair quotes are imprinted on my brain, and I need a dose of Aidan Turner and his tricorn to evict them.

I hit the button on my phone screen to return the call.

"Little Creek Animal Shelter, how may I help you?"

"Hey, Janice, it's Hayley."

"Oh, Hayley." Her voice drips with relief. "I'm so glad you called. When do you think you're going to be able to get here, sugar? The vet is running a little late, so we have some time, but we want the dogs clean and ready for her by the time she arrives."

Janice doesn't even bother to ask *if* I can make it or not, *if* I'm willing to help or not. She just assumes that I'll say yes and immediately come running. Because when have I ever said no? Not to the animal shelter or the church or the food bank or the senior center or anywhere else where I regularly volunteer.

My gaze swings over to my notebook, still lying on the passenger seat where I left it this morning before going into work.

I'm so tired. Physically, yes, because it's been a long day, but I'm feeling more soul tired than anything, and for the first time in maybe forever, I'm admitting it. Nothing I do will ever be enough. I know that. I've known that all along.

But I have to try, don't I? I can't just receive this amazing gift of life and not do anything to prove it wasn't wasted on me, prove that I was worth the sacrifice. Even if a million check marks in my notebooks can never make the scale tip toward an equal balance, at least I'm trying. That has to count for something. Doesn't it?

I pull my gaze away from the Moleskine. "I'm leaving the library now. I should be there in about five minutes."

"You're such a godsend, Hayley," Janice says before hanging up.

Her words soothe the raw edges of my emotions. A godsend. How can anything like a godsend be even a little bit wrong?

It only takes a few minutes to drive to the shelter. I step out of the car and wince as I look down and realize I should've swung by my house and changed first. Kitten heels and a three-quarter-sleeve, loose-weaved cable sweater aren't exactly the best choices for grooming duties. At least I have a pair of dress slacks on instead of a skirt.

Too late now. I pull my purse higher up on my shoulder and trudge toward the front door. The immediate smell of wet dog mixed with dry kibble greets me as well as a few woofs from farther back in the building where the kennels are.

Janice swivels around from behind the front desk at the sound of the door. When she spots me, her face lights up and she clasps her hands under her chin, beaming at me. "Anyone ever tell you what a blessing you are, Hayley dear?"

I smile at her, soaking in her words of praise like a balm. "I'm glad I can help."

"I already got all the supplies ready for you. Shampoo, washcloth, towels, that sort of thing. There's a pair of scissors there too. A couple of the dogs look like they have some poodle in them, and their hair is a bit matted. What they really need is a good shave, but since that's not possible right now, maybe you can just cut out some of the matted clumps. I'll look into getting a professional groomer to come in at a later date." Janice walks around and opens the locked door that leads to the back of the facility. "The new arrivals are in crates in the intake room. Dr. West should be here by the time you finish with the first dog, so just bring him or her back, and then the doc will look them over."

The phone at the front desk rings, and Janice bustles over to answer, leaving me on my own. I've put in enough volunteer hours that I'm familiar with the layout of the facility, so I go ahead and make my way to the intake room. Bright lights flood the four walls and shine off the stainless-steel exam table and veterinary equipment. Whimpers and yips sound from the five black wire crates settled along the far wall.

"Hello there, cutie pies," I croon, hoping my friendly tone of voice will put the most nervous at ease. I crouch down in front of the first crate. A midsized dog with overgrown fur tangled and matted with mud stares back at me with soulful sad eyes. "Oh, you poor baby. Let's get you cleaned up a bit, shall we?"

I lead the dog to the wash station in the next room and get him set up in the shower area. He blinks at me long and slow, and my heart breaks to see the shape he's in. The sound of the water turning on ignites a spark of fear in him, and he tries to lunge away from the spray. I'm as gentle and patient as possible, but I hadn't been exaggerating when I'd compared bathing shelter dogs to shower wrestling. By the time I finish rinsing out the last of the conditioner, I'm soaked with water and coated in a layer of fur so thick that I could IKEA-build a whole other dog if I wanted. I'm also utterly exhausted. And I still have four more dogs to go.

I quickly towel-dry the now-white fluffball in front of me and lead him back into the intake room. Dr. West looks up at my entrance and gives me a knowing grin.

"This one not a fan of baths, I take it?"

I push back a sodden string of hair that's adhered itself to my temple. "Not even a little. I'll make sure Janice notes it on his behavior checklist."

Dr. West takes the leash from me and lifts the dog up onto the exam table while I head toward crate number two.

A couple of hours later, with all the dogs bathed, examined, and processed, I slog my way out of the shelter, the straps of my heels hanging limply from my fingers. I groan as I open my car door and look down at the fabric seat covering. There's no help for it now. It's just going to have to get as damp and hairy as I am. I'll swing by the car wash and vacuum the seat tomorrow.

"This is Me" from *The Greatest Showman* belts through my speakers as soon as I start my car. I sing the lyrics with abandon and zip along the country roads that wind their way through the outskirts of town. I'm two houses away from my own when I notice a big truck parked in my driveway.

Levi?

As soon as I make the turn to pull in, he steps out of the truck and watches me drive the rest of the way forward and park beside him. My pulse is tripping in my chest, making my movements jerky as I stuff my notebook into my purse.

What's he doing here? My hand reaches to my hair on instinct, but no amount of primping or rearranging can make me look like anything but a drowned rat.

Oh well. Our relationship has always had its own timetable.

I guess we're fast-forwarding past the *I'm looking my best for you* stage and jumping headfirst into the *what you see is what you get* reality.

My door opens, and Levi's large palm comes into view. I remember the first time he offered me his hand to help me into his oversized vehicle. His long fingers were strong and warm and callused and swallowed mine whole. Of course, that impression had been quickly wiped away the second he'd let go of my hand and immediately scrubbed his palm roughly across his coveralls.

I grin. We certainly have come a long way in a short amount of time.

I slide my hand into his even though I don't need help getting out of the car. I appreciate his gentlemanly display of manners and cherish the small, considerate act. I smile at him. "If I'd known you were coming, I would've made myself more presentable," I joke as I lean forward to give him a hug.

Except he takes a step back and holds out a hand between us. "Hold on."

He turns and strides back to his truck. My smile falls. He comes back a few seconds later with a towel that he wraps around my shoulders and tucks in so that I'm a human burrito, my arms pinned to my sides. "There." He tugs me to his chest and squeezes me tight. "You smell like wet dog."

I bark out a laugh. "I'm aware." I pull back so I can look up at him. "What I didn't know was that you were waiting for me."

I want to hug this man back but my arms are caged in the towel, which I'm not sure is more for my benefit since I'm still damp or his since his senses are probably being attacked by the state I'm in. I wiggle a little until I find the gap in the fabric, then bring my hands free and rest them at his sides. "Have you been here long?"

He shrugs, which isn't really an answer but probably all I'm going to get.

"Do you mind waiting just a little bit longer? I really need a quick shower to wash off all this dog hair."

He lets his arms fall away from me as he motions toward the house. I lead the way, and he follows.

"What are you doing here anyway? I thought our date was later this week," I say over my shoulder.

"It is."

I glance back at him. "So . . . ?"

"Shower first." He points to my front door, then brings his hand back to scratch at his wrist. "You've got to be itchy and uncomfortable."

I grin mischievously at him. "C'mon, big guy. You drove all the way here and have been waiting who knows how long. Don't you want to cuddle up on my couch and talk about whatever it is that brought you here?"

"I do. After you shower."

I laugh, the exhaustion I'd been feeling falling away. I'm energized simply by being in his presence. "Help yourself to a drink or whatever you want in the fridge. I'll be out shortly." I hustle to my room and grab fresh, dog-hair-free clothing. I let the warm water of the shower wash away the transfer of dirt and grime from my skin as I scrub quickly. I try not to let my mind wander to the reason Levi is here. He'll tell me in his own time.

Finally feeling clean, I turn off the shower, towel-dry, and put on clean clothes. I run a comb through my wet hair but decide to let it air dry. Remembering Levi's comment about how I should never wear makeup, I forgo any cosmetics and step out of the bathroom, bare-faced yet secure in my appearance.

Levi's sitting on my couch reading a book when I walk into the living room.

"What do you have there?" I ask as I take a seat beside him and tuck my legs underneath me. He holds the book up so I can read the title. "*Successful Small Businesses in Rural America.*"

My nose scrunches. "Is your service station having financial problems?"

He sets the hardback down beside him. "No. Jack asked me to come to a meeting of the business owners in town."

I blink at him, remembering Jack's request that I talk Levi into attending. "And you're going to go?"

He shrugs.

"That's great, Levi."

He shrugs again.

"Is that what you drove out here to tell me?"

"No."

I wait a second, but he doesn't expound. "Are you going to make me guess?"

"No."

"Is it something to do with our triplets?"

"I said I wasn't going to make you guess."

I grin. "Yeah, but guessing is fun."

He shakes his head. "You can be exasperating at times, you know that?"

My grin widens, then I snuggle into his side, my head resting on his shoulder as I pat his chest. "Yeah, but that's why you love me," I tease.

But then I hear the words, and I go still. Levi tenses under me. I lift my chin so I can see his face. He's staring down at me, his golden eyes burning bright.

"I didn't mean—"

His hand covers mine on his chest, cutting off my retraction. My explanation. *I didn't mean it like that. I was just joking around.*

He squeezes my fingers. "I can't say if that's what this is yet. I've never been in love, so I'm not quite sure what it feels like. But maybe?" He shakes his head. "If this intense, all-consuming emotion inside me isn't love yet, then it's only a matter of time until it is. I'm falling, Hayley. I'm falling in love with you."

30

"What did you just say?" I ask on a breath that barely has enough power to make it out of my lungs. I couldn't have heard him right. Those words. That declaration. They had to have been an auditory hallucination. A figment of my imagination. My most suppressed desires tied up in my greatest fears.

"I'm falling in love with you," he says again evenly, simply, as if stating a fact. This conversation isn't rocking his emotional foundation at all. He isn't wrestling internally within himself, unsure which side should surrender—head or heart.

I guess that's just me.

I lick my suddenly dry lips. "You can't." My defensive response is weak, and I'm honestly not even sure if I mean he can't fall in love with me or that he can't be telling me he is.

Because, as stated, my defense is weak. Already I can feel myself crumbling under his sure and steady gaze. Of the affection and, dare I admit it to myself, love I see shining there.

"I am."

"But we've only known each other a couple of weeks." I grasp at the first argument like low-hanging fruit and hurtle it his way. The statement is true and easily volleyed. Much easier than grappling with the other problems he'd be adopting if he tethered his life to mine in the type of commitment that love demands.

He shrugs, the maddening man.

"Levi, I . . ."

I, what?

I don't know if I can do this right now.

I don't want to hurt you.

I'm falling in love with you too.

I don't want to lose you.

All true. Every one. Each thought and emotion wrestles with the other to come out on top. To be the one to be voiced into the world.

Levi gives me a soft look. One of understanding and a small degree of sheepishness. "You don't have to say anything, Hayley. I wasn't going to tell you yet, but . . ." He shrugs yet again.

"Levi, I . . ."

He brings his big palms to the sides of my face and leans down to press his lips to mine. When he pulls back, he looks into my eyes. "I read some of the entries of your notebook."

I blink. "My notebook?" How have we gone from *I'm falling in love with you* to talking about my notebook?

"I didn't mean to invade your privacy. I saw my name, and before my brain could tell my eyes to stop, I'd already read the page."

I wince, imagining what his reaction must have been. Anger? Confusion? Betrayal? "Levi, I hope you don't think—"

"I don't." His hands still cup my face, and his fingers flex into the back of my skull for a moment before they relax again. "Well, maybe for half a second I did. But then I remembered. I know the truth."

I'm falling in love with you.

I swallow the lump of emotion in my throat. He's giving me too much grace right now. He should be upset or feel used or have questions. It's what I deserve, and besides, isn't that how most people would react? But instead, he's calm. Not even asking for an explanation. Is he so secure in his feelings—in *my* feelings—that even when there's damning evidence in the palm of his hand, he only believes the best of me?

"How long have you kept track of your daily good deeds?"

I close my eyes, hot and prickly as my rising emotions seek a way out of my body. Grace, but not an escape from accountability. Levi is holding up that mirror once again, forcing me to look into it and examine my reflection. This is a question I don't want to answer. It's too telling. Too revealing.

And his voice. He's asking with compassion like a surgeon's scalpel, lancing my wounds open.

I blink my eyes open, owing him some type of explanation. Compelled to give him reassurance that he was right not to jump to any conclusions. That my notebook is just my way of bringing light to a dark world.

Or maybe I'm still trying to convince myself that's my single motivation.

He looks at me knowingly, as if he sees the parts of me that even I've been too fainthearted to study. It's too much. I slide my gaze away, ashamed because I know there are broken pieces inside of me I've kept from being healed.

"I've been thinking about it a lot," Levi's deep voice rumbles. I brace myself.

"You're really blessed, you know that?"

I tuck my chin to my chest, equal parts relieved and disappointed. I do know I'm blessed. Blessed to still be alive when I should have died. Blessed to be given these borrowed years.

It's a blessing I feel the weight of responsibility for every single day.

He crooks a finger under my chin, gently lifting my face back up into the light, then brushes my bangs out of my eyes. His Adam's apple bobs in his throat, evidence that I'm not the only one assaulted with the thickness of emotions this conversation is bringing.

"So blessed to have been given a personal perspective of redemption and the cross."

My brow furrows. Levi has jumped from telling me he loves me to bringing up my notebook, and now he's talking about the plan of salvation when we've never once mentioned our personal faiths before beyond sharing a premeal prayer. His grunting replies, I've learned to interpret. But this conversation? "What are you talking about?"

His golden eyes shine like the sun in a cloudless sky. "Think about it. If you grew up in a church, then all your life you've been told that Jesus died to give you life. And you've experienced that type of gift—being saved from an impending death by the ultimate sacrifice of another—in a physical way that not many people have."

I blink at his reasoning, slowly understanding how the conversation ended up here. "It isn't exactly the same."

"No, you're right," he concedes. "But there are similarities. Jesus gave his life willingly for all out of his great love for us. Your donor's life ended prematurely, but it was his or her wish or the wish of their family that they give the gift of life to another at their death. A gift, Hayley." He stares into my eyes as if willing me to understand what he's saying. "One that can never be repaid."

My gut twists and sours. "I know I can't ever repay the gift I've been given."

"Do you?" he presses, as if he doesn't believe me.

"Yes!" I shout.

Levi flinches but doesn't move away. Doesn't retreat even though I know that's his nature and instinct. This conversation is likely just as uncomfortable for him as it is for me, but he's not withdrawing. His care for me is making him stay.

"Then tell me. What is your notebook?"

I sigh, trying to get my emotions under control. I wasn't prepared for this. For facing the fact that our hearts are already binding us together in a way that makes the future even more complicated than it was before. For being confronted with my notebook and finally forced to take a good hard look at the uneasy questions about my daily acts of altruism. My head is spinning, my heart pulling in erratic directions.

"I'm paying it forward." That conviction, hearing it out loud, strengthens me. I lift my chin almost defiantly. As if challenging him to find fault with being aware and intentional, of doing good deeds. Of being a godsend to other people.

"Is that it? Or are you trying to prove you're worthy of the gift of life you've been given?" he challenges right back, no bite to his words.

No bite, but they land like a blow just the same.

Levi scoops me up and settles me on his lap, his arms banding around me in a secure hold, offering me his own strength as he forces me to not push these questions aside any longer.

"Don't cheapen the gift." His chest vibrates beneath my ear as he speaks.

"I'm not," I argue feebly.

He rests his cheek on the top of my head. "Aren't you?" he asks gently. "How many check marks do you think your donor's family would say their loved one's life was worth?" He squeezes me tighter as if trying to protect me, but he doesn't stop trying to help me see the truth even when he knows the truth is going to bring pain along with it. "You can't earn a gift of salvation by good works, sweetheart. No matter how many good deeds or how many notebooks you fill or how many volunteer hours you put in. You can't earn it, and you can never be worthy by anything you do either."

My heart constricts in my chest. It's what I never wanted to admit spoken into existence and no longer able to be ignored. Facing the fact that someone had to die for me to get a new liver, that someone else on the transplant list didn't receive the organ because I did, has caused a weight of guilt inside me so great that the only way I've been able to cope is with these notebooks. It's why I think I've already decided not to go on another transplant list when my liver starts to fail again. I've already been given the chance for a longer life once, undeserving that I am. It would be unfair to accept such a gift a second time and rob someone else of the opportunity for more years with their families and friends.

It's what makes this thing with Levi so hard.

I take in a shuddering breath, fist my hands into the front of his shirt, and bury my head in his chest. My thoughts and feelings are a tangled mess, all wrapped together in emotions that are just now identifying themselves as guilt, relief, anger, and anxiety. I should've talked to someone about these feelings a long time ago, but instead I let them tumble around inside me unchecked all these years. Now I'm one giant knot inside and I haven't the foggiest idea how to go about untangling it all.

I let out my breath and gentle my grip on Levi's shirt. His heart beats steady under my ear, his chest rising and falling in measured rhythms. Having spoken his piece, he now sits in silent support as I begin to process years of repressed truths. His firm, unwavering presence solid against my side continues his conversation even when words have left him. He speaks to my heart.

You don't have to go through this alone. I'm here. I'm not going anywhere.

31

There had to be something he was missing. Levi's mechanical brain laid out all the pieces, fitting them back together like parts of an engine.

He'd stayed with Hayley for hours the other night, talking. Or rather, listening to her talk once he'd said what he'd gone there to say. He hadn't known what words to use to make her feel better, so he'd simply sat there and held her tight, pushing down his own feelings of inadequacy and helplessness. This wasn't about him. It was about her. But that just made him want to help all the more.

Which was why he replayed her words yet again. Stripped down everything she'd said to their individual parts. Inspected them. Looked for some way in which he could step in and make things run smoother for her.

Call him selfish, but his mind kept tripping over one particular thread of discussion—the future. The reason she hesitated to be all in with him. The fact that her organ transplant had an expiration date and the confession that she wouldn't seek nor accept another donor liver. He understood her heart and her reasonings, and he couldn't help himself but admire her more for them, no matter how much pain the thought of losing her caused. She said she "didn't want to Nicholas

Sparks" him, but he'd rather spend and cherish the days she did have than live in fear and premonition of an uncertain future.

Frustrated, he ran his fingers through his hair and tugged on the ends.

"Whoa, what's got your panties twisted in a wad?"

Levi spun on his heel to find Jack standing just inside the open garage bay door. "What do you want?" he snapped. He sighed and let his shoulders drop. "Sorry." So much for improving on his social skills.

Jack waved off his apology. "Just wanted to let you know we have to postpone the meeting with the town business owners. May's daughter went into early labor, so she's heading over to Charleston."

Levi nodded, acknowledging the change.

"So, back to your panties and why they're twisted." Jack flashed a disarming grin.

Levi glared, unamused.

"Could your agitation have something to do with a certain librarian?"

Levi let out a grunt despite himself.

Jack's grin grew. "I'll take that as a yes. Trouble in paradise between the lovebirds?"

Levi folded his arms over his chest. Unfortunately, Jack had never found Levi's above-average size and bulk intimidating.

"Whatever happened, apologize. I've heard flowers go a long way in softening a woman's heart."

Levi looked away. A dozen roses weren't going to fix anything.

"Oh, it's that bad, huh? Well, tell me what you did and maybe we can figure out how to make her forgive you."

"I didn't do anything," he ground out.

"Would she agree with that assessment, or is that your stubborn pride talking? I mean, I've been told by womenfolk that men do stupid things all the time that we're not aware of."

Levi's hand made another pass through his hair. "We aren't fighting. I'm just . . ." Was he really going to talk about this with Jack? "Worried about her."

"Worried? About what?" Jack regarded him. "Wait. This doesn't have anything to do with why she needs to be on prescription medications, does it?" He quickly sobered. "I didn't realize it was anything serious."

"What do you know about it?" Levi growled.

Jack held up his hands in the universal sign to show he wasn't a threat. "Nothing. I just saw her take some pills from a prescription bottle. She seemed fine, though, so I didn't think it was a big deal, but maybe I was wrong."

Levi's head fell back, and he blinked up at the ceiling.

"Is that it, then? Why you seem stressed out of your mind?"

He pulled his chin down to look back at Jack. "I want to help her, but I'm not a doctor."

Jack scratched his jaw. "Have you talked to Dr. Smith? Maybe she has some insight."

Could Dr. Smith help him figure out what he was missing? It was worth a shot. "Anyone ever tell you you're a busybody, Jack?"

"Anyone ever tell you you're a sourpuss, Levi?"

The two men stared at each other, one grinning like a fool, the other hiding a small smirk behind his thick beard.

"Get out of here." Jack shooed him away. "I'll close up the shop for you."

Levi didn't need to be told twice. He grabbed the keys to his truck and marched out of the service station.

The road to Dr. Smith's house was more like two tire-worn paths with grass and weeds growing between them than actual road, not unusual for their neck of the woods. He pulled up in front of a barn that had been converted into a house at some point in time. He killed the engine and stepped out of the truck. The sound of a rocking chair moving over a loose board welcomed him from the direction of the front porch.

"Well, if it isn't Levi Redding as I live and breathe." An older Black woman stood from where she'd sat in the rocking chair. He recognized her as the doctor who'd pushed liquids and fever-reducing medicines at him when he'd been too sick to do much else than lie in bed. She gave him a kind smile and waved him over. "To what do I owe the pleasure of your presence on this fine afternoon?"

He mounted the steps, pausing when he reached the top. A breeze blew from her direction, bringing the scent of strong perfume with it. He fought against the grimace trying to freeze his muscles and forced his lips into a semblance of an answering smile instead. "I hope you don't mind me stopping by."

"On the contrary. I find myself quite curious as to what has brought you to my doorstep. Let me go get us some tea and we can have ourselves a little chat. Make yourself comfortable." She gestured to the second rocking chair, then went inside with the slap of the screened storm door following her.

Levi exhaled his pent-up breath and took in a long inhale of fresh country air as he walked over to the chair she'd indicated. The wooden slats of the rocker looked like they had seen better days, and Levi wasn't sure the frame would hold up under his weight. Maybe he should stand instead.

The screen door opened, and Dr. Smith stepped out, ice cubes tinkling in the full glasses of sweet tea in her hands. "Go ahead and have a seat. These rockers may be weathered with age, but they're stronger than they look."

Levi regarded the rocker dubiously but obediently sat. The wood creaked under his weight.

Dr. Smith cackled. "Don't you look like a giant in a doll shop. Here, sugar." She handed him one of the cold glasses, then sat in the other rocking chair. "Now, tell me what brings you to my neck of the woods. I know this isn't a purely social visit."

Levi rubbed at his neck, chastised to be called out on only seeking the woman's company when he needed something.

"None of that. I'm just giving you a hard time. My Earl isn't one to sit around chewing the fat either. In fact, he hightailed it back inside the second he heard your truck heading up the road."

Levi glanced through the window. "I didn't mean to scare him off his own front porch."

"Nonsense." Dr. Smith waved away his concern. "I'd been talking his ear off, so he's glad of the reprieve. But enough about him. I want to hear what's brought you out of hiding. Not feeling poorly again, I hope."

"No, ma'am." Levi sipped his tea. It was cold and sweet. "It's about a friend of mine."

She observed him with an air of open nonjudgment, as if her very presence created a safe space and invited confidentiality. He could picture her in a white lab coat, stethoscope around her neck as she gave patients the care and attention they needed.

"My friend received a liver transplant quite a few years ago when she was a young girl, and . . ." How could he succinctly describe all of Hayley's worries and concerns? And a thought he hadn't considered previously: Would it be a breach of her privacy and confidence to do so?

"I think I see." Dr. Smith hummed in a way that made Levi think she really did understand with so few words spoken. "You know, transplant science, especially in regards to the liver, has come a long way in recent years."

"It has?" Hope perked within the heavy weight inside him.

Dr. Smith nodded. "More and more living-donor transplants are being performed."

"What's a living-donor transplant?"

"Just as it sounds. Someone living who is medically compatible with the person needing the transplant gives a portion of their own liver."

Levi blinked at her in wonder. "That's possible? A person can function with only part of a liver?"

"Well, you see, in both the remaining portion of the donor liver as well as the recipient's liver, growth occurs. In the span of only a few short months after surgery, the segmented livers regrow to their normal size and capacity. Not only do living-donor transplants have fewer medical problems after the procedure, but they also have longer survival rates than a liver from a deceased donor."

This was it. The missing piece. He could give Hayley a portion of his liver if or when a need for another transplant arose. She wouldn't have to feel guilty taking a life-saving organ from someone on the transplant list, and she wouldn't have to live in fear of a future that might be stripped from her at any moment because of organ failure. Even if she ultimately decided the future she wanted wasn't with him, she could still feel like she had the time and space to make that decision.

He wondered why she didn't know this information already. Wouldn't it have been something she'd researched on her own or talked to her doctor about? Then again, she seemed to have been coping with this event in her life by ignoring every facet of it. Maybe in her refusal to face the unpleasant feelings her transplant had brought along, she'd also chosen to live in ignorance. She'd claimed that was the only way she thought she could hold on to any sort of contentment. If one didn't hope for more, one couldn't be disappointed.

"Before you start calling and getting on a surgeon's schedule, you'll have to find out if you're even a good candidate to be a living donor, and if you are, if you're compatible with your friend."

There was no holding back the reins now. "I have type O negative blood."

"An excellent start, but there are other tests that need to be done too. Blood tests to check your liver function and rule out any infections or diseases, chest X-rays, an EKG, an ultrasound of the abdomen, and possibly even a CT scan. As well as the physical, you will also have to meet with a psychologist to determine your candidacy."

Levi planted his hands on his thighs. Whatever obstacle, he'd overcome. Whatever hurdle, he'd jump over it. "Where can I go to get started on these tests?"

Dr. Smith smiled at him. "I'll give you the name and number to a doctor friend of mine. He can point you in the right direction at the very least."

"Thank you so much, Dr. Smith."

She stood, turning toward him. "It's a big thing, what you're contemplating doing. I hope you take the time to think it through. With your head as well as your heart."

"I hear what you're saying, ma'am." He looked up at her, his jaw set in a determined line. "But giving this woman a portion of my liver is a small thing considering she's already staking claim to my whole heart."

32

Levi pulled into Hayley's driveway for the second night that week. Unlike the other day when he'd been determined they have an open and honest discussion, now he parked his truck with an equal determination not to say anything about what he'd learned from Dr. Smith. Not until after all the test results came back, positive or negative.

If he ended up not being a compatible match, there was still the good possibility someone she was related to would be. Her future no longer had to be shadowed by ominous dark clouds. He felt a twinge of guilt that he was letting her continue to believe it was, but assuaged such feelings by arguing that she'd have to wait for the test results to come back regardless.

He wanted more than anything to do this for her. To give her a physical piece of himself. She'd already given him so much. More than he ever thought possible. A portion of his liver really did seem small in comparison. He hadn't been exaggerating when he'd told Dr. Smith that Hayley was already staking claim to his heart. In truth, he suspected she might already possess all of him.

And who knew, maybe his size would work to his advantage for once. Maybe his liver was in proportion to the rest of him and would make giving her part of it easier for him than for her parents or brother. A question he could ask the doctor.

Levi reached for the bouquet on the passenger seat. He would've had a pounding headache by the time he'd made it to Hayley's house if he'd gone with Jack's advice and brought her real flowers. But this was a date, and he hadn't wanted to show up empty-handed either. It had been Anna Leigh who'd saved him in the end. She'd pounded on his front door and declared she was there to check on the kittens and make sure he was doing a good job taking care of them. She'd taken one look at the mess he'd been making at his dining room table, shook her head, and declared him a hopeless case and *did she have to teach him everything?*

Apparently, yes. But thanks to her, he had a bouquet of paper roses made from the pages of a slightly damaged book that was headed to the recycling bin, now given a new and hopefully romantic second life. A librarian should appreciate flowers such as these. He hoped.

He walked up the concrete path to her front door, pulling on the cuff of his flannel shirt—the same one she'd mistaken as a dress and worn their first day together. It had since become his favorite shirt, although he would love to see Hayley wear it again.

The door swung open, and Hayley stood on the threshold, smiling widely at him.

"These are for you." He thrust the book-page flowers at her.

Her fingers encircled the twigs he'd hot-glued the paper petals to, her eyes growing round. "Levi Redding, did you make me a bouquet of roses out of the pages of a romance novel?"

Heat climbed up his neck, but he didn't waste words confirming when the evidence was already in her hands.

She held the paper roses to her nose even though the only

smell she'd find there would be eau de paperback. "These are the most thoughtful flowers I've ever been given. Thank you."

She lifted up on her tiptoes while tugging down on his collar. She planted a soft kiss on his lips, then lowered the soles of her feet back down to the ground. Threading her fingers through his, she tugged him into the house. The smells of ginger, garlic, chili, and miso wafted warmly and welcomingly from the kitchen.

"Something smells good."

"It's a spicy miso ramen recipe I found last winter that I can't get enough of. There's extra garlic chili sauce or sriracha you can add to your bowl if it's not quite spicy enough for your taste. I know you like your food hot enough to set fire to your mouth."

Trinity said that was one of his sensory-seeking traits. To him, it just made food taste good.

"Before we eat, I wanted to show you the cutest thing I saw online earlier today." She pulled out her phone and tapped the screen a few times before turning it to show him. She bit her bottom lip, but even that didn't contain the magnitude of her joyous smile.

He smiled back at her before shifting his focus to the picture on her phone. He barked out a laugh before he could swallow the reaction down. On the screen, a cat sat with a cloak around its shoulders, the Hufflepuff crest prominent on the side, a black tie and white collar around its neck. He'd had no idea cat costumes were even a thing.

"Isn't it adorable? We have to get them for the triplets. Although, do we try to decipher their houses based off their personality or based off their names? Meowfoy to Slytherin and Harry Pawter and Dumpurrdore to Gryffindor?"

"They're cats." He highly doubted their issue of offense would be being put in the wrong house.

"Your point?"

He shook his head, chuckling. "Absolutely no point at all. We should get them a Hogwarts cat tree while we're at it," he joked.

Her eyes went wide. "Do they make those?" She bent her head and typed on her phone. "Oh my gosh, they do."

"What else do the kittens *need*?" he asked in jest. He wouldn't put it past her to see if there was a cat bed in the shape of a hippogriff.

She glanced up from her phone. "A vet appointment. They need some vaccinations and dewormer."

"Already on it. Scheduled for the day after tomorrow with Dr. West."

"I've worked with her at the shelter. She's really good."

"Her office is also here in Little Creek. A place I'm planning on spending a lot of my time."

Hayley flushed, her freckles becoming more prominent. Levi bent down and kissed one on the tip of her nose. She swayed into him, then seemed to force herself to sway back.

"We should eat before the noodles get overcooked and mushy."

He'd rather keep kissing her but followed her into the kitchen instead. She handed him a bowl and ladled broth and noodles into the dish. Baby bok choy, sautéed mushrooms, boiled eggs, and seasoned crunchy tofu were set out as toppings as well as the container of garlic chili oil and bottle of sriracha. He took a little of each topping and added a healthy portion of both hot sauces before following Hayley into the dining room. She took a seat at one end of the table, and he set his bowl down at the other.

"Really?" She gave him a bemused shake of her head.

"I'm falling in love you." He pulled the seat out and sat down. "But that doesn't mean I want to listen to your chewing sounds while you eat." An involuntary shiver ran down his spine. If someone wanted to torture him, making him listen to people chew would do it.

He eyed the spot beside Hayley, now uncertain. Maybe he should sit there. Force himself to endure and try to ignore the discomfort and irritation. There shouldn't be an *I might love you, but . . .* right?

"Stay where you are, big guy." Hayley cut through his second-guessing. "I was only teasing. Plus, this way I can appreciate your manly good looks all through dinner. A little eye candy with the entrée." She winked at him.

"I, uh . . ." Levi's face felt on fire. He wasn't quite sure how to respond to that.

Hayley let out a peal of giggles. "I'd take pride in rendering you speechless, but it's not an uncommon occurrence."

"For this reason, it is," he mumbled, pulling the collar of his flannel away from his neck.

Hayley laughed some more, then asked Levi to say a blessing over the food. He kept the prayer short and to the point, picking up his spoon as soon as he said amen.

"So, how was your day?" Hayley asked as she pinched a stalk of bok choy between her chopsticks.

He swallowed his spoonful of broth, loving both the temperature and spicy heat on his tongue. "Good."

"What did you do?"

Discuss a surgical procedure that would make it possible for her to entertain thoughts of living beyond a world of seizing the day but seizing a long lifetime. Where she didn't have to fear losing her contentment in order to dream of tomorrow. Hopefully with him.

"Work."

She wiped her mouth with a napkin, her smile dancing in her eyes. "Ever with the eloquence. Now ask me, and I'll show you how this type of conversation is supposed to go."

"The type of conversation between two people who care

for each other and have been apart for the long hours of the day and can't wait to hear about all the things that transpired while they were separated? Is there a reason why I need to get better at that particular type of conversation? Like, say, there are a lot of them with you in my future?"

She rolled her eyes playfully, but that becoming blush overtook her cheeks once again. "Oh, now you say more than one word."

They held each other's gazes, a wholly different conversation going on. One where Hayley reminded him of her uncertainty and Levi reassured her of his.

Letting her off the hook, he asked, "How was your day, Hayley?"

She visibly relaxed, happy to go back to their playful banter and leave more weightier discussion for another time.

"Cletus and I went to Talikwa and spent the morning at the senior center."

His shoulders tensed. "Any mechanical issues?"

"Not a one. Almost like someone had recently spent a great deal of time under the hood making sure things ran smoothly." She flashed him a grin.

"Good."

"You know, I cursed Mayor Breckenridge for foisting that hunk of junk on the library, but I think I need to revoke my ill will."

"Oh yeah?"

"I had a lot of fun today meeting everyone and bringing books and connection to communities that sometimes feel cut-off. I didn't think I'd like the circulation part of being a circulation librarian, but I actually love driving the bookmobile around."

"I'm glad."

"Although maybe you fixed Cletus up a little too well."

"How's that?"

"Well, now when I want to be stranded in Turkey Grove with you, I'm going to have to pull a play out of the nun's handbook from *The Sound of Music* and steal the distributor cap."

"And here I thought I was the only one to come up with that plan."

33

My emotions going into the doctor's office on routine test days could be represented with the yin yang symbol— opposite yet interconnected feelings that swirl inside me. At least, I think that's what the symbol means. My aunt Missy tried to explain the ancient Chinese philosophy to me one night while we gorged ourselves on chocolate chip cookie dough, but I think she got her information from Wikipedia when she was trying to learn more about her biological roots, so it's quite possible we're both off base.

Either way, that's how getting these regimented tests done feels. On the one hand, I push back the worry and invite in the positive thoughts. The tests have only ever come back with good, normal results. I haven't been experiencing any symptoms that would lead anyone to believe that today's results will be any different. I'm healthy. I'm happy. I have a lot to be grateful for. On the other hand, today's results *could* be different. There's always the possibility that they will be, and quite frankly, it's only a matter of time.

The swirl of emotions circles, so it doesn't matter how many times I relegate the negative feelings to the recesses of my mind; they still niggle their way to center stage, demanding a chance to audition for the lead role. A constant rotation of positive and negative. Honestly, I'm surprised these days don't leave me a nauseous mess.

"Hayley?" Joan smiles at me from the threshold of the door that separates the waiting room from the exam rooms. There are other nurses who work here, but for some reason Joan has been the one to initiate each of my visits over the years. The familiar sight of her makes me feel both comforted and anxious.

I grab my purse and sling it over my shoulder as I follow her to the back, reminding myself that this visit will be like all the others. No need to worry.

"How've you been?" Joan asks kindly as we make our way down the hall.

"Doing well. What about you? How's your husband?" Last time I was here, her husband had been in the ER a few floors down getting a fishing hook taken out of his hand and then a tetanus shot for good measure.

She rolls her eyes. "Would you believe me if I said he's on a fishing trip with his buddies right now?"

I laugh at her exasperation.

"Boys, beer, and bass: a dangerous combination." She shakes her head. "If I get called away because of an emergency, you'll know why." She stops in front of an open door. "You'll be in exam room three today."

I turn to enter through the open door but pull up short when a large figure farther down the hall captures my gaze. I know the broad expanse of those shoulders, the corded muscles of those forearms. I've kissed that bearded jaw.

"Levi?"

He stoops and disappears into the last room at the end of the hall, unaware that I've called out to him.

I blink. I hadn't imagined him, had I? Like a Big Foot sighting but in an Appalachian doctor's office instead of the wilds of the Pacific Northwest? My brow furrows. What is Levi doing here?

"Hey, Joan, was that Levi Redding going in for labs?" I point in the direction he'd gone, the room where all the blood draws are done.

She turns to look down the hall. "You know I can't tell you the name and information of other patients."

I chew on the inside of my bottom lip. "I know, but he's my . . ."

My what? This isn't a Mad Libs, but I am desperately looking for a noun. Except there aren't any defining titles for what we are to each other. He's more than simply the man I'm dating. Levi is . . .

The man falling in love with me.

My chest expands. Unsure as I am about what is the right thing to do with handling Levi's heart, I cannot contradict nor belittle his professed feelings. Whether they happened fast or slow, convenient or unexpected, leaving me conflicted or lighthearted. I could never do him such a disservice as to dispute what he says he feels for me.

What I know I feel for him in return.

Joan urges me into the exam room, but my feet are as heavy as my mind as I force them to carry me inside. I don't want to jump to any conclusions that Levi is sick, but he's also not the kind of man who goes to the doctor unless something is seriously wrong.

"Let's get your vitals, shall we?" Joan wraps the blood pressure cuff around my upper arm and clips the oxygen monitor to my index finger. The cuff tightens around my bicep, but I pay it little mind. I'm still stuck on seeing Levi and what the implication could mean.

"Hmm. That's a little high." She frowns at the digital numbers on the machine. "Let's get the rest of these questions answered, then I'll take it again and see if it's gone down any."

She asks me the same questions I've been answering for almost two decades now. I consciously focus on my breathing while I answer, and when she retakes my blood pressure, it's back in normal range.

"I'll go let Dr. Pender know you're ready for him." Joan smiles at me as she shuts the door behind her.

I wait a few seconds, then tiptoe to the door, open it, and peek my head out. HIPPA may prevent any of the employees from telling me that Levi is here and why, but I'm not above taking this unsupervised moment to get him to tell me himself.

I feel a bit like Scooby-Doo and the gang as I creep down the hall. I don't want anyone to spy me before I can unmask this Levi-sized mystery and get some answers, so I try to be as quiet as possible. My stealth is pointless, however, because when I turn the corner into the lab room, the phlebotomist's chair that I expected Levi to be sitting in is empty.

Derek, the nurse who always draws my blood, looks up from a vial he's placing a sticky label on. "Oh, hi, Ms. Holt. Has Dr. Pender sent you back for labs already?" He turns to his computer, presumably to check for the doctor's order.

"Uh, no, not yet." I eye the chair again and then lean back on my heels so I can peek past the doorway and down the hall. No Levi. I straighten and look back to Derek. "The man who was just here . . ." I begin.

Derek grins and retrieves a piece of paper from the counter behind him. "Yeah, he said you might come looking for him. Asked me to give this to you if you did."

I take the paper from him. I want to consume his words right here, right now, but I make myself thank Derek and walk back to exam room three first. As soon as the door snicks closed behind me, I drop my gaze hungrily to the words penned there.

Hayley,
  Don't worry, I'll explain everything soon. In the meantime,

I know I'm not a doctor, but my prognosis is that everything is going to turn out more than okay.

Levi

P. S. I'm sorry that I don't have another clue to give you, but if X marks the spot of my treasure, you'd be the 24th letter of the alphabet.

I don't know whether to laugh, roll my eyes, or say aww. Somehow, I manage a combination of all three, choking on a chuckle as I shake my head and grin like a madwoman. The line is both incredibly cheesy yet incredibly tender. The last thread of my shaky resolve to maintain any sort of emotional distance in order to safeguard his heart is snipped completely through. My heart, now untethered, soars into realms of blissful euphoria. I'm tempted to jump down from this exam table, reschedule my appointment, and find Levi right now to tell him that I won't stand in the way of us any longer. If he would rather savor every day we have together and live with those shared moments after I'm gone, then I want to make as many memories with him as possible, living each day without regret.

The door to the exam room opens, cutting off my escape plans and putting a damper on the joy of finally allowing myself to accept Levi's unrestricted affection. I straighten my shoulders and clutch his letter closer, wishing it was his hand I held instead.

"Hayley, it's good to see you again." Dr. Pender comes in, and we shake hands. His gaze snags on Levi's note. His eyes twinkle in a way that I've seen before. It's the same look he gets whenever he has good news to give his patients.

I look down at the note, then back up at Dr. Pender. "Would you happen to know something about this and why Levi Redding is now a patient of yours?"

"Of course I do." He breezes past my skewering look and accusing question. "But you also know I'm not going to tell you. Now, let's talk about how you're doing."

"I'd be doing better if I knew why Levi was just here," I say a bit petulantly. Dr. Pender has seen me at my absolute worst and has been my doctor for more than half my life. He's comfortable and familiar, so it's easy not to put on any sort of front with him.

Dr. Pender leans back and studies me. "Is that so?"

I squirm a little under his scrutiny.

"Before we go any further in this exam, do you have any questions or concerns you'd like to discuss?"

Now it's my turn to study him. He always asks me this at every one of my appointments, but the way he poses the question seems different than before. "No?"

He sighs and nods. "Give me a moment." Without another word, he exits.

I shift, the thin white exam table paper crinkling under me. I consider leaving Dr. Pender my own note letting him know an emergency has occurred and I'll call and reschedule. No need to add the emergency is that I can't wait another second to see Levi and tell him that I want to be with him fully, no holding back.

Before I can even begin to look for a pen, the door opens. Dr. Pender walks in, a looming Levi behind him.

"No one can accuse me of not putting the well-being of my patients first." Dr. Pender grins. "You said you'd feel better if Mr. Redding were here, Hayley. Well, here he is. Feel better now?"

Levi and I stare into each other's eyes. Can he see the shift in me? Every wall torn down, every door to my heart open to him?

"I can see that you do." Happiness is laced in Dr. Pender's voice. "Now, I'm going to ask again, and I want you to answer me honestly this time. Hayley, do you have any questions or concerns? About the longevity of your liver and what comes next if it begins to fail again, perhaps?"

His question is so pointed, so specific, that I realize he must have some insider information. The answer to why Levi is here begins to take shape. But the picture is still fuzzy. Even if he came to let Dr. Pender know of my fears, that doesn't explain why he went to have his own blood drawn.

"Hayley." Dr. Pender takes my hands in his, forcing me to give him my attention. "I wish you'd come to me with your concerns when you'd first started worrying, and I'm sorry for my dereliction in not anticipating such and providing you the information you needed to put your fears to rest."

My gaze flicks to Levi before resetting back to Dr. Pender. "To rest?"

He squeezes my hands and glances up at Levi. "I'll let you two talk."

He leaves, and it's just Levi and me in the room. I slide down from the exam table as Levi takes one long stride, eating up the distance between us. He cups my face and tilts it up, peering down into my eyes.

I hold up his note. "Is this when you explain?" I ask, emotion making my voice wobble. We both have so much to say, and yet, for me, I want to tell him everything in my heart without the use of words.

Levi's Adam's apple bobs in his throat. "I'm having the doctor run some tests."

I take a step back, and his hands fall away from my face. Blood drains from my cheeks, leaving me lightheaded. "Tests?" Tests means they're looking for something wrong. I should know. I've had so many medical tests done. I rake my gaze over Levi, looking for any sign that he's unwell. So many conditions aren't visible to the eye, though. He could be dying, and I wouldn't know.

266

I rush forward in a tackling hug, gripping him in a constricted embrace as if I can keep him with me by my physical force and sheer willpower. I will fight tooth and nail for this man. To be with this man. Is this how he's felt all this time and I've misguidedly put reservations between us? I hold him tighter in silent apology, hoping he'll let me make it up to the both of us.

His thick arms settle around my back, pulling me close in the safety of his embrace. "Not like that. Sorry. I didn't mean to scare you." He grunts. "I'm messing this up."

I shift so I can crane my neck back and look at him but don't loosen my hold. This position is not exactly comfortable, and I foresee needing a lot of neck massages in my future. He mumbles something under his breath, and without so much as a by-your-leave, he hoists me off my feet and settles me back onto the exam table. He hooks a rolling chair with his foot and drags it over, settling his hulking frame onto it so he's sitting right in front of me, eye to eye.

His large palms rest on the tops of my thighs, as if he needs the physical connection between us at this moment as much as I do. "Hayley, there's no reason why you can't have as bright of a future as you want."

I tilt my head, trying to make sense of what he's saying.

"The tests I'm having them run, it's to see if I'm a good candidate to give you a portion of my liver if you ever need it."

A portion of his . . .

He goes on to explain living donations, and that even if he isn't a match, someone related to me probably will be. There are still risks, as there are with any medical procedure, but the success rate and prognosis are both highly encouraging. It's more hope than I've had in a long time.

My vision swims as tears pool. I remember Aunt Missy trying to bring up transplant science one evening when our two families got together for dinner at her house about ten years ago. She's always reading about new studies and possible cures for Tai's asthma—some from actual medical journals but more often than not untested, home remedy claims—and I'd politely told her I didn't want to talk about it. No text messages with links to cocktail recipes of liver cleanses or how basil essential oil is linked to improving liver health. In fact, I'd told everyone in my family that night to never bring up my liver or health in general unless I broached the subject first.

Have they known about living donations all this time and never told me because they were respecting my wishes? Could I have really saved myself years of uncertainty and denial if I hadn't been so stubborn about clinging to my ignorance and perceptions?

"I want you to know, if we're a match, my liver is yours without condition. I'm not doing this because I want you to choose me. I mean, I do want that, but that's not why I'm doing this." He looks down, breaking eye contact. "I know I'm not an easy person to get along with. I'm particular and exacting. Grumpy and strict. I'm not easy to live with and definitely not easy to love."

My nostrils flare, and I reach out and cradle his rough jaw, forcing him to look at me. "That's where you're wrong, Levi. I have a feeling that loving you will be the easiest thing I'll ever do in my life."

He growls low in his throat, his fingers flexing and curling into my thighs. His nose nuzzles down the length of mine, and then he captures my lips in a searing kiss, unfettered and unhindered. If we were still making notes about the ways I like being touched, this would go to the top of the list.

And now I can have it. I can have Levi and contentment and joy and gratefulness. I can have an endless supply of tomorrows, sunrises and sunsets, stars glittery like diamonds in a blackened sky, and the first blush of dawn pinkening iridescent dewdrops. Comfortable silences watching fireflies dance in the dusk from the front porch and long talks on lined paper that start with *Dear Hayley* and end with *Love, Levi*. Surviving storms in the solace of each other's arms and finding delight in the antics of a trio of kittens.

Endless possibilities lay before me, along with the priceless gift of time to explore them all. None of it would've been possible without this lovely, grumpy man in front of me.

EPILOGUE

I can't believe he's doing this again," I say to Evangeline and Martha, who are standing on either side of me, the library set to open in fifteen minutes.

Mayor Breckenbridge is smiling wide for the camera that Peggy Sue is pointing his direction, Cletus directly behind him. Apparently, our illustrious leader intends to have a full-page one-year anniversary write-up about the bookmobile in the paper. Some things never change.

Then again . . .

I let myself think back over the last year. Maybe not everything has stayed the same. I know I've experienced growth over the last twelve months. For one, Levi and I have learned together what a real relationship looks like. It hasn't been all paper roses and rainbows. We've weathered our storms, but I also think we've both come out the other side stronger.

He may not be exactly thrilled about the expansion on his social calendar since Jack wrangled him into a board position for the newly developed Turkey Grove Small Business Association, but I also know he feels pride in watching his neighbors start to thrive as they diversify their clientele and shore up their bottom lines. He's also taken some advice from Trinity and listened to what she's learning in her occupational therapy classes. Some of the strategies she's suggested he try have helped him to cope more, but not all. He still has days when he gets overwhelmed by sensory input and needs to take some time alone to decompress.

As for me, I started going to therapy. And, as predicted, Dr. Brown has had a field day with my good deeds journals. She's helped me work through a lot of the guilt I've been carrying around, along with feelings of unworthiness. I still like to volunteer and help people, but there are boundaries on my time now. I have standing volunteer hours each month with the animal shelter, the food bank, and the senior center, and I no longer drop everything to rush over if they call. I'm no longer compelled to keep a list of everything I do either.

There are other changes as well. Even physical ones. Like Levi sporting a similar scar on his abdomen that I have on mine. Turns out he wasn't a match for me as a liver donor, but he did perfectly match a husband and father of three from Sweetwater. We're planning a camping trip with them next month.

Well, we'll see if it actually happens.

Because that's another change, and this time not such a good one. My most recent lab results came back with some concerning numbers. I have to go in next week to run more tests, but the day I've been dreading may have finally arrived—my secondhand organ may be failing me.

I'm not alone, though. And hope isn't lost. In fact, when my family found out how I'd been living in the dark about my future for so long, a riot almost broke out. Somehow Aunt Missy made her voice heard above everyone else, and I've had to endure her repetition of *"If you'd only listened to me . . ."* more times than I can count. She's right, though. I should've listened to her.

If I had, I would've known that every member of my family was tested years ago to see if they could be a donor match. Both my brother and father are, though my brother insists that he will be the one to go under the knife for me. He says it's so he has something to hold over my head for the rest of our lives, which I absolutely believe is a motivating factor. But so is the fact he knows he'll have an easier time recovering than Dad since Elliot is younger and in perfect health.

"You have the keys, don't you?" Evangeline asks. "I say you end this now by simply driving away."

"Here." Martha shoves a pigeon stuffed animal into my hands. "I thought you could use a copilot. But whatever you do—"

I laugh. "Don't let the pigeon drive the bookmobile?"

She grins. "Exactly."

Just last week she'd had a whole day dedicated to Mo Willems. She'd even played some of his Lunch Doodles YouTube videos so the kids could learn how to draw a few of his characters. Now the children's section is covered with pictures of Knuffle Bunny, Pigeon, Piggie, and Gerald.

"Let's fly this coop, Pidgie," I say to the stuffed animal, then fan my fingers out in a good-bye to my friends before I dig Cletus's keys out of my pocket.

Mayor Breckenbridge doesn't even notice as I make my way to the other side of the bookmobile and slide into the driver's seat. The engine cranks easily—Cletus hasn't had a single mechanical issue since his epic breakdown in Turkey Grove—and I can see Peggy Sue's amused expression as she waves me off. Mayor Breckenbridge is as ripe as a tomato in the rearview mirror. I should probably feel ashamed at my rude behavior, but I can't find it within myself. The mayor was delaying my departure, and my route today takes me to Turkey Grove. If his basking in the limelight wasn't cut short, who knows how far behind schedule Cletus and I would be.

The two-lane winding road leads me farther from civilization. Autumn is hitting the area sooner than normal this year, the tops of the mountains already showing off their colorful array. It won't be long until every tree is decked out in vibrant hues of red and gold. Like every autumn when I witness the change, the song from The Byrds pops into my head. I'm singing "turn, turn, turn" under my breath as I take a left off the main road and onto the dirt path that leads to the heart of Turkey Grove. My gaze scans the mountainside, looking for any sign of a rockslide, but everything is still and stable. I pass the last remnants of boulders that are evidence of the natural disaster that catapulted my own personal change in season.

"A time to every purpose under heaven." I sing the lyrics that originated from the book of Ecclesiastes.

It takes another good ten minutes of driving before the hollow of Turkey Grove comes into view. I pull into the General Store's parking lot, my brow knit in confusion. There's usually at least one or two people waiting for me on scheduled route days, Levi at the head of the line to greet me. But the parking lot is deserted.

I kill Cletus's engine, then climb down from the driver's seat and make my way to the other side of the bookmobile to get started in opening him up for business.

"Special delivery."

Jack's voice has me turning around, a welcoming smile on my face.

He holds out an envelope to me, and I immediately recognize Levi's chicken-scratch handwriting.

"He has you playing mailman again, I see."

Jack just grins, watching me with barely concealed excitement. I give him a funny look because he's acting strange, then scan the parking lot again.

"Where is everyone?"

"Busy." He stares pointedly at the letter in my hands. "Aren't you going to read that?"

I glance down at the envelope, then back up at Jack. I want to read it, but not with an audience. Besides, I need to get the Wi-fi going, the book cart unloaded, and make sure everything else is in place for the first patron.

I wave my arm behind me. "I need to get Cletus set up first."

Jack breezes past me, heading in a direct line to Cletus's side door. "I'll do it. You read the letter."

I stare at Jack's back before he disappears inside the van. Is it just me, or is he acting stranger than normal?

Another sweep of the parking lot tells me there still aren't any people waiting for the bookmobile. Giving in to curiosity, I slip my finger under the envelope's flap and peel it open. I love that Levi and I still exchange letters. I hope that we never stop.

There's only a ripped piece of paper inside. No salutations or greeting of any kind. The few words there stare up at me, kicking my pulse into high gear. It's a clue.

I bite my bottom lip, torn. I want to drop everything and follow this trail, figure out what game Levi is playing. But I'm also working and have to be responsible.

"Just so you know, no one is coming." Jack steps out of the bookmobile and shuts the door behind him.

"Excuse me?"

"Turkey Grove is boycotting the bookmobile today. Not a soul is going to stop by, so you might as well get." He crosses his arms over his chest and juts his chin in the direction of Levi's, a smile gracing the lower portion of his face.

"The whole town is in on this?" I hold up the paper.

He shakes his head at me. "I'm not saying another word except to tell you again to get out of here."

I grin at him, then bolt toward Levi's house, the words on the paper burned into my mind.

"What woman has a lover more truly in love; what queen a servant more ardent."

Which of course is a quote from *The Three Musketeers* written by Alexandre Dumas. Levi often refers to our feline triplets as the three musketeers despite their wizarding names, so I know the clue, while on the surface a romantic quote, is pointing me to our cats.

I haven't bothered knocking on Levi's front door for a while now, so it's not weird when I barge inside. "Levi? You here?" I call, not expecting a response.

Sure enough, he doesn't answer. Dumpurrdore does, however, with a meow and a brush against my leg. I bend down and pick him up, my gaze snagging on the piece of paper safety-pinned to his collar.

"Did your daddy make you an accomplice to his shenanigans?" I ask as I nuzzle his head and unpin the next clue.

"My dear Jerusha," it reads. *"Please be thinking about me. I'm quite lonely and I want to be thought about."*

I once told Levi I wanted to be wooed by a mysterious pen pal because of Jean Webster's *Daddy-Long-Legs.* Jerusha was the name of the heroine, even though she preferred to go by the name Judy.

It takes me longer than I want to admit to figure out where I'm supposed to go from here, but it's the name Jerusha that finally clues me in. The matron of the children's home Judy was raised in selected the name from a tombstone.

I kiss Dumpurrdore on the head and set him down. Off to the church cemetery I go.

Once I'm there, I look around. At some point, I'm expecting to find Levi. I was the last one of us to lead the other on a little treasure hunting adventure like this. At the end of his clues, he found me and a candlelit dinner set up in the gazebo at the park beside the library. So while I don't know exactly what these clues will lead me to, I'm pretty certain he'll be there.

But he's not in the cemetery. I meander through the tombstones looking for another clue. Levi is too big to be able to hide behind any of the marble slabs. Sure enough, a bouquet of paper flowers rests atop a particular marker, a note hidden within the petals.

I unfold the paper and read.

"If you live to be a hundred, I want to live to be a hundred minus one day so I never have to live without you."

My heart clenches at the words. How has he managed to find quotes that are romantic, speak to us and our relationship, while also pointing me forward to the next clue? He is the sweetest, most adorable man I've ever met.

The quote is from *Winnie the Pooh*. He wants me to go into the woods behind his house. Anna Leigh and I were exploring back there a few months ago and imagined it was the Hundred Acre Wood. We imagined we found the treehouse where Piglet lived, and then Anna Leigh told me how Fancy and Jolene would never live in a tree. Levi had teased her, saying it was actually my treehouse since I was really a woodland sprite—one of the nicknames he calls me on occasion.

I smile at the memory and collect the bouquet of paper flowers as I make my way toward the wooded hillside. The tree with a hollow section at the base is near a hedge of wild mountain laurel. In the spring, the flowers are a snowy white with purple markings and give off the scent of grape soda.

Leaves crunch under the soles of my shoes as I blaze a path through the underbrush. My pulse ticks steadily against my ribs, picking up speed with each step that I take. Intuition thrums within my veins. Kind of like how I knew the first time I laid eyes on Cletus that my future was about to be changed forever. It's not ominous this time, however—the intuition.

More like a happy knowledge that something good is waiting for me right around the corner.

Levi steps out from behind Piglet's tree at that exact moment.

I was right. Something good was waiting for me.

No, something amazing.

Levi's gaze captures mine, and his golden eyes melt at the sight of me. I don't think it will ever get old, being looked at in this manner. I've never had to guess, never had to doubt this man's love for me. And that's the greatest gift he could have ever given.

He steps forward and takes my hands in his. "You made it."

I quirk my brow mischievously. "Did you doubt me?"

"Not even for a second." His smile spreads wide. He dips his head and captures my lips in a sweet kiss, as if he couldn't hold himself back another second. "Sorry," he says when he pulls back.

"Never apologize for kissing me like that," I say dazedly.

He grins for a moment, then sobers. His throat works as he swallows hard. "Hayley, I love you."

My heart melts. "I love you too, big guy."

"I'm not always good at expressing myself, though I wish I could tell you all the things you mean to me. All I can say is that I love you. I've loved you even before anyone thought it was logical for me to do so. Maybe at the first sight of you or the first touch, I don't know. But I do know I'll keep loving you for the rest of my days." He lowers himself to the forest floor until he's down on one knee. "Will you marry me?"

A velvet jewelry box materializes, a dazzling engagement ring nestled inside. His heart is in his eyes as he looks up at me, and my vision begins to swim with happy tears.

"Yes!" I shout, then launch myself into his arms.

The impact punches the air out of him, and he loses his balance because of my attack. He falls to the ground, and I land on top of him, peppering him with kisses anywhere my lips can touch. His chest rumbles with his laughter, and his arms come around to band behind my back, squeezing me tight.

I lean back to look into his eyes. "One day at a time."

"Every day. For the rest of our lives." Then he seals the promise with a kiss.

AUTHOR'S NOTE

Currently, sensory processing disorder (SPD) isn't included in the *Diagnostic and Statistical Manual of Mental Disorders* (DSM-5), the handbook that healthcare professionals use to diagnose mental health conditions. This means that there isn't a universally accepted diagnostic set of criteria for an SPD diagnosis. Sensory processing difficulties can often come alongside other neurodivergent conditions, like autism spectrum disorder and ADHD. Because of this, the medical community continues to research and debate whether SPD is its own distinct disorder or a symptom of other conditions.

It was when my son was being assessed for ASD and ADHD that we were referred to see an occupational therapist for his sensory difficulties. The occupational therapist asked us a list of questions, then handed me a pamphlet for SPD. I didn't realize at the time that it isn't a disorder with an official diagnosis, so I asked her if SPD was something he had. She winked, nodded, and said most definitely. After reading over the pamphlet, I realized that I could put more check marks beside the symptoms than he could! I finally had a name and an explanation for why I wanted to peel off my skin any time my husband would lightly caress my arm or why it felt like my blood pressure was rising whenever I was in an environment with multiple sources of audio input or why I felt like I was about to go into a rage whenever someone chewed beside me.

There are different types of sensory processing disorders. A person can be overly sensitive to sensory information, or they can be under responsive. They can be sensory seeking as well. SPD can also affect your movement and coordination. Yes, clumsiness can actually be a symptom of SPD.

For Levi Redding, I gave him a mixture of some of the sensory difficulties that I face as well as some my son experiences. Not everyone who lives with SPD is going to have these same experiences.

Occupational therapists can help both children and adults with SPD. They can offer coping techniques and strategies to help with overstimulation and self-regulation, address motor skill functionality, and overall enhance an individual's quality of life.

DISCUSSION QUESTIONS

1. *Hearts in Circulation* begins with the library acquiring a bookmobile. What is your opinion on the need for mobile library services to rural areas?

2. What was your initial reaction upon learning that Hayley keeps a journal of all her good deeds and makes sure she does at least one good deed a day? Did your opinion on Hayley's journal change after you learned why she keeps track of her acts of kindness?

3. Levi is terse and grumpy when Hayley meets him for the first time. However, instead of jumping to conclusions about his character, she wants to give him the benefit of the doubt. She thinks "fictional characters sometimes get a better deal than people in real life because readers are allowed to see the conflicts and motivations on the page, the reasons they are the way they are. Real people are too rarely afforded the same consideration even though we all have backstories of our own." What are your thoughts on this belief? Do you agree or disagree?

4. Hayley and Levi begin to write each other letters even though they are living in the same house. In what way

do you think those letters progressed their relationship? Was this an aspect of the book that you enjoyed? Why or why not?

5. Levi is an adult before learning that a sensory processing disorder could be the cause of his feeling overstimulated all his life. He is eventually open to learning coping strategies but doesn't ever seek a formal assessment. Do you agree with his decision? Why or why not?

6. Hayley thinks that if she allows herself to dream of tomorrow, then she's robbing herself of today's contentment. What words of advice would you give her on this topic?

7. Levi and Hayley fall in love in a very short timeframe. Do you know of anyone who had a whirlwind romance in real life? Do you prefer the insta-love or slow burn trope?

8. Which character did you most identify with? Why?

ACKNOWLEDGMENTS

I think the first acknowledgment here really needs to go to you, sweet reader. Without you, books would be nothing more than tattoos on dead trees. Instead, you help give them not only a destination but a purpose. So thank you. Thank you for lending me your time as well as your tender heart and open mind. And thank you to any and all who have reached out with motivating support and kind words. I appreciate them more than you know.

As always, I owe a heartfelt thanks to my agent, Rachel McMillan, who works tirelessly on my behalf. Thank you for being in my corner.

To the talented editors at Bethany House who helped hone this book into what you hold in your hands, Jessica Sharpe, Jennifer Veilleux, and Bethany Lenderink. Thank you so much for all that you do and for pouring your energy into both myself and my stories.

Toni Shiloh, you're the best cheerleader and critique partner I could ask for. Just knowing how much you adore Levi and Hayley means the world to me.

I couldn't write without the support of my husband, who

works so tirelessly to provide for our family. Thank you, José, for your loving sacrifice.

And most importantly, thank you to the supreme Author of all our stories. Our happily-ever-after is with You.

Read on
for a *sneak peek* at
the next book in the

CHECKING OUT LOVE

series.

Available Summer 2026

CHAPTER 1

If I had a choice, a black-and-white cow onesie, complete with pink udders hanging from my lower belly, is not exactly what I'd pick to be wearing when called into my boss's office. But here we are.

It's five minutes until pajama story time begins, and Ryan is looking at me with his brows raised, waiting on my answer about whether I'm free for a "little chat" once I send my tiny munchkins back home and into bed.

I pull the hood of my onesie over my humidity-inflated curls and feel the fabric horns flop to the side as I force a carefree smile to my lips, even though my stomach is threatening to swoop down to my toes. If I'm going to be the cow that jumped over the moon in *Goodnight Moon*, then by golly I'm going to commit to my character. And a nighttime bovine track-and-fielder wouldn't be concerned about the deep crease between her boss's eyes or the resigned slump of his shoulders.

"I'll stop by after the last 'goodnight to noises everywhere,'" I assure him, still holding my pitched-up smile.

His gaze drops to the bundle in my arms—a couple of books I'm planning to read aloud and the sock monkeys I made myself because they are surprisingly expensive to buy and I'm trying to save the library money.

289

His lips twitch north but fall almost immediately as his gaze meets mine, then bounces to the group of preschool and early elementary kids who are starting to get a little rowdy. He nods and pivots without another word, trudging across the library like he's making his way through a bog instead of walking over well-worn, low-pile carpet. He disappears behind the door that leads to the space he uses as his office whenever he makes the commute from the main regional library, where his actual office is.

We're a tiny blip on the map here in Little Creek, but along with the other librarians, Evangeline and Hayley, we make sure the library runs as smoothly as possible. Evangeline has a weekly video call with Ryan to discuss business and trouble-shoot any issues that arise. Plus, he comes in-person once a month as well. But no one expected to see him today. He's not scheduled to work from this location for another two weeks. The cloud of tension hanging around him is thicker than the dust billows that follow Pig-Pen in the *Peanuts* comics.

"Bluey's stupid. She's for babies." A little boy's snide tone jerks me back to the present.

Right. Story time. Before the tiny troops mutiny.

"You're a baby if you like Bluey," he continues to taunt.

I march to the front of the round rainbow rug all the kids know to sit on during story time. A little girl with wispy pigtail braids wearing a Bluey nightgown glares at the boy beside her.

Derrick. Of course it's Derrick. And of course his mom is leaning against the wall in the back corner with her face buried in her phone, oblivious to the fact that her son is about to make a little girl cry. Or, nope, he might be the one to cry if her tiny balled-up fist is any indication.

"I love Bluey." I swoop in with a smile and a distraction, stealing their attention in the nick of time. "And I'm not a baby, am I, Derrick?"

His expression immediately transforms, his pinched features going lax as he looks up at me with big brown eyes. "No," he agrees, "you're a cow." He says this the same way he would if he'd just declared I was a fairy princess instead of a rotund farm animal. With awe and childlike worship. Evangeline teases me that I have the kids of Little Creek under some sort of spell with the way they hang on my every word, but I remind her it's the stories that captivate them, not me.

"And you look like a real paleontologist with all those dinosaurs on your pajamas." I tweak his chin and give him a genuine smile.

He scrunches his nose. "What's a pale-toe-la-lo-gist?"

My smile stretches, charmed at his mispronunciation. "A paleontologist is a scientist who studies fossils like dinosaur bones."

"Do you need a volunteer today, Miss Martha?" Amara tugs on my onesie and peers up at me with pleading puppy-dog eyes. A slight pout of her lips is the cherry on top of her cute manipulation to get me to let her participate in the stories.

I take her hand and have her stand beside me. "It just so happens that I do. I need six volunteers for our first book, in fact."

Hands pop up as if they are all spring-loaded. I choose five more volunteers and watch as each child comes to the front with wide, proud smiles on their faces. I pass out the five sock monkeys and place a toy stethoscope around May's neck, who is the youngest reader.

"Any guesses what book we're going to read first today?"

"*Five Little Monkeys!*" a couple of them shout.

"That's right."

I've placed a Nugget Play Couch that was donated to the library on the floor to act like the bed the monkeys jump on. After a few instructions to the kids holding the sock monkeys, I begin to read. The helpers up front act out the story with the monkeys as I hold the book up so all the kids in the audience can see the pictures. Predictably, each child tries to make their monkey jump the highest. The laws of gravity mean nothing when the imagination is involved.

When I get to the part about the doctor, I point to May.

She pulls her thumb out of her mouth with a loud pop. "No monkey jump bed," she says in her little three-year-old voice.

There's a few *awwws* from the parents in the audience and a couple of giggles from the kids. I turn the page and keep reading. The sock monkeys are now doing flips and summersaults as the kids launch them into the air. Thankfully, they've managed to keep their landing pad on the Nugget instead of on another child's head.

At the end of the book, we quietly and calmly tuck the monkeys into bed. Amara kisses her monkey on the forehead, and the other four children follow her lead, each smack of the lips growing a bit louder as they try to outdo one another.

"Okay, I think the monkeys are ready to get some sleep. Thank you so much for your help, but you can go sit back down on the rug."

While the kids lower themselves back into their spots, I pick up the next book. *Five Little Cows*. I make my eyes as round as I can, dramatizing a look of surprise, and give a little gasp. "Oh, look! It's a book all about me. Mooo!"

The kids giggle, and I open the book. Every time the word *moo* is on the page, I point to it, and the kids all do their best cow impersonations. *Five Little Ducks* was checked out, and the library doesn't have *Five Little Fireflies* or *Five Little Hummingbirds* to continue our "five little" marathon, so I've chosen to end with the classic *Goodnight Moon*, which even the adults will likely enjoy.

I settle back in my chair, signaling silently the tone of the book before I read. For *Five Little Monkeys* and *Five Little Cows*, I sat on the edge of my seat, a constant smile on my face, projecting the fun and energy the story within contained. But now it's time for calm. For the lulling that only a good bedtime story can bring.

"'Goodnight noises everywhere.'" I close the book in my lap. "Good night, May," I say in the same soft, lilting voice I'd used while reading. "Good night, Rosa. Good night, little Jordan, and good night, Derrick. Good night, Theresa and Evelyn and Carter." I wish them all a good night and wave as parents hold on to hands and lead their children out of the library to drive them home and tuck them into bed.

"You forgot to whisper *hush*," Hayley says with a grin after Amara is led out the front door and there aren't any more kids left.

I stand up from the rocking chair that does resemble the one in the picture book. "Are you implying that I'm the quiet old lady?"

"Who me?" Hayley touches her chest in mock innocence. "I would never." She bends down and collects the sock monkeys for me, then begins to fold the Nugget to go back to the storage closet. She pauses and smirks at me. "I might have heard one of your munchkins guess at your age though."

I wince. "I don't think I want to know."

Hayley straightens. "Let's just say that that many candles on your next birthday cake might be a fire hazard."

"I'm not surprised, considering they think anything before the year 2000 is 'the olden days,' when pictures were only in black-and-white and we didn't have television."

"Ouch."

"So, depending on who you overheard, Laura Ingalls Wilder and I could've been childhood friends."

"I guess you know how to milk yourself, then, huh?" Hayley cackles.

I look down at the udders hanging from my belly. "Ugh. Don't remind me."

"Any idea what he wants to talk to you about?" She's jumped

to Ryan's unusual presence here, which, even though she and Evangeline often help me clean up from story time, was probably why she'd come over in the first place. Not to taunt me about how much farther ahead on the number scale of life I am than her. The big four-oh might be just one skip count by twos away, but hitting middle age is the least of either of our worries right now.

"Not a clue."

"Yeah, Evangeline didn't know either, which I find odd. She's practically the boss without the official title, but Ryan hasn't told her anything." Hayley hefts the Nugget into her arms. "I'll finish up here if you want to go figure out what's going on."

I bite my lower lip, sigh, then nod, accepting that there's no use putting off the inevitable. "Thanks."

Evangeline is helping a patron at the circulation desk as I pass. Our eyes meet, and she gives me an encouraging dip of her chin. When I reach Ryan's closed door, I pause. My heart is thumping against my ribs, and even though I don't know why he wants to talk to me , I feel like my subconscious has picked up on some subtle foreshadowing and is warning me that whatever the news is, it isn't good.

Not that it makes an ounce of difference to projecting any sort of professionalism while wearing a cow onesie, but I reach up and tug the hood off the top of my head. I may still have udders, but at least now I don't have horns. My head falls forward in resignation, inadvertently thudding on the door in front of me.

"Come in," Ryan calls.

The knob turns in my sweaty palm, and now I'm not only a cow, I'm a sweaty cow. Perfect.

"Have a seat, Martha." Ryan indicates the chair that he's placed on the other side of his desk that isn't usually there. His office isn't large. There's not much room for things like chairs. Or other people, for that matter.

I squeeze into the seat that's wedged between the wall and his desk. Or I try too. My udders, which I had very much not wanted to draw attention to, are making it difficult to maintain any sort of poise. Especially when they flop onto the top of my boss's desk and no amount of tugging or pulling on my part—all while struggling to maintain a nothing-to-see-here strained expression—gets them to budge.

"Martha."

I sigh and admit defeat, threading my fingers together and placing my clasped hands over the pink fabric teats. Very demure, very mindful.

"Let me start off by saying what an amazing children's librarian I think you are. You've created programs here in Little Creek that other libraries in the region are adopting. You're dedicated, hardworking, and the children and parents love you."

I give him a moment, allowing him time to continue. Except he doesn't. He seems just as hesitant to say what he needs to say as I am to hear it.

Feeling a little bit bad for him, I break the silence. "Thank you, but I'm sensing a *but* coming."

"Did I mention you're also very intuitive?" He forces out a chuckle meant to ease some of the tension.

It doesn't.

He sighs. "*But*, unfortunately, we've run out of money."

I blink at him. "What do you mean?"

"We didn't get the grants."

My heart sinks. A bad storm a few weeks earlier had caused a lot of damage to the library's roof, to the point where the whole thing needed to be replaced. Because of the type of insurance the library carried, they would only issue a check for the value of the old roof. Which turned out to be a drop in the bucket after estimates from roofers came in. We'd filled out applications for a few federal grants, hoping those funds would cover the additional costs that weren't in the library's current budget. Without those funds . . .

"It's going to take the rest of the levy money to cover the cost of the new roof."

The levy money that had previously been allocated for the library's youth programs. The money that paid my wage. While everyone calls me the children's librarian, technically I'm only a librarian's assistant. I don't have a library science degree like Evangeline and Hayley. I'm a part-time employee who volunteers just as many hours.

"What about the new levy?" I ask weakly, already knowing what his answer will be.

Ryan shakes his head. "It didn't pass. I'm sorry."

"But . . ."

"It's not fair, I know. We've all been very excited about the programs you've implemented, and no one wants to see the funding cut and those programs put on hold, nor do we want to lose you, but the money has to come from somewhere."

Put on hold? He can't put the programs on hold. If Ryan pauses Budding Authors, then what will happen to Bethany and Andi? They're both at pivotal parts of their stories, not to mention journeying through the valley of doubts about creativity, craft, and community. And Sam. Sam just started to open up. To find a place with like-minded peers when she's been searching for so long. If Ryan pauses Budding Authors, Sam might not know that she belongs. That she's not an outsider and that she does fit with other girls.

Lego Builders? Yes, the hour is loud and takes time to clean up, but the response since starting a dedicated time for young Lego enthusiasts has been more than we ever expected. Some families can't afford the increased price in Lego sets and so the library is the only time their kids get to play and create with the bricks. And Lego is so much more than a toy. Lego helps with social skills, problem solving, spatial awareness, creativity and experimentation, fine-motor development, focus, anxiety, and so much more. Ryan can't get rid of Lego Builders.

Community Connections? Crafternoon? Homework Help? STEM Time? Story time? Every program meets a need. Pausing these programs isn't an option. We must find a way to cover the costs.

"There's got to be something we can do. I can volunteer more." My brain has switched to solution mode.

"Unless you're independently wealthy, I hate to be the one to remind you that you can't work for free if you also want to pay rent and eat."

Well, there is that. Rent isn't an issue since I work on the Anderson property in exchange for living in the apartment above their horse stables, but I would like to continue to have food in my pantry, and that does require some source of cashflow.

"How much money do we need for the new roof so the levy funds don't get reallocated?" I ask, knowing whatever number he gives me, I have no way of paying. My contribution to Friends of the Library is buying a few books here and there. I'm not a big donation tier.

Ryan looks away, not meeting my gaze. I'd think that was it, all doors closed, if it wasn't for the rhythmic strumming of his fingers on the desk. After a few moments, he turns back and looks bleakly into my eyes.

"We'd need a big donation," he hedges.

"How big?"

He winces "A hundred thousand dollars."

Definitely more than the paltry sum currently sitting in my bank account. More than in any bank account in Little Creek, if I had to wager a guess. Which means local fundraising would only be a splash in the bucket when what we need is a downpour.

I close my eyes and draw in a deep, slow breath. Lucky for

me, I know where to find a thundercloud. "I might be able to get the library that donation."

All I have to do is go back on a promise I made myself. The one in which I swore to never step foot in Mr. King's office ever again.

A Carol Award finalist and Selah Award winner, **Sarah Monzon** is a stay-at-home mom who makes up imaginary friends to have adult conversations with (otherwise known as writing novels). As a navy chaplain's wife, she resides wherever the military happens to station her family and enjoys exploring the beauty of the world around her. You can follow her at SarahMonzonWrites.com.

Sign Up for Sarah's Newsletter

Keep up to date with Sarah's latest news on book releases and events by signing up for her email list at the website below.

SarahMonzonWrites.com

FOLLOW SARAH ON SOCIAL MEDIA

Sarah Monzon, Author   @SarahMonzonWrites   @MonzonWrites